EVERY UGLY WORD

DISCARD

EVERY

UGLY

WORD

All characters appearing in this work are fictitious. Any resemblance to real persons, living or dead, is purely coincidental.

Every Ugly Word © 2014 by Aimee L. Salter

All rights reserved. No part of this book may be reproduced or transmitted in any form or by any means, electronic, mechanical, photocopying, recording, or otherwise, without prior written permission of Alloy Entertainment. If you would like to use material from the book (other than for review purposes), write to permission@alloyentertainment.com. The publisher does not have any control over and does not assume any responsibility for author or third-party websites or their content.

alloy**entertainment**

Produced by Alloy Entertainment
1700 Broadway
New York, NY 10019
www.alloyentertainment.com

First edition July 2014

Cover design by Liz Dresner
Mirror photo © Kittibowornphatnon under license from Shuttershock.com
Landscape photo © SNEHIT under license from Shuttershock.com
Legs photo © Catalin Petolea under license from Shuttershock.com
Hands photo © Robbi under license from Shuttershock.com

ISBN 978-1-939106-38-4 (ebook)
ISBN 978-1-939106-44-5 (paperback)

LINCOLN LIBRARY
SPRINGFIELD, IL

To Alan.

You're the handsomest guy in the room of my life, and way more important than doing the recycling.

Thank you.

God makes dreams come true, but He used you to fulfill mine.

LINCOLN LIBRARY
OF R. I.

CHAPTER ONE

AS THE PSYCHIATRIST enters the room, he offers me a patronizing smile. I return it in kind.

He indicates for me to take a seat, then sinks into a worn leather chair, looking just like a doctor should: graying hair, well-trimmed beard, and wire-rimmed glasses I suspect he doesn't actually need.

We face each other over a glossy, mahogany coffee table. While he flips through my file, I scan the room. Shelves of creased paperbacks line the walls. The single window is framed by subtle drapes. There are doilies under the table lamps and two doors on opposing walls. This office resembles a living room—if I ignore the bars over the shatterproof windows. Kind of kills the good-time vibe.

Doc clears his throat. I take a deep breath and turn back to him.

"How are you, Ashley?" His voice is too loud for the muted tones of the room—all earthy browns and soft corners. The quietly ticking clock in the corner tells me it's 9:34 a.m. That gives me about five hours to prove I'm normal and get out of this place once and for all. Five hours until *her* life goes to hell, if I don't make it home in time. I focus on him, try to smile. It's already been a rough morning, but I can't tell him that, not yet.

"I'm okay." I shrug, then freeze. My stitches are only memory now, but searing pain lights up along the hard, pink lines spider-webbing across most of my upper body. I breathe and wait for the jagged bolts to fade. My surgeon says I'm healing. But he forgot to mention that to the layers of mangled nerve endings beneath my fractured skin.

"Pain?" Doc's eyes snap to mine. The benign disinterest was an act. He is measuring me.

"It's fine. I just moved wrong," I say breezily.

My physical scars aren't the reason I'm here. He can't fix those. But he can help me by letting me out. As head of this facility, no one leaves without his approval.

I mentally shake myself. He *will* let me out today. He must. If I can get home in time, I can fix . . . *everything*.

Doc's lips press together under his perfectly trimmed mustache. After a second he smiles again.

"I see you brought your bag."

The duffel bag my mother packed before dumping me here six months ago sits on the floor like a well-trained dog, as ready to go as I am.

"Yes."

"So you're confident about today?"

"I'm confident that I'm not crazy."

Doc's smile twists up on one side. "You know we don't use that word in here, Ashley."

There are a lot of words they don't use in here. *See you later*, for example.

I take another breath. Cold. Calm. Sane. "Sorry."

He returns my stare, face blank. "I'm glad you feel confident. However, I do have concerns."

"Concerns?"

He smiles in a way I'm sure is meant to be reassuring. But when he sits that way, with the overbright anticipation in his gaze, it kind of makes him look like a pedophile.

"Ashley . . . you've changed therapists three times during your stay. Do you know what I think when I hear that?"

I think the question is rhetorical, but he waits, expectant.

"Um . . . no?"

He hasn't looked away. "I think as soon as anyone gets close to the truth, you flee."

I can't break my gaze without confirming his suspicions. So I swallow and wait.

His calm is maddening.

When he speaks next, it's in the cool tone of a professional shrink. "I've read your file, spoken to your nurses, and been briefed by your therapists. Now I want to talk to you. About this."

He makes his way to a closet in the corner, then pulls out a massive full-length mirror. It stands taller than I am, with a wrought-iron frame that is hinged in the middle, allowing it to pivot. He rolls it in front of the shelves in the corner of the room, far enough behind me that I can't see into it without turning my head.

A kindness? Or a challenge?

Doc returns to his chair and I force myself to follow him, to keep my eyes away from the glinting surface.

"I have a hunch if we examine whatever it is you see in the mirror, we'll find the truth about the rest, Ashley," he says. "I'd like you to stand before it and tell me what you see."

Panic lights up my veins. "What? Now?"

Doc raises a brow. "Unless you have a better idea?"

I don't. I'd expected this session to be like all the others—a glib exploration of my past, patronizing questions about my psyche, along with self-congratulatory compliments when I make a "breakthrough." I was prepared to do whatever it took to get out of here by 2:30, but I can't look in that mirror—not now.

What if she's there? She won't understand why I'm ignoring her. She's been through enough today already. We both have. And breaking her heart is breaking mine.

"The mirror won't make any sense without the rest of the story," I say, trying to buy time. If I can get him talking, show him how normal I am otherwise, maybe he'll decide I don't need to look.

His face remains impassive, but his head tilts to the side just a hair. He's onto me. "I know the story you've fed your previous therapists. If there's more, I'm willing to put the mirror aside for a time—"

I slump with relief.

But he raises a single finger. "—*if* you tell me everything. There's only one route to getting my signature on your release forms, Ashley. And that's it."

His patience is a marble rolling along a slim edge, precariously balanced between hearing me out and sending me back to that cell they call a bedroom.

Swallowing again, I try to make myself pitiful. I drop my head into my hands. "Okay," I breathe into my palms.

"Okay, what?"

"I'll tell you the truth." As much of it as I can, anyway. I'll let him think he's gotten through where others failed. Hell, I'll even consider what he has to say if it means he won't make me look in that mirror.

"Excellent."

"So . . . where do you want me to begin?"

He crosses his leg over his knee, pulling up his pant leg slightly. "Nothing too dramatic. Start with the night you planned to give Matt the letter."

I feel the grin slide off my face. Nothing too dramatic. *Right.* I can't help glancing sideways at the mirror. Doc follows my gaze, and when he sees where I'm looking, he frowns. For a moment the magnitude of what I'm trying to achieve is overwhelming. I cannot breathe. But I force my muscles to loosen. I swallow my fear—and begin to speak.

CHAPTER TWO

THE HEADLIGHTS OF my mom's ancient Civic cut across the deep black of the Oregon countryside, turning the grass silver and bringing the post-and-rail fence into sharp relief. The engine whined as I downshifted and took the corner too fast into my best friend Matt's long driveway.

"You know, in moments like these I'm grateful I never have to actually ride with you," a familiar female voice said.

"Stop scowling. You're giving me wrinkles," I replied, adjusting my rearview mirror so I could see her better. In the small, rectangular frame, it almost looked as though she were in my backseat, arms folded across her chest, her too-long reddish hair falling limply across her shoulders. But she wasn't there, not *really*.

She appeared five years ago, the same day I lost all my friends. I'd run home from school, refusing to cry until I was alone. When I made it to my room, I caught sight of my pathetic self in the mirror. Except, it wasn't just me staring back—Older Me was there, too.

"Are you in the bathroom again?" I asked.

She nodded. "My roommates are home." She'd moved into an apartment a few months before. She didn't seem to like her roommates much, but then, she didn't seem to like much of anything.

As I braked in front of Matt's huge brick house, she frowned again, worry lines creasing her forehead.

"I told you I don't need you tonight," I reminded her.

Tonight was about me and Matt.

If you'd asked me twelve hours earlier if tonight would be That Night for us, I would have laughed. But that was before art class this morning. Matt had grabbed my elbow as the bell rang. He'd shifted his weight and avoided my gaze.

He was . . . nervous. Twitchy.

Matt was *never* nervous with me. And I'd only ever seen him twitch when he was talking to a girl he wanted to ask out.

"What's up?" I said.

"We need to talk." He glanced over my shoulder. "But not here. Can you come over tonight, before the dance?" His Adam's apple bobbed.

"Of course."

When he left, I'd almost floated to the cafeteria.

Matt was nervous. And he wanted to *talk* . . .

Older Me's voice yanked me back to the present. "Look, I know you like Matt, but he's your best friend. Dating would just make everything . . . complicated."

I sighed heavily and killed the engine. I'd gotten used to Older Me being around, popping up in mirrors and glass surfaces, always listening, commenting, offering advice. Usually it didn't bother me. But tonight was big.

I'd hidden in the library after school and written Matt a letter that confessed everything—my feelings for him, and what I saw when I looked in the mirror. Then I'd tucked it deep in my purse where there was no chance she'd catch sight of it and try to talk me out of it. She'd always sworn upright and sideways that *no one* could know about her and me. Especially Matt, though I was pretty sure she'd said that because he was the only person I would tell. She hated it when I went to other people for advice. And she was *full* of advice. Always. You'd think that'd be awesome, right? Advice from your future self. A literal glimpse into the future.

I wish.

I'd learned years ago that asking her about my future would be met with stony silence and pursed lips. *You and me . . . we're taking different roads, Ashley. How can I tell you what your future is when it might be different from my past?*

She cleared her throat. "What about just giving it some time?" she suggested. "You don't have to tell Matt how you feel tonight. I mean, you guys are so close now. Wouldn't it be better not to risk the connection you have?"

Before I could comment on the irony of my older self asking *me* about the future, my phone pinged with a text, no doubt Matt asking where I was. I picked up the phone from where I'd left it on the passenger seat . . . and dropped it immediately.

HEY FATTY R U COMIN 2NITE? DONT 4GET UR BRIDLE—FINN WANTS 2 GO 4 A RIDE

"What is it?" Older Me asked, the irritation gone from her voice.

My cheeks burned. The caller ID said UNKNOWN, which meant it was Terese. She was the only one with a private number because her mom was the local district attorney.

I could just picture Karyn and Brooke peering over Terese's shoulders, cackling, telling her what to type. With shaking fingers, I deleted the message. My stomach hardened into a knot, the bitter taste of bile rising in my throat.

How had they gotten my new number?

"Ashley?" Older Me said cautiously.

"It's just Karyn and Brooke and Terese," I muttered. "Forget it."

Older Me frowned. "Ashley, forget them, okay? Their cruelty says a lot more about *them* than it does about you."

Yeah. I'd heard that before. Funny how it didn't change that *they* thought *I* was a complete loser. "I'm not talking about this now," I said, gathering up my purse and dropping my phone into it. "Tonight is supposed to be fun."

Tonight was supposed to be more than fun. Tonight was supposed to be *epic*. The beginning of everything finally going right. A day I looked back on and said, *There. That's where it started.* Because I hadn't felt this way about a guy ever—not even Dex, the guy I'd dated last year. Kind of.

"I'm going in now," I said.

She went very still. "Is his dad home?"

"I hope not." Matt's dad was . . . difficult.

"Be careful," Older Me murmured as I opened the door.

"Geez, he's not an ax-murderer."

Silence echoed around me when I let myself into the house. The Grays' foyer had immaculate cream walls and hardwood floors, and was so big it could have just about swallowed my entire house.

"Hello?" I called, the word reverberating.

"Up here." Matt's voice floated down the curving flight of steps.

Downstairs the house was shiny and cold—like a showroom in a modern architect's portfolio. But upstairs the hardwood floors gave way to carpet, the walls were dotted with family pictures, and the beds were covered with colorful quilts and surrounded by painted furniture. When the Grays had moved in, I'd told Matt it looked like they'd taken his mother's house and sat it on top of his father's, then linked them by a stairway.

He hadn't laughed.

I found Matt sitting on his neatly made bed, head in his hands. His fingers made claws in his sandy hair. He still wore the T-shirt and jeans he'd had on at school, though there was now a rip in the right sleeve. I perched next to him on the edge of the bed and laid a tentative hand on his back.

"What happened?"

"I told Dad about the competition." His deep voice was hard. Rough. Like someone had taken sandpaper to his throat.

I dropped my head to his shoulder and let out the breath I'd been holding. Matt and I were in AP Art. Somehow we'd both qualified for National Young Artist of the Year. I mean, I'd known Matt would get in. He was incredible. But I was floored when I got the letter, too. The top twenty artists would be displayed in New York next December, and the winner would be awarded a full-ride scholarship to the College of Fine Arts in the city. But all the finalists had a shot; between the judges—who were usually professors at top schools—and the gallery opening, most ended up with scholarships somewhere.

The problem was, according to his dad, Matt wasn't supposed to be an artist. Last year, when he'd won a local competition with an impressionist watercolor painting of his cousin blowing bubbles on the beach, Mr. Gray took one look at it and accused Matt of being gay. As far as his father was concerned, Matt was going to MIT to be an engineer, just like him.

"I knew he'd get mad. But I thought he was under control. I thought I'd shown him he *couldn't* hit us anymore." A shudder rocked the length of Matt's six-foot-two frame.

My throat tightened and I took his hand. "Tell me."

I'd always known Matt's dad had a temper, but I learned what a monster he really was when we were fourteen. Matt had gotten in trouble for sassing his mom at the breakfast table, and when we got back to his house that afternoon, Matt's entire comic book collection was gone.

Mr. Gray had burned it.

I was there when Mr. Gray told Matt what he'd done. I'd watched Matt's jaw clench and his eyes strike sparks—even though all he'd said was, "Yes, *sir*."

After his dad left, Matt put his fist through the bedroom wall.

Later, Older Me told me to help Matt talk it through whenever things went bad—so he wouldn't boil over that like.

Or worse.

"He got angry," Matt said. He was squeezing my hand so hard the tips of his fingers had turned white. "Mom tried to get him to calm down. But he went crazy. Shoved her into a wall trying to get to me. I had to . . ." He swallowed. "I punched him.

Put him on the floor." He turned his right hand over. Two of his knuckles were split, the skin swollen and red.

"When he got up . . . Ash, even *I've* never seen him like that before. He just screamed, and came at me." He stopped, his face pale.

"Matt? What happened?" I was whispering now, afraid of what he would tell me. Suddenly afraid of the awful silence in this cold house.

He let go of my hand and stood up. "I need to change if we're going to make it to the dance."

I gaped. "You can't be serious. Matt, we can't go to the dance after this. Let's just watch a movie. I'll even play that ridiculous *Apocalypse* game with you if you ask nice." I tried to smile.

Matt scowled. "I'm not staying here." He turned away from me and pulled his T-shirt over his head. I was left juggling the fierce desire to protect him from himself with the dry-mouthed awareness of his muscled back.

"Matt—"

"We're going." He punched one arm into a blue-checked shirt, then the other.

I glared. Matthew Thomas Gray was my best friend, and the nicest guy I knew.

And he was stubborn as a mule when he wanted to be.

I got to my feet, ignoring the tingle of nerves. If he didn't want to talk about it, it had to be *really* bad. "Matt, you can't just stop halfway through that kind of story."

"We're going to the dance," he said. "We can talk about it tomorrow."

"I don't want to talk about it tomorrow—and you won't want to, either. You're just trying to make me stop asking."

12

"So take the hint!"

"No!"

"Fine!" Matt yelled, whirling to face me.

The button-down shirt hung open over his chest, revealing two angry, oval marks. It took me a second to realize they were bruises. *Thumbprints.*

Right at the base of his neck.

The line of his jaw flexed. I knew my mouth had fallen open, but I couldn't seem to close it. I reached for Matt, but he stepped back and snapped his shirt closed.

"I put him on his ass. He isn't going to do it again."

"That's what you said last time!" My voice jumped an octave.

"Well, this time I'm right." He grabbed his wallet and shoved it into the back pocket of his jeans. Checked his phone, then put that in the other pocket.

When he started messing with his hair I realized he was serious. He was going to show up at this stupid thing. He was going to dance and flirt and pretend his life was completely normal.

I didn't move. "He could have killed you."

Matt jerked to a stop, tension radiating from him. "No," he said quietly. But the word lacked conviction. "It was never that bad. He never . . . I could always breathe."

"I didn't say he *tried* to kill you. I said he could have."

He stared at the floor, swallowed hard. "I get it, okay? But I handled it. I handled *him.* And I told you the truth." He turned back to me. "Now I want to go be normal."

"Let him go." The words were a whisper, floating out of the mirror behind Matt. I glanced at the shining surface, but from this angle I could only see copper-colored hair, a shade darker than my own. "It's hardly the night you want to declare yourself anyway."

I shook my head. That wasn't the point. Not anymore. "Fine. Let's go."

Matt started for the door, then hesitated. When he turned his face was screwed up and he cursed under his breath.

I stopped. "What?"

"I forgot. I need to talk to you," he said. He ran his palms down his thighs.

He was twitchy.

Despite everything, hope rose in my chest.

"Look, Ash, I'm really sorry about this. The thing with Dad just took my head out of the game and . . . I wouldn't normally do it this way. Okay?"

"It's okay," I told him softly, laying a hand on his arm. "Whatever it is . . . this is *me*."

"You're my best friend. You know that, right?" he said.

"Yeah." *And I want to be so much more.*

Matt took my hand and cleared his throat. "Right. Okay. I need to tell you . . . do you remember that youth leadership conference thing I went to a couple of weeks ago?"

"Um . . . yeah." Random.

"Well, while I was there, we had to do this assignment and we all got paired up. The only other person from our school was Karyn. So she and I worked together."

I froze.

Suddenly, I saw him through a different filter. The nervous energy. The inability to look at me. The twitchiness.

"I told her you were my best friend," Matt rushed on. "That

I'd never date someone who hurt you. But she said she didn't have a problem with you. She said she feels terrible about how things have been between you. That it started because she thought *you* didn't like *her*."

He smiled a little and shook his head, apparently warmed by the memory. I wanted to smack the grin off his face. Stupid, gullible, *idiot*.

"Ash . . . Ash, are you listening?" Matt squeezed my hand.

"Of course." My voice sounded dead, even to me.

"Nothing's going to change, okay?" he promised.

I nodded because I had to. "Yeah, sure." *Like hell.* I took my hand back, resisting the urge to wipe it on my jeans. "It's just . . . why Karyn?"

Why my ex-friend, the girl who'd made my life hell since eighth grade? The girl who'd told the guys in PE that I didn't wear underwear. The girl who'd told Gerry Henkins I liked him—when all he wanted was someone to sleep with. The girl who whispered to her friends that I'd hit on their boyfriends, setting them on me like well-trained dogs, then stood back and laughed.

Why couldn't he see what a witch she was?

But the answer was obvious: He was a guy. All he saw was her platinum hair and flashing baby blues. And her dimples—everyone loved those stupid dimples.

Matt stared at his feet. "It's just . . . she helps me forget," he said. "She doesn't know anything about my dad. She doesn't care if I'm on student council, or if I make honor roll . . . She doesn't care about anything. She just wants to be with me. And when I'm with her, I don't care about that stuff either."

The expression on his face was a mallet to my frozen heart.

"This is okay, right, Ash?" he asked quietly. "We can all be friends. It'll be great."

I nodded, for his sake. But it wouldn't be great. At all.

As Matt smiled and started for the door again, I took a step back and looked right at the mirror. At Older Me. At her hunched shoulders, and her hands buried in the pocket of that hoodie. At her wide eyes.

Wide with guilt. Not shock.

She knew. She knew this was coming and she didn't tell me.

CHAPTER THREE

DOC CALMLY EXAMINES his thumbnail. While I'm grateful for the lack of histrionics, part of me is offended that he can listen with such detachment. I've just told him my high school sweetheart was almost killed by his father, and, oh, by the way, I talk to myself in the mirror. To my *other* self.

Then again, if he's read my file, he knows where this is going.

"Karyn?" he says to his thumb. "The same Karyn who was involved in your . . . incident?"

"Yes." I spit the word. It's the wrong way to respond.

Doc looks up. "It must be hard, looking back."

I cross my legs, tipping my weight so I don't stretch the scars on my side.

"You were friends with Karyn?"

"Yes, at least in the beginning. She moved to town in seventh grade. Back then I was friends with her and all of the girls, Doc. I was popular until the end of eighth grade. Sort of."

"And Matt?" he asks.

"He went to a different middle school," I explained. "His dad sent him to some private, rich-kid one in the next town over. He didn't go to school with us until freshman year."

Doc looks at his notes, frowns. "So, what changed for you? What happened in the eighth grade?"

I flap a hand to pretend I'm unfazed. "Just kids being kids," I say. "What's your point?"

He sighs and removes his glasses, holding them up to the light. "Ashley, I can assure you that none of my questions are pointless. If we're going to get through this today, you're going to have to trust me to identify what is important and what is not."

Trust.

Now there's a word.

Doc returns his glasses to his nose and stares at me.

Okay, fine.

"I'd been friends with all those people for years—Finn and Brooke were in elementary school with me and Matt. But by the eighth grade Matt was off at his fancy school and I was alone with the rest of them. I got sick of the games. Sick of feeling like I was always on the verge of being *out*. I wanted to impress the girls. I thought maybe they'd make me a real part of their circle if I did. So I told them a stupid lie."

Pause. "What was the lie?"

I pick at the cuff of my hoodie. "I said I slept with Finn. He was dating Brooke at the time, but they were always fighting."

One Monday when I knew Finn and Matt had gotten together over the weekend, I told Terese I had snuck over to Finn's house. I "proved" my story by telling them about a little birthmark Finn had in a place you could only see when he was naked. He told me and Matt about it one time when we were playing Truth or Dare.

Brooke heard about it and asked one of the guys if the birth-mark was real—which it was. Next thing I knew, the entire school was talking about it. Brooke broke up with Finn. Told the other girls he was a cheater. Blamed me. To get back at me, Finn told everyone we *didn't* sleep together because when I showed up I was all mental and sex crazed. That I was lying to cover myself. Between them they turned everyone else against me. Once I real-ized no one thought I was cool for sleeping with him, I tried to apologize and admit it was a lie. But my *proof* was too good. No one wanted to believe the truth.

Doc frowns. "Why did you start a rumor that cast yourself in such a negative light?"

I throw up my hands in exasperation. "Because I was thir-teen and stupid. Back then everyone was kind of in awe of the girls who slept with guys. I thought they'd think I was grown-up and cool, and then the whole thing would blow over. But they never let it go. *Never.* From that day on, I was the slutty freak."

"What did Matt think of all this?"

I squirm. "Matt didn't know the real story for a long time. I never told him why I stopped hanging out with Finn. And I guess Finn didn't say anything, either. Matt didn't notice until fresh-man year. When he came to high school, he realized me and Finn didn't get along anymore."

"What did he do?"

"He asked Finn what happened and Finn told him to talk to me. I told Matt it was just a fight and to forget about it. So he did."

He frowns harder. "How did that make you feel?"

Oh, *please*. I look up so he can see I'm serious. "I felt relieved that Matt was still my friend since I'd lost everyone else."

"*Ah*," Doc says, in that infuriating, knowing way shrinks have.

"What?" I ask, too sharply.

He eyes me over the frame of his glasses. "It just seems like Matt dating Karyn might have made you finally feel like you'd lost your last friend."

"Maybe." I shrug, pulling at another loose thread on my cuff. Suddenly the whole hem comes undone.

I drove Matt to the dance in silence. The whole car was filled with the smell of his aftershave, a crisp, piney scent that normally made me want to do nothing but close my eyes and inhale. Instead, I gritted my teeth and ground the gears.

It wasn't just the fact that Matt had a girlfriend—he was always dating someone. But usually I could tell it was coming. He'd ask about a girl. Find out if I knew anything about her. He'd work up the courage to ask her out, then I'd help him plan his first date so he could impress her. I'd listen to him gush about her for a few weeks. Then something would change. He'd stop talking about her as much. Hang out with me more. Start complaining about whatever she was doing that irritated him . . .

It was a cycle we'd been repeating since freshman year. But now he'd broken it. He'd said nothing. Hidden her completely. So what was different? Was he more serious this time? About *Karyn*?

Just get him to the dance. Then you can claim a headache and go home, I told myself. *No questions, no declarations.* Older Me would be thrilled.

In ten minutes, we were there. Black Point High (*"Home of the Bears!"*) took up two whole blocks in our tiny town. It was bordered on all four sides by tall fences. Like a zoo. Three entrances—one at the front door, one at the cafeteria, and one at the gym—let seven hundred animals in every day. Rumor had it, the original building was an insane asylum, and Principal West's office used to be the electric-shock room. I figured it was just a way for kids to freak each other out. But there *were* a large number of outlets behind West's desk . . .

I pulled into a parking spot and killed the engine. Matt started to open his door, but he paused, looking at me over his shoulder. "Ash? Are you coming?"

Before I could reply, his door swung wide. "There you are!" sang an irritating little-girl voice.

Karyn.

Matt grinned. "*Hey.*"

My heart squeezed painfully. That one syllable held more desire, more *passion* in it than every kind word he'd ever said to me combined.

"You're late," Karyn squealed.

"Sorry, got held up." Matt pulled himself out of my car and wrapped his arms around her, his chin dropping to rest on the top of her head.

You got held up by your abusive father, Matt. Tell her that. Oh, wait . . . mopping you up then watching you fall all over someone else is my *job.*

I knew I was being unfair, but I could practically feel the letter nestled in my purse, never to see the light of day. *Time to get home and burn it.* I put my hand on the key, ready to turn it.

21

"Hey, Ashley," Karyn squeaked.

"Hey, Karyn," I said without looking up. But I guess my flat tone was the only clue she needed.

"You told her? Finally!"

"I told you I would," Matt murmured sheepishly. "Don't worry. It's all good."

All good.

Yeah, Matt. Sure. It was brilliant.

"Great! So let's go in and tell everybody else!" She tripped around the car and opened my door, like we were suddenly best friends. I was taken so off guard, she had me by the elbow and half out of my seat before I found my voice.

"I actually have a bit of a headache—"

She shook her head. "C'mon, Ashley, it'll be fun. The three of us can hang out."

I turned, openmouthed, to Matt, silently asking *Can't you see through this?* But he was too busy smiling at Karyn, and a moment later, she had each of us on an elbow, and we were crossing the parking lot to join the other students walking toward the main lobby entrance.

A wave of panic trilled down my spine. *It'll be all right,* I told myself. As soon as Matt and Karyn had everyone's attention— which would take all of five seconds—I'd slip out the back door of the gym. Matt could get a ride home from his new *girlfriend.*

"Hold my hand when we're walking in so everybody knows," Karyn said in a low voice, her cheek against Matt's bicep. I stifled a groan.

The second we walked through the main doors, everyone— and I do mean *everyone*—stopped what they were doing and turned to look at us. They looked from Matt, to Karyn, to their entwined hands, back to their faces.

Brooke immediately stopped flirting with Eli, a lacrosse goalie with calves the size of watermelons. "I knew it!" she called, patting her glossy black waves.

Karyn squealed again; Matt grinned like the farmer trotting out his prize hog as Brooke and Terese crowded around Karyn. Eli and a couple of other guys gathered in behind them, talking to Matt.

"And I see you two brought your puppy!" Eli flicked his hair out of his eyes and clapped me on the shoulder. The entire circle laughed.

"Says the guy wearing a choke collar," I muttered. Eli wore the same wooden bead necklace every day. He swore it was good luck because the night he bought it, he'd lost his virginity.

"Lay off, dude." Matt shoved him good-naturedly.

"That's no *puppy*," Brooke said quietly to Karyn and Terese. "That's a *pony*." Then she smiled at me. "Did you bring your bridle, Ashley?"

I glanced at Matt, but he was too busy high-fiving Eli to notice the barb.

Screw this. Ignoring the girls' hushed voices and giggles, I turned on my heel and shouldered back through a crowd of freshman gawking at Matt and Karyn. I was out the front doors and almost to my car when I noticed Finn Patton leaning against the fence of the parking lot with several friends, discreetly sucking on a flask.

Everything about Finn was angles and hard edges: the way his elbows poked out of his shirtsleeves like the ends of wire hangers. The spiky peaks of his intentionally messy dark hair. The sharp jut of his cheekbones. At first glance he seemed lanky, almost skinny. But when he curled his arms, ropes of granite muscle twisted under his skin.

Finn pushed away from the fence and gave me an awful half grin. "Hey, C! You made it!"

His gaze locked with mine, and I imagined plowing my fist into that smug smile. "C" was the first letter in the word he'd been suspended for calling me the semester before. "What, were they out of dog food at home? I'm sure I saw a couple of biscuits around here somewhere."

"Grow up, Finn." I pulled my chin up and stalked toward my car.

At the last second I saw his foot sliding out to catch mine. I twisted, tried to step over it. But he just lifted it higher to catch me at the ankle. Muttering a curse, I grabbed his shirt as I toppled and pulled him down, too. I landed hard on my tailbone. My purse skittered across the cement, the contents bursting out like confetti. Half a second later, all the air left my lungs as Finn landed on top of me.

Wolf whistles, applause, and laughter echoed in the darkness.

"Get a room!" someone called.

Finn's face was barely an inch from mine, black eyes glittering. He reeked like an ashtray. He swore and rolled off me, landing a vicious elbow in my ribs in the process. Then he was on his feet, shouting, "I've been molested! Call the police!"

My tailbone throbbed. It took a second to get to my hands and knees. Laughter still bubbled from the guys as Finn knelt down over the scattered contents of my purse—my keys, a tube of lip gloss, a few receipts—and came up with a tampon.

"So, it's true," he said, holding up the purple tube. "You really are a chick."

I grabbed it from him and shoved the items back in my bag. As soon as I was upright, Finn stood too.

"I already told you, Ashley, I'm not interested," he said too loudly. "Go bark up someone else's tree."

The laughter and whooping behind Finn snapped up a notch. He held my stare, upper lip curled. I let him see the waves of hatred rolling off me like heat. Yet I had nothing; no quip, no pithy remark. It was moments like these that always left me wondering why, when faced with someone who clearly despised me, I lost all ability to think.

I took a breath and shoved Finn out of my way, striding for the parking lot and my car. Air rushed past my cheeks, cold and damp. I pushed my bangs from my face, and shook off the laughter still breaking up the night behind me. I cranked open the car door and got in behind the wheel. For a moment I gripped it, my fingernails digging into the hard plastic, imagining plowing the car up onto the walkway and over Finn and his arrogant crowing.

But instead, I put the car in gear and reversed out of my spot. I heard someone yell my name and glanced in the rearview mirror. Finn had his hands cupped around his mouth. His words reached me even through the closed window.

"This night just got a whole lot better, bi—"

I turned my music up, loud, and gunned for the exit.

CHAPTER FOUR

DOC IS PAYING attention now, leaning forward, elbows on his knees, stroking his moustache. "Did you tell anyone about these events? Maybe your mother?"

Hell, no. I shook my head.

"Why not?"

"Because all Mom cared about was that I didn't embarrass her."

Doc frowns, but I can see the light turning on behind his professional reserve. A dysfunctional mother-daughter relationship is his bread and butter. "What made you feel that way?"

Seriously? "Just little things."

"Like?"

"Like . . . she wasn't interested in understanding how things were for me. She wanted me to conform. Be like everyone else. Be normal."

"And how did she define 'normal'?"

I scoff. "Wearing the right clothes, belonging to the right groups. Being popular. You know, high school stuff."

The finger on his moustache freezes. "I see."

"Do you?"

He nods. "Yes, I think so."

An awkward silence descends. I don't believe him, and he can tell.

He sits back in his chair. "Can you give me an example? From around the time of the letter?"

I snort. "Take your pick."

"Just tell me the first one that comes to mind."

That's easy.

When I walked in the door at home, still tense from the events at the dance, I was already composing a sketch in my head. Not one for my class workbook, but one for my personal collection. One in which a cartoon Karyn was pregnant and chased a fleeing Matt, pleading with him to look at her dimples. I was debating whether the cartoon Matt should be demanding a paternity test or crying, when I walked into the kitchen and found my mother in her robe, sitting at the dining table. That was odd. Mom owned a flower shop, which meant she left the house every morning before five to go to the markets. Even on the rare occasions I went out, she was usually in bed by eight.

She sat, rigid, her almost-black hair sleeked back into a ponytail. She'd taken out her contacts, so her glasses were perched at the end of her nose. She stared through them at her phone, frowning.

Had Dad called? Doubtful. We hadn't heard from him in months.

I tried to keep my voice casual. "Mom, what are you doing up?"

Mom held up the phone, screen bright with a text message. A message that said FROM BROOKE.

My heart thumped painfully. "Why is Brooke sending you messages?"

"She isn't. She's sending them to you," Mom said evenly.

I furrowed my brow. "On your number?"

Mom sighed. "You changed your number twice in the last six months, Ashley. I wanted to know what was going on. I had the technician add . . . Look, it doesn't matter. I'm receiving copies of whatever is sent to you, and I want to know why you're getting messages like these!"

"You're *what*?"

Mom's face remained impassive. She turned the phone to herself and began to read. "'OMG. You're so fat and stupid. Stop throwing yourself at guys. Everyone hates you. Why don't you just die?'"

Mortification started at my hairline and cut through every nerve ending on its way down to my toes. My phone had beeped several times during the drive home. I hadn't bothered checking it.

"Mom—"

"'Bow wow. Go home, dog.'"

I swallowed, but she wasn't finished.

"'Hey, Fugly. If you really want some, you can have this.'" She looked at me over the frames of her glasses. "There's a picture attached of a boy's penis. At least, I think that's what it is. He isn't the best photographer. And frankly, in a year or two, he'll realize what he's got isn't really anything to be proud of."

I knew I should laugh. She was mocking whoever had sent it. But I couldn't move, couldn't breathe.

"What's going on, Ashley?" Mom's voice was cold.

"I . . . uh . . . it's just a joke."

One of her brows slid higher. "Do teenagers routinely send photos of their genitals to each other? I thought that was just a *Dateline* special."

I shook my head. There was a reason I'd changed my number. *Twice.*

Mom dropped the phone to the tabletop and sat back, chewing the inside of her lip. "This is so disappointing. You have to learn to stand up for yourself, Ashley! I mean, life isn't going to get easier out of high school. You know that, right?"

The back of my throat burned.

Mom flailed one hand. "No one's going to *offer* you respect. You have to earn it. Demand it! You can't walk into a room of teenagers looking like last year's leftovers and expect them to admire you." She gestured to my stretched-out jeans. "It starts with how you look, then you tell them what to think of you, then you act like you own the world. That's the only way to get through this life without being a loser. Don't you want people to like you?"

I closed my eyes. "Yes."

"So why do these kids feel like they can do this? Why aren't you on that phone giving it right back to them?" She indicated the phone and my jaw dropped.

"You think I should send insulting texts to my classmates?"

"Unless you want them to keep doing this." Her face didn't change.

I stared at her, disbelieving. "You think I *want* this?" I stormed past her, headed for my room.

"Ashley, I'm not finished!"

"Well, I am."

I ran to my room and slammed the door with a satisfying bang. I grabbed my phone out of my purse and threw it as hard as I could. It smacked against the wall and tumbled to the floor, the screen a starburst of cracks. But the cover stopped it from falling apart. It just lay on the carpet, green light blinking to let me know yet more of my classmates had taken the time to get in touch.

I looked around at my unmade bed, the white dresser and desk I'd had since I was twelve, the faded yellow wallpaper I hated and had covered with as much of my art and Matt's as I could. One huge piece I'd done the year before hung over my bed. It was a meadow in perspective, tall blades of grass crystal clear in the foreground, fading to a hushed, blurry green blanket in the distance. I'd done it to try and make my room peaceful, because this room, with the door closed, was my only safe space.

But they always managed to ruin it anyway.

Pinching my lips together, I grabbed the phone, tore the SIM card out of it, and squeezed hard until it snapped into two pieces. Then I gathered up my pencil bag and sketchbook and dropped into the chair at my desk. Art was cathartic, the only way to exorcise my demons.

Using acrylic crayons, I rubbed Karyn into existence on a sheet of heavy cartridge paper. The bold colors and shiny effect suited her. Her hair came out more gray than the platinum I'd been aiming for, but her eyes were perfect—scraped out of the waxy crayon with a razorblade.

Finn emerged next, also in crayon. I discarded two false starts before I got his rodentlike features right. I made his too-wide lips an acidic blend of red and purple. By the time I'd worked over his cheekbones and the sharp angles of his face, there was too much black on the paper, but the effect was perfect: He'd dirty anything that touched him. Just like in real life.

As evening passed into midnight, I tried to draw Matt, in pencil this time. But it was impossible to get him right. His eyes looked dead, his face just a flat copy of the real thing. So I drew pieces of him instead—the way his shoulder fed into the muscles at the base of his neck. The way his hair flipped at his temples when it got too long. A profile of his nose, and one eye—downcast, so I didn't have to get it *right*. Piece by piece, the different images of Matt came to life on the paper. Finally I drew my favorite part of him—his hand. I drew it grasping a pencil, the tendons on the back standing proud.

When I was done, I put the pencil aside. I couldn't resist running my finger along the soft gray lines. I closed my eyes, imagining he was really there, remembering how he'd held my hand earlier that night. How he'd *needed* me.

Until Karyn showed up.

With an angry cry, I crumpled the drawing and threw it on the floor. I leaned forward on the desk and put my head in my hands.

Who was I kidding? Matt was never going to love *me*.

CHAPTER FIVE

DOC'S FACE IS blank. When I close my mouth, he doesn't move immediately. And when he does, it's a simple tilt of his head, as if he's listening to something I can't hear.

Then he takes a breath. "Did your mom ever confront you about the phone again? Or mention the texts?"

I shake my head. "A couple of days later, she left a new card for my phone with a note telling me to change the number and not give it to anyone except Matt."

"Did you do that?"

"No. It was just another way for people to taunt me, so I stopped using it entirely. I closed all my online accounts, too."

His eyebrows climb almost to his hairline. "At seventeen years old, you stopped using a cell phone *and* social media?"

"What choice did I have?"

His inability to come up with an answer is satisfying. But it also lowers my defenses. I find I'm suddenly desperate for him to tell me those texts were awful. To tell me I was strong.

Instead what he says is: "I'm sorry that happened to you."

I tip a shoulder. The fire in my scars makes me wish I hadn't.

"Ashley," he says quietly. "I'm here to help you, no matter what else happens. You know that, right?"

They are simple words, but a well of emotion springs up in their wake. I am suddenly hopeful and afraid in the same breath.

No matter what. Does he mean it? No one's ever said that to me before.

Well, almost no one.

After balling up my drawing of Matt, I'd intended to get changed and just go to bed. But when I turned away from my sketchbook, I found Older Me in the full-length mirror on my closet door. She wore a heavy green hoodie, zipped all the way up to her chin.

She peered at me. "Hey, Ashley. How are—"

"You knew about Karyn," I spat, stomping across to my dresser to dig out my pajamas.

She blinked. "It wasn't—"

I cut her off by slamming a drawer. "Did you know Matt was going to date her, or not?"

"I thought maybe." She frowned. "But things . . . things are a little different for you, so I wasn't sure . . ."

"How could you not have told me? I almost made such a fool of myself!"

Her face was pained. "I guess I hoped, for your sake, that I was wrong," she said quietly.

I sank to the floor and let the tears come. "He looked so happy with her," I said into my hands.

"Ashley . . ."

"It doesn't matter what I do, or what I say, he just doesn't *see* me. Not like that."

Older Me heaved a sigh, but didn't respond. Anger burned in my chest again. How could she be so calm when *everything* was going wrong?

"Ash, can't you see that if he doesn't realize how wonderful you are, that's his problem?"

I rolled my eyes. "You sound like an after-school special."

She shrugged. "So?"

"*So?*" I stabbed a finger toward her. "So, you could have helped me—if not to get him for myself, at least not to get my hopes up!"

She blinked. "I tried. You wouldn't listen."

Not for the first time, I wished I could reach through the stupid mirror and shake her.

"If you'd said to me, 'Ash, don't get excited, he's dating Karyn,' I promise, I would have listened!"

"I didn't know for sure—"

"Take a stab at it next time. I'll cut you some slack if you're wrong, okay? If you can't at least give me a clue, why are you even here?"

She scowled. "I'm here to help you."

"Right."

"Ashley, you can't blame Karyn, or me, or even Matt for this. People do what they want. They love who they love. No one else can change that. It's like with Mom—you can't change the way she is. The only thing you can control is you. You can't let her—or anyone—get under your skin that way."

"Are you kidding me?" I raked my hands through my hair.

34

"I'm getting texts that tell me to kill myself. How can that *not* get under my skin?"

Older Me placed her hand on the mirror, as close as she could come to touching me. She kept her voice to a whisper. "I know. I do. But you have to keep going. You just have to. If you push through this, you'll show them. You'll show them you didn't deserve this."

Those words . . . *you didn't deserve this* . . .

I chewed them over. I wanted to believe them, but I just couldn't.

Older Me kept talking. "You think the way these people treat you is the end of the world. But I can tell you, it isn't what happens to you in your life that destroys you. It's what you do about it."

"Are you trying to say it's my fault everyone—"

"No." Older Me put her hand up to stop me. "I'm saying that you've had crap thrown at you. You can either keep going and prove everyone wrong—show them you didn't deserve to get it in the first place. Or you can roll around in it and think you deserve it, and start acting like you do."

"Is that what you did?"

She leaned closer. "Ashley, if I had the chance to go back and live it again—to be in your shoes—I'd do it in a heartbeat. To learn that I wasn't who they thought I was."

I couldn't look away from her. "But everyone *else* thinks it is me! Even if I believed what you're saying, it wouldn't change what they thought."

"Look, there's nothing I can say that will make this easier." She ran a hand through her hair and looked as tired as I felt. "You just have to keep going. Because . . . because if you can believe that the problem is theirs, you won't end up like me, or Mom. You'll be better. Stronger."

"I don't know . . ." She was telling me to fight. And I was so tired of fighting.

She gave a watery smile. "It's a hard road for us. But maybe you can find an easier path. And if you do, let me know."

I gaped at her. "Really? You're the one who's supposed to have all the answers."

"Ash, I told you, no one has *all* the answers," she said, frowning. "Not even someone who's lived the problems already."

"But you must know."

"Some, Ash. I know *some.*"

"So tell me!" I groaned.

"And lead you down the same path I took? No. No way." She shook her head. Emphatic.

I slumped back onto my bed and the smell of detergent rose from the comforter. "What point is there to having a future self, if your future self won't tell you—"

"I'm here to help you do it better!" she snapped.

I rolled over to glare at her. "So do that!"

"I am!"

We were both silent. She sat at the mirror's surface, visibly panting.

"You don't get it, Ashley. You just don't. And you won't until you're on this side of this stupid glass." She flicked her finger at the mirror.

I swallowed hard. "I don't think—"

"Would you just listen, for once? Please!" She took a slow

breath. When she spoke again, her voice was softer. "Somehow . . . somehow I'm here. And even if it doesn't feel like it, I am helping. As far as I'm concerned, it's my job to help you avoid the mistakes I made. Everything I tell you, or don't tell you, is intended to help you make better decisions than I did when I was your age." She stopped, biting her lip. "When you're in my shoes, you can make different choices, if you want. But I'm doing the best I can."

I hated those reminders that she'd once been on this side of the mirror. She'd only admitted it once before—that she had an Older Me when she was a teenager, too. But if she was reluctant to talk about my future, she flatly refused to talk about her own past. As much as I wanted to know everything, part of me understood. I'd hate being her, having to recount—to *relive*—the most humiliating moments of my life. But I'd do it. I knew if I was ever on that side of the mirror, I'd tell my younger self everything. Warn her about everything.

Suddenly, she cursed under her breath and her face paled.

"They heard me." Her voice caught.

"Your roommates?"

She nodded, blinking rapidly. "I'm sorry, Ashley. We're going to have to finish this later."

A moment later, the only reflection in the mirror was my own.

CHAPTER SIX

DOC HAS BEEN scribbling frantically on his notepad while I talk. I hate that thing. Every therapist here has one and they write things about me without telling me what they're writing. Sometimes I fantasize about reading it. But then I think, *I probably don't want to hear what they have to say.*

Finally he looks up. "Your other self was very ingrained in your life, wasn't she?"

He's finally talking about it. About *her.* If only I could figure out what he was aiming for. "How do you mean?"

"I mean, you spoke to her about everything—you were very open."

I snort. "When she'd let me. We didn't always see eye to eye, and sometimes it was easier to just not talk about something than to keep arguing. Hard to escape your own reflection."

Doc nods slowly. "Were you always honest with your other self?"

If I'd been taking a drink at that moment, it would have flown out of my nose. As it was, I choked on my own spit and had to blink back tears. "Wha-what?"

Doc's face is blank, but he won't break eye contact. "I think you heard me, Ashley. I want to know if you were always honest with your other self—if you ever lied, or exaggerated, or deceived her."

I keep blinking and hope he'll think it's because my eyes are still watering from the coughing. "Um . . . no. But I wasn't *always* honest with anyone back then. There were things I just didn't want to get into."

"Like what?"

"Like my problems."

Doc's lips tip down at the corners and he makes another note. "You didn't want to talk about the things that were causing you problems? Why not?"

I try hard not to roll my eyes and instead, with one finger, I follow the thread of the pattern on the arm of my chair.

"The only person I could open up to was Matt. And if I had, he would have just tried to fix me."

"And that's a problem because . . . ?"

"Because I'm not the one who needs to be fixed."

He looks like he'll argue with me, but I plow on before he can speak.

I waited to leave my house until the last possible second Monday morning, hoping Matt would pick me up. I had no idea if he'd tried to call since I'd killed my phone. He certainly hadn't called our home line. It was raining, but Mom was sleeping in—Mondays were her day off—so I walked the fifteen minutes to school in a steady drizzle, cursing my hair for never being able to decide if it was straight or not.

By the time I pushed through the doors to get inside, I wasn't the only one who looked like a mess. The main hallway was steamy and damp. Wet feet made muddy tracks away from each door, and everyone's raindrop-frosted hair glittered under the fluorescent lights.

It was one of those mornings when I just couldn't focus. In second period trig, Mr. Henderson stood in front of the board in the same gray slacks he always wore, waving his marker in the air. My classmates whispered, shuffling to lean into each other whenever he turned his back. But I was having trouble seeing anything except Matt's face when he looked down at Karyn.

That is, until there was a scuffle at the seats next to me and someone whispered a frantic, "No!"

A folded piece of paper fluttered over my elbow, landing on the desktop in front of me.

I looked around. Brooke was two desks over, Terese hovering—as always—in the seat behind her. Brooke stared intently at Mr. Henderson, nodding along with his lecture. Her glossy black hair fell in gentle waves just past her shoulders—no frizz for her. But her cheeks were tense and her lips kept twitching. Terese had ducked her blond head and was examining the textbook in front of her like she actually understood what it said.

I slowly unfolded the paper, bracing myself for whatever it was and willing myself not to react.

The paper was white with blue lines—torn from someone's notebook. It had been folded in four, flattened, and refolded haphazardly a couple of times.

Math Tutoring was scrawled across the top. I held my breath and looked at the rest.

Someone had drawn two stick figures. Going by the short hair and lack of any distinguishable features, the first—seated in a chair—was male. The name *Mr. Henderson* was written above it.

The second stick figure knelt between what would have been the knees of the first. This one had on a skirt and messy hair drawn in with red pen. *Ashley Watson* was emblazoned on the paper, with an arrow pointing at my stick-figure head, which was bent forward into "Mr. Henderson's" lap.

Excellent. Freaking wonderful.

Word got around quick. A couple of condoms landed on my desk during third period, accompanied by giggles and notes like "Trig Homework." I ignored them, then hung around at the end of class, letting everyone else leave first. No point inviting further humiliation. Once the hallways stopped echoing with voices, I walked in virtual isolation to the creative wing. When I finally made it into the art room, Mrs. Driley gave me a pointed look, but didn't break stride. She was lecturing. Her favorite.

Matt's eyebrows slid up as I dropped into the seat next to him. Avoiding his gaze, I pulled out my notebook and pencils, leaned my head on one hand, and started to doodle. In half a minute, a hunched figure came to life on the paper—bent forward over a desk, with a wicked smile.

Matt nudged my arm. I glanced up, and he was frowning a question at me.

I just kept drawing. But somehow he knew.

A minute later, Matt's hand, holding a pencil, appeared next to mine. He moved it in short, confident swipes, our hands jumping and cutting across the paper in a duet that made my heart ache, because I knew what he was drawing. His hand curved up, above and behind my nameless tormentor. A long, low hill was quickly exaggerated, given ears, flattened against an angular skull, and wide, hateful eyes with dilated vertical pupils.

Teeth and claws came next, jagged and bloodied.

His demon cat pounced, caught in the split second before it drove the bully into the floor and devoured him.

The first time Matt had drawn me the demon cat, I was nine. It was the day after my dad visited. I'd arrived at school that morning already wrung out. At recess, I'd stayed at my desk to draw. My picture was unpracticed and jagged, but it was obviously of a man.

Matt appeared beside me. "Who's that?"

I stopped drawing, but didn't look up.

"My dad," I said.

"He looks mean," Matt said.

I just nodded.

Without another word, Matt picked up my pencil and began to draw. At first I wanted to stop him. But then I saw that the long body and tail leaping through the air had paws. And claws.

That very first demon cat devoured my father, and my bad mood along with it. Since then, it had pounced on teachers who gave me detention, my mother when she was irrational, Dex . . .

Now I rolled my eyes, but I couldn't hide my smile.

Suddenly, Mrs. D clapped her hands. "I want the drawings by next Tuesday. Come see me if you have questions or need help."

The assignment. Right. Probably should have been listening for that.

All around us chairs screeched and voices rose, and Mrs. D appeared at the other side of my table.

"Okay, you two." She noticed the drawing and shook her head. "Perhaps you should try to use your powers for good next time, Matt," she said in a resigned tone.

He gave her his best innocent expression. "We were just—"

Mrs. D held up her hand. "I want you two working on your portfolios. Find a way to fit one of your pieces into this assignment. We don't have any time to waste. In fact, how would you feel about coming in on Saturdays for the rest of the semester, if I were to open up the room for you?"

I closed my mouth and glanced at Matt, who was nodding.

Last week, spending every Saturday with Matt would have sounded like heaven. Now it felt like walking to the gallows. But even as I recoiled from the thought, I knew if I could get into art school—any art school—I'd be free. It didn't have to be the best school if it meant I could leave this hellhole.

"Thanks," I said. "That sounds great."

Matt agreed.

"Excellent," Mrs. D said. "I'll discuss the details with you on Friday. Now, get to work."

Matt and I grabbed our sketchpads and headed to the easel room, a small nook with a steel sink for washing brushes, a dozen bar-height stools stacked in a corner, and easels leaning in neat lines against the wall. One wall was almost completely windows, drenching the space in natural light.

Matt set up immediately, right at the front of the room, his easel tipped to pick up the sunlight. I'd always admired Matt's fearlessness. When I was just starting a piece—and usually getting it wrong—I couldn't stand the thought of someone else *judging* it. I always kept my easels facing the back of the room, preferably a corner, so no one could see what I was doing.

When I finished pulling materials from my cubby, Matt fixed me with a stare. "Are you okay?"

"I'm fine, why?"

"You've been really quiet," he said.

"Didn't sleep well." I flipped through my workbook. Mrs. D had left a project list with my name scrawled on the top. She'd crossed off the pieces I'd already completed.

ASHLEY WATSON

All works should demonstrate a common theme or subject. Use workbooks to plan. Keep all sketches and studies, even for works not included in the final portfolio. Date and sign every page.

Extra credit for works outside these requirements will only be considered once all required elements are complete.

Each portfolio must include:

- ~~Still life~~
- Self-portrait
- ~~Reproduction of a classic artist~~
- A multimedia work
- ~~Use of impressionism~~
- ~~Use of realism~~
- Use of cubism

- Diptych: one panel in style of artist's choice, second to reproduce the first in abstract
- Three other works in theme, demonstrating the artist's range

Mrs. D wanted me to start the self-portrait. So far I'd tried twice and hated both efforts so much I'd painted over them. She was already pressing for my next attempt. But with the mood I was in, I'd end up painting roadkill and calling it *My Life*. I did have an idea for the diptych—a two-paneled work. But I had to make a final decision on which picture I would use.

A hand flattened the page I'd been about to turn. "I like that one."

Matt leaned over me, holding the page down. I could feel the heat from his chest on the back of my neck. A blush flooded my face, so I pretended to examine the paper.

It was a planning sketch for a self-portrait. In the foreground I'd drawn myself from behind, from the shoulders up, looking in a mirror. In the reflection, I had crossed arms. Older Me stood behind me with a half smile. Mom hunched deeper in the background, scowling.

I cringed. Mom had caught me drawing it a couple of months earlier and freaked out. I got a huge lecture about how she thought I'd "finished that phase." We fought over whether or not I was mental, then never talked about it again. Why had I left it in my workbook?

"Um, it's just something I'm playing with."

Matt stood up straight, his fingers brushing my shoulder. "It looks awesome—like you're seeing yourself as you age, right? That last one makes you look like your mom." He chuckled.

I forced a laugh, nodded, and turned the page, praying he didn't notice my shaking hand.

He buried his hands in his pockets and swallowed audibly. "Are you mad about Karyn?"

I looked up. He smiled, but it didn't reach his eyes.

Yes. "No. I'm just trying to figure out what picture to do next."

One of his brows rose in trademark skepticism, but I pretended to be dense. "What?"

He shook his head. "There's something I want to talk to you about."

Again? I was coming to dread those words out of his mouth. "What's that?" I unzipped my pencil bag, my heart thumping.

"I've been thinking," he said carefully.

"Always dangerous," I muttered.

He grinned, but shook his head. "Ashley, I think you should spend more time with me and Karyn . . . and everyone else. Especially Finn. I feel like everyone's holding on to ancient history. But if we all just hung out, I know it'd be okay again. What do you think?"

My pencils clattered to the floor. I slid off the stool and knelt to pick them up, my knees shaking.

"I think that's about the stupidest thing you've ever said," I said, placing the pencils back in the bag.

"Hear me out." Matt bent down to help. "If we give them a chance to talk to you when it's not pressured—when you're relaxed—they'll find out they like you. You're way more interesting than most of the girls we hang out with."

Except Karyn, apparently. Anger fizzed in my chest. I bit my lip to keep the comment inside. "It won't work."

"Sure it will," he said hopefully, as we both stood. "Finn's having a party at his place on Friday. You should come."

Party at Finn's place? Right. Sure.

"So?" Matt said, leaning in close, one hand hooked around the top of my easel.

"So, what?"

"C'mon, Ash. I'm trying to help you."

"Well, don't." I couldn't keep the anger out of my voice.

"Why not?" Confusion marred his features.

I grabbed my workbook and tossed it onto my bag with a *whump*, unable to believe he was so dense. "You tell your friends to talk to me, and while you're there they will. But as soon as your back is turned, they'll be rolling their eyes—at me *and* you."

Matt stared at me. "I'm telling you, you're wrong. And Karyn agrees with me."

I almost threw my pencils at him. "Well, clearly I misjudged the situation. I guess I should think about it, then," I said scathingly.

"That's all I ask." Matt brightened, the sarcasm apparently lost on him. "You're always complaining that your life is boring, so come hang out. They'll get to know you, and you can . . . I don't know, make more friends, or something? We'll get to spend more time together . . ."

His obliviousness was astounding.

"Ash, please. I think . . . Things with Karyn are really cool. It would be awesome if we could all hang out. And the other guys are with us all the time. So, give it a shot. For me?"

His face was so close that I could have kissed his soft, broad lips and run my hands through his hair. Instead, I saw Karyn doing those things and Matt, eyes closed and smiling with the pleasure of it.

I turned back to my canvas, and for the first time in my life, I told Matt what he didn't want to hear.

"No."

CHAPTER SEVEN

DOC WATCHES ME like a cat watches a sparrow. "Why wouldn't you accept Matt's help?" he asks carefully.

"Weren't you listening? It would have made my problems worse. And I didn't want to be a charity case. I didn't want to turn Matt into a target, which is what would have happened."

"How so?"

I cross my legs and wonder how to explain it. "Clearly you were never bullied."

"Let's assume not."

Right. "Well, it's hell, okay? And it isn't just hell on you, it's hell on anyone who's brave enough to admit they don't hate you. I lost almost every single friend I had in the space of a week when I was thirteen—not because what I'd done was so awful. But because the people everyone *wanted* to be friends with decided it was awful, and they'd crucify anyone who didn't agree. So, sure, Brooke and Terese back off because they're pissed. But all the other girls? First, they're turning down hallways to avoid me, then they're joining the whispers in class, because if they didn't, Brooke and Terese, and Finn and Eli would be chewing pieces out of them almost as badly as they had out of me."

When I stop talking, I realize I am breathing too quickly. I pause to regain control.

Doc waits, his hand resting on his notebook. "But Matt continued to be your friend? Why didn't they turn on him earlier?"

"It's one thing for Matt to have hung out with me on his own," I explain. "Bringing me into the group was an entirely different situation."

"How so?" Doc asks.

"Just trust me," I say quietly. "In the end, I learned that it was better to protect the people around me from whatever firestorm I was in. High schoolers don't really appreciate being dragged into social leprosy just because they let you borrow a pencil. And when push comes to shove, most kids will turn on you to save themselves."

He chews on this for a moment. "So, you wouldn't accept Matt's help in case his friends turned on him. Instead, you did what?"

"Instead, I planned to stay under the radar. Avoid those people as much as possible."

"And did that work?" he prompts.

I drop my head back and stare at the ceiling tiles. "No."

I can hear him shuffling papers, but I don't look down.

"Why not?"

I rub my face. Remembering makes my skin feel too tight. "It all comes back to that damn letter," I murmur.

* * *

I thought Matt would forget the conversation about me making nice with his friends, but I was wrong. All week, he pestered me to come with him and Karyn to the rec room. By Friday, I was about ready to scream. So at morning break, instead of heading to my locker and the inevitable argument with him, I turned the corner in the hall and pushed out the door to the courtyard.

The library was a huge, old building, completely separate from the main school building. Hardly anyone went there, and that Friday, it was empty. It was a beautiful day after almost a week of rain—even the nerds were outside.

Upstairs there were fewer windows and a lot more shelves. I hid in my favorite section, the one with all the historical commentaries, where the books were leather bound, the old kind with gilded spines and vintage lithographs. I'd just unzipped my bag to get out my sketchbook when I heard a giggle.

Footsteps sounded lightly on the carpet, coming from the direction of the stairs.

More giggling.

"*Shhhhhh . . .*"

A moment later, Karyn stepped partially into view.

She had her back to me and was half hidden by one of the floor-to-ceiling shelves. A large hand curved around her waist, and I froze. Karyn went in for the kiss and made a tiny noise that threatened to bring up everything I'd eaten in a week.

I was watching Matt and Karyn make out.

My heart thumped against my ribs. I couldn't breathe. But when Karyn pulled Matt closer to her, I realized it wasn't Matt at all

It was Finn.

I gasped audibly, and they broke apart like rubber bands under tension. They turned to look at me, horror washing over their faces.

Oddly, I was reminded of the moment Dad walked out on Mom and me—how, in some ways, it was great, because I wouldn't have to worry about them fighting anymore, or Mom blaming me for his moods. But there was also the sick feeling that came with knowing it was wrong and would never sit easily.

Finn was almost vibrating with anger. "You stupid b—"

"Actually, I'm pretty sure I'm the most intelligent person in this room," I said. "If I was making out with my best friend's girlfriend, I'd do it in the privacy of my own home."

While Karyn looked on in stunned silence, Finn strode forward and grabbed my elbow. "If you say one word . . ."

My heart pounded against my ribs, but there was a calm that came with knowing that, for once, I had the upper hand. "Let. Me. *Go.*"

He didn't move. For the span of three breaths, we just stood there, locked in place. There was a strange kind of honesty in the moment. I felt great. Certain. *Solid.* I didn't care if Finn finally cut loose and pummeled me senseless. When I regained consciousness, I was still going to tell Matt that his girlfriend was cheating on him with his second-best friend.

But then the corners of Finn's lips tipped up. His shoulders relaxed, and his fingers loosened on my arm. "Go ahead, do it."

Karyn let out a strangled cry.

I smiled. "I will."

"He'll never believe you," Finn said.

"Wanna bet?" I reached for the strap of my bag where it was slumped on the floor.

"Sure. But just keep in mind, if you tell him, I'll show him this." I looked up as Finn pulled something out of his satchel: a piece of white, lined paper, folded into a rectangle. With the name *Matt* written on it.

In my handwriting.

My purse scattering in the parking lot on Friday night. Finn kneeling to "help" . . .

I gasped and grabbed for the note, but Finn yanked it away easily. He held it over his head, far above my reach. Karyn moved to stand behind him. But her eyes were wide and her hands were clasped together so tightly her knuckles had turned white.

"Finn . . . *please* . . ." I knew I sounded pitiful, but I didn't care. If Matt ever saw that. If *anyone* ever saw it . . .

He clucked his tongue. "Tsk, tsk, C. Sloppy leaving your *precious* letter sitting around where anyone could find it."

"Who else has seen it?" I demanded, my voice shaking.

"Only Karyn. For now."

I glanced at her. Her face was pale but the ghost of a smile played on her lips.

"You know, it's funny. I thought about just e-mailing it out so everyone would know how sick you are in the head. Glad I kept it for a rainy day." Finn stepped right up to me then, leaned in so I could smell the peppermint on his breath. "You and your ugly face already screwed up my life once. I'm not letting you do it again. You say one word to Matt, and he'll find this in his locker."

I blinked. "But . . . but you could do that anyway."

"I guess that's a risk you'll have to take," he snapped.

I felt like I was being torn in two. Matt *needed* to know about this. But if that letter got out, my life would be over . . .

I had to get it back. No matter what.

Finn tucked the letter back into his bag. "Something to keep in mind." He winked, then turned away, taking Karyn with him. He didn't look back, but Karyn glanced at me over her shoulder, a mix of anger and unease on her face.

I should have said something. Should have told them what I thought of them both. But instead, I stood glued to the site of what was supposed to be the turning point, the place where everyone—where *Matt*—should have learned the truth about who Finn and Karyn really were. So why was I the one left staring at the ground, wishing I'd done things differently?

CHAPTER EIGHT

DOC FROWNS AND makes another note on his pad, then stares out from behind those suspiciously clear lenses.

"What?" I say, harder than I intend.

He glances at his notes, then back at me. "Did you consider telling Matt about the letter?"

I cough to cover a cold laugh. "*No.*"

"Why not?"

I hope the expression on my face conveys my incredulousness. "Because this isn't the movies, Doc. In the real world, when a seventeen-year-old guy gets a *love letter* from his best friend, he doesn't suddenly decide to love her back. He runs screaming."

"Possibly," Doc concedes. "Or perhaps he learns something about who his real friends are."

Whatever.

"So not telling him . . . did it make things better?"

I cross my arms, my scars burning beneath my hoodie. "Maybe for a second."

But then, as usual, things just got worse.

* * *

I managed to avoid talking to Matt in art that day, but he followed me to my locker at lunch. I tensed, worried that the truth was written all over my face. I'd spent what was left of our morning break in a handicapped bathroom calling for Older Me, desperate to ask her what I should do. But she never came.

Matt leaned up against the locker next to mine and didn't even say hi. "No more excuses, Ash. You're coming to the rec room with us."

"*No*," I said, loudly enough to turn several heads. I pulled a book I didn't need out of my locker to give myself something to look at. "Are you cracked?"

"Don't you trust me, Ash?" he said quietly.

He tipped his head down so we were almost nose to nose. His brilliant blue eyes locked on mine, and my heart sank. He trusted me. And I was keeping a secret that hurt *him*. My resolve to get the letter back before I told him crumbled. Whether he read my letter or found out I'd lied about his girlfriend cheating, he was going to hate me anyway. Maybe it was better to tell him the truth and pay the consequences. At least then Finn and Karyn would pay too, right?

I cursed Older Me for disappearing just when I was in crisis.

"Look, Matt," I started. But before I could say another word, the silver piglet arrived and launched herself into his arms.

"There you are!" she squealed. "What are you guys talking about?" Her voice was bright, but she kept darting wary looks at me.

"Hey, babe." Matt's gentle tone, combined with the way he put his arm around her, clearly reassured her that I hadn't told.

Her face lit up, and Matt took her hand as we turned together down the hallway. She clutched his arm like it was a life preserver.

"Ashley's going to start coming to rec room with us," he said, like she might get excited about it.

"I never said that," I muttered, as we passed out of the English wing and into the main hallway.

"Don't make her do something she'll hate, Matt," Karyn said casually. "I wouldn't want to walk into a room where no one wanted me, either. I don't blame you, Ashley."

Oh, no freaking *way*.

Game on.

"Actually, maybe I *will* try it." I cut Karyn a glance. "Once."

"You will? Awesome!" Matt high-fived me. Karyn stiffened and had to rearrange her face when he looked at her. "What made you change your mind?"

I shrugged. "I had this big realization lately that made me rethink everything."

"What was that?" Matt looked genuinely interested. Karyn glared at me.

I glared back. "Nothing too interesting. I guess I just realized that no one else is better than me, you know? So why should I let them win? It kind of feels like if I do, I'm helping them, well, *cheat*."

Matt frowned, and Karyn sucked her cheeks in.

"At the game of life," I added.

Matt looked puzzled.

"Karyn knows what I mean," I told him, gesturing toward her.

"You two talked?" He looked down at Karyn, a hopeful smile

on his face that made me love him and want to punch him in the nuts at the same time.

Karyn's gaze—hot enough to weld steel—slid from my face to meet his, morphing into self-conscious adoration in the process.

After a beat she replied, "Only for a minute," then blinked prettily. She sounded, of all things, *humble*.

I seethed. How did she *do* that?

When we reached the rec room, Matt's phone buzzed, chirping the opening beats of "She's So Honey." I was the only person who knew that was the ringtone he gave his mom. He'd once admitted he was embarrassed that she called him after practice all the time, so he gave her a ringtone the team would think came from a girl.

"I've gotta take this," he said without a smile. I noticed he didn't tell Karyn who it was. "You guys go in. I'll be there in a sec."

I opened my mouth to say I'd wait, but he'd already turned his back and was striding down the hall.

Karyn peered at me expectantly. "Well? Are you coming?" The half smile told me she didn't think I'd do it without Matt. And I definitely didn't want to. Then again, the little chat with Karyn had given me a taste for torture. Maybe this was my chance to make Finn squirm, too.

"After you," I said.

"Oh, no, I insist." She stepped back to give me a clear pathway to the door and folded her arms.

I took a deep breath and turned the handle.

I'd only been in the rec room twice before. The carpet was threadbare and the faded furniture looked like the early nineties got drunk and threw up. Kind of smelled that way, too. The blue walls had faded to almost-gray behind a long, low mirror and several motivational posters—most of which had been altered. My favorite: REFUSE TO BE ROADKILL! DON'T GET IN A CAR WITH A DRUNK DRIVER. Underneath someone had scrawled *Take a few pills and fly home instead.*

Cam O'Neal, the basketball center, was flopped on a bean-bag, his long legs stretching across the floor. Brooke and Terese sat on a love seat on either side of Eli, who was fiddling with his lucky necklace. Karyn made a beeline for the long couch and plopped down next to Finn, then looked straight at me.

I had to hand it to her, she had lady-balls.

"Take a picture, C." Finn sneered.

Heat rose in my cheeks. I was sorely aware that the volume in the room had dropped. Brooke exchanged a questioning look with Karyn, who rolled her eyes. I shuffled toward an empty chair. The old vinyl was split and it looked like it might give way if you sat down too fast, but it was set slightly apart by a coffee table on one side and a magazine holder on the other. Perfect. I settled myself in the old chair carefully and pulled a browning banana from my bag, letting the conversation pick up and swirl around me.

". . . should have seen it man, it was a thing of beauty."

". . . and then she said—you won't believe this!—she said *I* was the one who needed to go on a diet!"

". . . McPherson is going to kill me. He's already given me an extension once . . ."

". . . it's like she's *practicing*." That was Karyn's voice.

I paused halfway through taking a bite of the banana.

"Yeah, or advertising." Finn laughed.

I looked over and met Finn's flinty gaze. Then I bit off the banana, hard.

Finn winced and grabbed his crotch. "Oh, bad idea, C. No one wants your *teeth* involved."

Several chuckles rose from those seated nearby.

"Should have told that to the chick who circumcised you, Finn," I snap.

A chorus of "*Oooooo*" went up in the room, along with mocking laughter. Finn threw his arm along the back of the couch—behind Karyn—and looked like he was about to say something else. But then, Matt walked in and dropped into the seat next to Karyn, still staring at his phone. He put his arm on the couch behind her shoulders, just as Finn yanked his back to his side.

Karyn wiggled closer so she was practically in Matt's lap. The banana turned to sawdust in my mouth.

Matt leaned forward. "So, Finn, are we on for tonight?"

"Yep." Finn nodded. "Mom and Dad headed out this morning. Keg's arriving at seven."

"You're coming, right, Ashley?" Matt said.

Karyn inhaled sharply. Finn snapped his head around to look at Matt. Matt looked back, expressionless.

"To Finn's house?" I said, my voice climbing. Matt nodded. "I don't think . . ."

"Don't you think she should come, guys? Karyn?" Matt prompted.

"Yeah, Ashley," Karyn said through clenched teeth. "You should definitely come."

Finn looked at her like she'd grown a third head.

"Um . . ." I was about to say *no freaking way*, when it occurred to me: This could be the perfect chance to get the letter back. Finn's parties were notorious. Surely, in that kind of chaos, I could find five minutes to search his room?

"Okay, then. You convinced me!" I said brightly. And despite the twist of fear, it was funny to watch the entire room go still.

Geez, people. I'm unpopular. Not an alien life-form.

Finn slumped back in his seat. The little muscles at the back of his jaw thumped like arteries on overload. His chin was shoved forward and he stared at me with an edge that made the hair on the back of my neck stand up.

Matt smiled. "Great. We can give you a ride. Right, Kar?" Matt nudged her.

"Right!" She made it sound like a swearword.

"Cool," I said.

"Excellent," Finn muttered.

The bell rang, and everyone got to their feet. Brooke stomped on my bag as she huffed across the room toward the door. Of course.

"Sooo-rry," she sang without looking back. Matt and Karyn left together, hand in hand. Finn wasn't far behind. I let Eli and Cam pass, then pulled my bag over my shoulder and prepared to enter the fray out in the hallway.

"Are you suicidal? *Finn's* house?"

The voice was so unexpected that at first I thought someone was still in the room with me. But when I spun around, I saw Older Me in the mirror behind the couch, staring at me like I'd just decided to pickle small children. Her face was pale, and there were dark smudges under her eyes.

I glanced around to make sure I was alone, then whispered, "Matt will be there. It'll be fine."

Her expression said otherwise, but I didn't have time to argue. I exited the room with a grim smile.

She was right. It was a huge risk. This could all end very, very badly.

Or, for once, I just might win.

CHAPTER NINE

"IF YOUR OLDER self told you not to go to a party, why didn't you listen?" Doc asks, without looking up from his notes.

Duh. "I had to get the letter back. I couldn't let Finn use it to turn Matt against me."

"Yet, your older self—"

"Wasn't always what I would call *forthcoming*," I mutter.

Doc tips his head. "So, then, wouldn't it have made more sense to listen to what advice she gave?"

How can I answer that without giving too much away?

"Here's the thing, Doc. If my life—my *situation*—has taught me anything, it's that it doesn't matter who's giving advice—or even what advice they give. What matters is how much you trust them."

Doc's brow furrows. "You didn't trust your other self?"

I scoff. "More like my other self didn't trust me."

"Interesting."

For a moment the only sound in the room is his pen rolling across the paper. But then he drops it and looks up, as if something has just occurred to him.

He watches me until I start to wonder if I've ruined everything. "So, given everything that has passed, and knowing everything you know now, if you could go back to that day, what would you have done differently?"

I sit, silent.

What would *I* have done? That's easy: I wouldn't have gone.

Finn lived just outside town, in an imposing stone structure with pointed eaves that had always made me feel small and messy. Fairy lights pricked the gathering dark, strung through the trees and bushes lining the house. The front door was wide open, and thumping bass and the babble of voices drifted into the gray light of dusk.

Matt parked on the grass just across from the door. He ran around to open both Karyn's door and mine at the same time. But it was her hand he took to walk toward the house. I reluctantly followed them, feeling like the puppy Eli had accused me of being.

Being inside Finn's at-once-familiar-yet-strange house took me back to when I was twelve, when Matt, Finn, and I would hang out together. The entryway still smelled like Mrs. Patton's favorite cinnamon candles, and there was a framed photo of Finn on the wall with a hairline crack down the glass; the boys had knocked it over one time when they were wrestling. But some things had changed, too—like the stairs. They were hardwood now, and the walls of the living room were a soft blue.

"Matt, you've gotta come see this!" called Eli, who wore his lucky necklace over a gray T-shirt emblazoned with the words GOT MILF? He motioned Matt and Karyn into the living room, where music blared and several of Matt's teammates stood huddled around a phone, no doubt watching someone make an ass out of themselves on YouTube. Opposite the living room was a farm-style kitchen, where Finn stood messing with a keg. Layla Jameson and Caitlin Grace stood on either side of him, red Solo cups in hand, touching his arms and laughing at everything he said.

Then Finn looked up, saw me, and sneered. "Hey, C."

Layla smirked and pulled out her phone. She was the unofficial class paparazzo. No doubt my face had just appeared on every form of social media known to man, with the hashtag #losercrasher.

I shoved past them, already feeling fragile and questioning the wisdom of this plan. How was I going to survive tonight long enough to find the letter?

Suddenly, there was a hand on my shoulder. I whirled around, ready to do battle, but I found myself facing Samuel Oster, a lanky, curly haired junior with a sweet smile. He'd been an outcast in middle school, when I wasn't. But he'd had his growth spurt before freshman year, and now, despite still looking like a colt who hadn't grown into its legs, he was part of the football team.

He looked at me with a cautious smile. "If you want, I can get you a drink when I'm up there?" He tipped his head toward the keg.

"Oh, I don't need—" A great burst of laughter from where Finn stood startled me. I jerked to look. By the time I turned back, Sam was already walking away. "Sorry, Sam. I just—"

"No worries." He pushed up next to his teammates. One of them said something that made him grin. I stared at his back, wondering if I should have said thanks, or whether it was a lucky escape from someone trying to trap me. Again. I'd learned the hard way not to trust any of my classmates when they were being nice.

Older Me's voice rose from a little mirror hanging off the refrigerator. "Don't scowl like that. Sam is sweet. He probably remembers what it's like to be at your first party with these people." I glanced over as she shook her head.

"He caught me off guard," I said, trying not to move my lips.

"If you're going to be here," she said, "you should make the most of anyone being friendly. Just a thought."

I wanted to snap at her to keep her thoughts to herself, but suddenly Sam was in front of me again, a red cup in each hand.

"Last chance for liquid courage?" he said.

This time, I returned his smile and thanked him, taking the offered cup.

He shrugged and downed half his beer in one go. "Just stay under the radar. You'll be fine." He clapped me on the shoulder and headed back to the keg before wandering across to the living room.

I sipped the beer carefully. It tasted fine, and the fizz in my chest was comforting.

"Not what I meant," Older Me sighed from the mirror. But I ignored her.

Ten minutes later, having drained and refilled my cup, I headed into the living room. The beer was already settling in a tight, not entirely unpleasant feeling in my stomach and a decidedly floaty feeling in my head. My fear and anxiety waned with each sip.

"Where have you been, Ash?" Matt asked, coming up to me, his arm around Karyn's shoulders. "You disappeared the second we got here."

"Just got a beer," I said, holding up my cup.

"I could use one of those. You want a drink, Matt?" Karyn said, wiggling out from under his grip.

Just then, Finn shoved past us, bumping my arm. Beer sloshed over the side of my cup and straight onto my chest.

"Oh, sh—!" I jumped back, brushing·frantically at the sticky liquid on my chest.

"Drunk already, dude?" Matt said, grabbing some napkins off a nearby table and handing them to me.

"What? Oh, *sorry*, Ashley! I didn't see you there." Finn stood to my right, a broad smile on his face. Beside him, Karyn struggled not to laugh.

I glared at him and patted at my shirt, but it was useless. I'd worn a white tank top under a crop cut, deep V-neck sweater. My white top had plastered itself to my chest and my bra was already showing through the fabric. Finn's eyebrows rose when I brushed at it again. Even Matt glanced down from my face to my chest.

"You might want to get that seen to," Finn drawled. "Or not. Maybe you'll be more popular tonight than I thought."

"Finn!" Matt barked.

"What? I'm just joking."

"Not funny, man," Matt warned.

"I'll be back in a minute," I muttered, glowering at Finn, who was making no effort to hide his laughter.

As I turned to find the bathroom, I saw Matt pull Finn aside.

Finn wasn't laughing anymore. I could feel him watching until I was around the corner.

Pushing through the growing crowd in the hallway, ignoring the stares and laughs as I went, I made it to the stairs and ran up. There was a large bathroom just a couple of doors from the top. Mrs. Patton had renovated since I was last in the house. The bathroom now had two sinks, a mirror that spanned the entire wall, and a shower large enough to house a party of its own.

I locked the door behind me, yanked my sweater off, and turned to assess the damage in the mirror. My top was a disaster. The white cotton looked like it had been peed on, and my lacy white bra was showing through, somehow making me look *more* naked instead of less.

Suddenly, Older Me appeared next to my bedraggled reflection. "I can't believe you're here. Have you completely lost your mind?" She stood in the mirror, arms crossed under her ample boobs, staring at me like I was insane.

I fixed her with a pointed look. "You tell me."

"Ashley . . . ," Older Me started. But the tone in her voice was gentle. Pitying. "You should go home. Now."

I shook my head. "I can't."

Her frown deepened. "Why not? What aren't you telling me?"

"Nothing! It's just . . ." Since I couldn't tell her about the letter without getting a huge lecture, I settled for the next best truth. "Karyn's *cheating* on him! I can't just let her get away with it and pretend it's nothing."

She took in my soaked shirt and the determined expression on my face and shook her head. "So tell him. Don't put yourself in situations like this on the off chance you'll catch her doing something. It's not like she's going to pin Finn against a wall when Matt's in the room."

"I know . . . but . . ." Tears bit at my throat. I swallowed them, holding on to the fuzzy warmth from the alcohol that was beginning to spread from my chest into my arms and legs.

With a frustrated growl, I grabbed my sweater from the floor where I'd dropped it. But when I put it on, it hung open at the front since it only had one button. Glimpses of my bra still peeked through. I could walk through the house holding it closed, but that seemed like a recipe for trouble. My head spun a little as I dug through the drawers that lined the countertop, then pushed aside some old makeup tubes. There was a small safety pin I could use to keep the front of my sweater closed.

"Where are you going?" Older Me asked urgently.

"Calm down. I'm leaving." *Soon.* Once I got the letter.

There was no one in the hall outside the bathroom. Music and voices drifted up the stairs, but so far everyone was too sober to have spread out. If I was lucky, I had a good half hour before anyone started looking for privacy.

With one last glance at the stairs to make sure no one was on their way up, I made my way down the hall to Finn's room. His door was closed, but when I tried the knob, it turned.

Finn obviously figured he'd be bringing someone up here. Apart from his school bag on the chair at his desk, the room was spotless. His massive bed had been made with crisp corners. He'd closed the curtains, but left a lamp on next to the bed.

I closed the door noiselessly, then darted across the room to his desk. I tried his bag first, but the leather satchel held only a few pens, his tablet, and a couple of books. No loose papers at all. Doing my best to leave everything as it was, I rifled through the long drawer in the middle of his desk. It was crammed with trash, pens, and broken pencils. But the second drawer down on the right . . .

As soon as I opened it, I knew that was my best shot. It was full of printed e-mails, notes, cards—obviously the spot he threw everything girls gave him. And judging by the piles in here, there had been a lot of girls in his life. I pulled out stacks of paper and printed photographs, flipped through them, looking for anything with my handwriting. When I'd removed most of the contents of the drawer, I discovered the little box in the back.

It was nothing important looking—an old, oversize match-box. But right on the top, over a pile of notes, was my letter. I grabbed it out with a little cry and was about to shove the box back and get out of there, when I noticed what had lain beneath it. It was a blue Post-it. In pink pen in a loopy hand with a heart to dot the *i*, was written:

next saturday at 4 at our spot. M has practice.
don't be late.
xoxo

It was from Karyn.
Proof.
My heart beating a rapid tattoo, I grabbed the Post-it and slid the box back into its place, then scrambled to pick up the piles of envelopes and notes and pictures, returning them to the drawer, praying I'd gotten the order right. My fingers felt slightly numb as the alcohol seeped into my bloodstream. It was harder than it

should have been to grab the piles. I was just shutting the drawer when I heard a click behind me and whirled, cursing.

Finn stood just inside, his upper lip pinched into a sneer.

"Hey, C. Whatcha doing?" Then he slammed the door behind him and flipped the lock.

CHAPTER TEN

"JUST TAKING WHAT belongs to me," I said, standing on wobbly legs, the letter and note clutched in my fist.

Finn covered the space between us in three long strides, grabbing for the letter. I held it behind me and shoved him off with my free hand. "Back off, Finn!"

"You little thief!"

I barked a laugh. "*I'm* the thief? You stole it from me!"

His gaze trailed down my body.

"You know, I liked you when we were twelve. You could have been normal. Like, with friends. What happened to you?"

I put my hands on my hips. "If being normal means cheating on my best friend, I'll stick with what I've got."

Finn scowled and leaned in close to my face. "Cheating, lying, what's the difference? Doesn't seem to bother you." His breath was hot on my cheek, washing me in the tang of half-digested beer. "You think Matt would ever look at a fatty like you when he's getting *everything* from the hottest girl in our class?"

Matt and Karyn were sleeping together? No, no. Please, God, no.

"I wrote it before I knew he was with Karyn." Beer churned in my stomach, threatening to push its way back up.

Finn scoffed. "So? I can't believe you thought he actually liked you. Matt feels sorry for you. He's only nice to you because his parents told him it would be wrong to dump you when you don't have any other friends. He laughs about you when you aren't there. Did you know that?"

"No. He doesn't." Tears pressed at the backs of my eyes. I swallowed the lump and shook my head to push them away. "Finn—"

"Give me the letter," he snapped.

"No!"

The rest happened fast. He grabbed me by both arms and threw me sideways. I landed heavily against the edge of the bed and the whole room tilted. Both his long arms circled me, pinning me as he tried to grab the letter. I struggled, but he just clamped his arms around mine.

"Finn! Let me go!"

Finn grunted and his hand closed on mine. I twisted onto my side, pulling the hand with the letter under me, even as he wrestled for it. I was trying to turn over, but he was too strong, and the beer had made me slow.

"You're so predictable, C," he said through gritted teeth.

"Let me go!"

"Not until you give me that letter." He used his weight to pin me even harder.

"Finn, *please*." My breath came in pants, echoing the pounding of my pulse. The feeling of his fingers on my skin turned my stomach. Then one of his hands closed over mine. Over the letter.

"No!" I cried and twisted hard. Finn grunted, but I ended up on my belly, the hand with the letter pinned under me. Our struggle became a gross parody, him behind me, pressed into my backside, me bucking beneath him. Finally I managed to flip onto my back, but I still couldn't get free.

"It's never going to happen, C," he hissed in my ear, shifting his weight just slightly, to release one of his hands. "I'm stronger than you. And faster. Not to mention prettier." He snorted.

"Let me go!"

"Although, I don't have *those*," he said silkily. Finn's finger traced a line from my collarbone, down my sternum, dipping into the middle of my bra. My sweater pulled wide, the pin stretched almost to the breaking point by our struggles. The middle of my bra was clearly visible, and the tops of my breasts rose out of the fabric.

"Get your hands off me!" I screamed and bucked again, suddenly hyperaware of his greater strength, his hateful smile, how he would do *anything* to win.

The door clicked, then thumped.

"Hel—!" I tried to scream, but Finn's mouth came down on mine to muffle it.

I panicked and twisted, brought both my hands up to shove at his chest.

And just like that, he grabbed the letter and pulled it from my grip.

"Yes!" He sprung off me and took two steps back, leaving me sprawled against his bed, sagging almost to the floor before

I caught my own weight. My head spun and I sucked in a huge breath, ready to scream again. But the door jiggled and a high voice rose behind it.

"Finn? You in there?"

It wasn't Karyn. Must have been one of the girls hanging off him at the keg.

Finn glanced at the door, but didn't respond. Just ran a hand through his hair and waved the letter at me.

"Better get moving, C. I'd hate to have to tell everyone you got drunk and attacked me in my room. Again."

I stood up, my entire body trembling. "Give it back," I said, but it came out on a breath, barely more than a whisper.

"Not. Even. A. Chance," he spit at me. "And after this stunt, I'll be making copies. So even if you do get this back, it won't matter. You say one word, and everyone will *still* know what you are. Who you *want*." Finn flashed a sharp grin and took a step closer. "Did you need some help with your sweater?" he asked, reaching toward me.

"Don't!" I gasped and lunged for the door.

He stopped, laughing, as I fumbled with the knob, turned the lock, threw the door open, and ran out, past a drunk-looking girl who turned when I burst through the door.

"Finn, whaddyer doing with *her?*" rose up behind me as I ran for the stairs.

But Samuel and Josh Levins were just coming up with a couple of sophomore girls whose names I didn't know. They all stopped when they saw me.

Samuel frowned, but before he could speak, Matt elbowed his way to me, Karyn at his side. "Ashley, what's going on?"

I whimpered.

Behind him, Samuel, Josh, and the girls with them kept staring.

I looked at my feet. "Please take me home. Now."

"Are you crying?" Matt took me by the arm. "What's wrong?"

"No-othing," I said. My tongue took too long to make the word.

Karyn sank into one hip. "She looks drunk, Matt," she said in her little-girl voice.

Matt's brow creased. "Are you?" he asked me.

"No!" I snapped, then swallowed hard as nausea rose in my throat. If I threw up, he'd never believe me.

Finn appeared in the hallway then, arms folded. "She's wasted, Matt. I told you this would never work. She's making a complete ass out of herself and it isn't even ten o'clock yet."

Matt said something I didn't catch to Finn—he didn't sound happy—but Finn just shook his head. "I told you, man. She's certifiable."

"Can you just take me home, Matt? Please?" I begged. Then the tears started for real. I couldn't tell Matt the truth about what had happened, not with Finn right there. He'd just whip out the letter.

"Are you going to leave, Matt?" Karyn pouted, flicking her blond hair off her shoulders.

Matt looked torn. "Just to give Ashley a ride home. But I'll be back in half an hour, okay? Sorry, babe."

He leaned forward to kiss her. She jerked back, glaring, first at him, then at me. But then Finn sidled up beside her and threw his arm over her shoulder, and her expression suddenly lightened.

She waved a hand and shook her head, a slow smile spreading on her face. "It's fine. You're right. She's drunk. Get her out of here."

"I am not drunk!" But they all ignored me.

Finn smirked, squeezing Karyn's shoulder. "Yeah, don't worry. I'll make sure your girlfriend doesn't get into too much trouble while you're gone."

"Thanks, man," Matt said. My mouth dropped open. Karyn looked at me and her smile got broader.

Uneasiness swirled over me. "But—"

"Just walk, Ash," Matt muttered, pulling me toward the stairs.

I stopped, yanking back on Matt's grip. "But, Matt, can't you see? She's going to—"

He cursed. "Keep walking!" He shoved his way down the stairs and through the last of the people in the hall, with me trotting in his wake. Then he yanked the door open and stomped across the driveway like he was crushing bugs.

"Matt, seriously, we should go back. Karyn and Finn—"

"Ashley, seriously, it is time for you to *shut up*."

That's when I realized he was seething. Absolutely livid.

It was rare for Matt to lose his temper with me. I caught his arm.

"I'm sorry—"

"*Shut up!*" Matt stopped in the middle of the driveway and whirled on me. "I got you here to try and make things *better*, and you just—" His lips clamped down over the words.

"I'm sorry." I breathed. "Really, Matt."

Matt stared at me, his brow furrowed, jaw twitching with tension. But it wasn't only anger painted on his face. There was something else in there. Something that I couldn't define.

"I told you it wouldn't work," I said softly.

"It might have if you hadn't gotten drunk."

"I'm not drunk!" *Just a little fuzzy around the edges.*

"Well, it looked like you were. And that's all they're going to care about," he snapped, pointing back toward the house.

"What a surprise that you'd care more about what *they* think than what really happened!"

"I do *not*—" He cut himself off, eyes screwed shut. "If I cared more about what they thought, I wouldn't be helping you, would I?" he said through his teeth. Then his eyes snapped open and fixed on me. "And what the hell you were doing with Finn?"

"Mind your own business."

Matt huffed out a breath. "You don't want me to mind my own business."

"Yes, I do."

But he was right, and he knew it. I didn't want him to stop caring. I didn't want him to be mad at me. But I couldn't tell him what was going on.

Matt shook his head, walking toward the car. "Sometimes you're a real piece of work, Ash," he muttered.

I shivered. "Glad you finally noticed."

CHAPTER ELEVEN

I AM SURPRISED by how affected I am, recounting that story. I take a deep breath as Doc removes a tiny cloth from his pocket. He cleans his glasses as he speaks.

"So, your *incident* wasn't the first physical altercation with Finn?"

"No, but the night of the party was the first time I actually felt . . . threatened."

He puts his glasses back on. "Ashley, I know that the legal ramifications of your story have already been dealt with. But given the emotion clearly still attached to this, there is something that I think might be important to say at this point."

I wait, prepared to hear about how I should role-play confronting Finn, or write him a letter or something. I've been through this before.

Doc clears his throat. "I want you to know that what Finn did to you that night was nothing short of despicable. It was intimidating, violating, and horribly disrespectful."

"I know," I said.

"No, I'm not sure you do."

I frown at him, because I'm confident that I know Finn's a pig better than anyone else. But Doc leans forward.

"Ashley, what he did was wrong. You didn't deserve that on any level. He used his superior strength and social status to *threaten* you. I have no doubt that your reaction after the fact was actually shock. For a young man to do that to a young woman simply because he can? I am sickened by it."

I swallow. "T-thank you."

Doc shakes his head. "This story goes much deeper than I was led to believe. I find myself . . . disturbed that these events went unaddressed for so long."

I shift in my seat.

"Tell me, did you report these events to your mother? Or a teacher? Any responsible adult?"

I shake my head.

"Why not?"

I sigh. "Because it all kind of got lost in the shuffle of what happened after that. By the time things had calmed down, it felt like it was too late to tell anyone. And I didn't want them to know about the letter, so . . ."

Doc frowns. "What events could possibly have overshadowed *that*?"

I woke the next morning to a tectonic shift in self-loathing.

I couldn't stop seeing Matt's stony face when he'd dropped me off. How he'd shaken his head. How he left the party to *deal* with me, then returned to Karyn . . .

I buried my face in my pillow. It was really happening. After ten years, Matt was finally sick of me. He was finally going to dump me forever. And it was totally my own fault.

I dragged myself out of bed and got in the shower, stood facing the hissing stream, praying that somehow things weren't as bad as they seemed. Praying Matt would come pick me up and be his nice, caring self, making sure I was okay, tell me the fight last night was no big deal. Praying Karyn had gotten really drunk and cheated on him with Finn, and Matt had found out.

Afterward, I got dressed and twisted my wet hair up into a bun; I needed to get to the art room by 9:30. Then I heard a knock on the front door. It had to be Matt. Nerves and relief hit in equal measure. I practically ran for the door. The dark shadow behind the glass had his back to me as I approached. I took a deep breath and twisted the knob.

"I'm so glad you're here! I'm so sorry ab—"

The six-foot-two frame in front of me turned, but instead of sandy brown hair and blue eyes, I was faced with light hair and brown eyes and *oh for the sake of all that is holy . . .*

Dex stood in the doorway, early morning sun filtering in behind him. At least, I *thought* it was Dex. The Dex I'd known had had a shaved head, bad skin, and hooded, glazed eyes. This one had a mess of golden hair, a perfect complexion, and a clear gaze. Underneath a gray cotton T-shirt and a leather jacket, his lanky limbs had filled out with hard muscles.

He smiled. "How are you doing, Ashley?"

"I'm . . . What are you doing here?" I blurted, managing to swallow the follow up: *Where the hell have you been—and when did you start looking like* that?

"I tried to call, but it said your old number wasn't connected anymore . . ." His Adam's apple bobbed. "I know this is weird, but . . . I'm back. I wanted to see you before school on Monday, especially after the way things went down."

"You left without a word," I said through clenched teeth, mad as hell to feel my throat tighten. That's when everything came flooding back—how I'd thought he and I would be together . . . how he never cared as much about me as I had about him . . . how he just left without even saying good-bye. How angry and humiliated I'd been.

Dex and I had dated . . . sort of. He'd asked me to prom, then two days before it, he just disappeared. One day, he was in class—the next day, he wasn't. And that wouldn't have been so crazy, if his phone hadn't been turned off. And if he'd answered any text messages. Or e-mails.

No one could tell me where he had gone or what had happened. I even went to the school office on Friday afternoon, before the dance, to ask if they knew where he was. All they could tell me was that he was no longer registered as a student. The next morning, when I realized I had to tell my mom, she accused me of making the whole thing up just so I could get a new dress.

"I know." He swallowed again, hunched his shoulders, hands buried deep in the pockets of his jeans. "I came here because I wanted to explain. I wanted you to know . . . everything. And I want to say sorry. For real."

"Where *were* you?" I'd heard his dad had gotten a job in Ohio, or somewhere random. I'd heard his mom had cancer and they had to go to California for her treatment. I also heard Dex had decked a teacher and gone to jail.

Dex took a deep breath, his feet shifting on our cement step. Then he looked right at me and said, "I was in rehab."

After that little bombshell, I brought Dex to the living room and put him on one end of the couch. He didn't want coffee, but he took a glass of lemonade that he held on his knee and kept turning while he talked. I sat at the other end of the couch.

"That day . . . ," he said to his glass, "I came to school high. I'd been doing that more and more. Or just skipping."

I nodded. Toward the end, I'd never known if he was going to be around or not. And when he was, he'd sometimes walk right past me, joking with his friends, skateboard tucked in his big backpack.

Dex shoved out a breath. "So, after school, I was under the bleachers with Wade. He'd gotten his hands on some stuff. I don't really know what it was, but it felt like the top of my head was about to blow off. When Mr. Goodrich found us and said he was going to suspend us, I just . . . lost it." He clenched his hand into a fist. "I swung at him. Got him in the chin. It wasn't that hard because he ducked, but . . . well, my dad made an agreement with the school that I couldn't come back until I'd been clean for a year. Then my parents sent me to rehab." He trailed off, looking sheepish.

There was still a lump in my throat I had to keep swallowing. "I had to hear you'd left town from *Brooke*."

He put the lemonade on the coffee table, fiddled with the coaster for a second. "I won't make excuses, Ash. I just . . . I was all messed up and I made terrible decisions. By the time my head was clear enough to realize what I'd done, I wanted to wait until I was clean and could tell you the whole story. There was a lot I had to make up for. My parents . . ." His jaw twitched. "I'm sorry," he said quietly. "Seriously."

I gaped. Dex didn't apologize. He didn't own up. I used to watch him flat-out lie—to the teachers about where his homework was or why he was late for class, or to me about why he'd stood me up.

"You were a good girlfriend, Ash," he went on. "And I just . . . took you for granted."

"You thought I was your girlfriend?" I squeaked, hating myself for the surge of pleasure that came with the word.

Dex frowned. "Of course you were my girlfriend. Did you think I was dating other people?"

"No. I mean, I didn't know. I had no idea what we were . . . or what you thought. I just . . . I just wanted to be with you . . ." I trailed off, blushing, and hugged my knee to my chest. I couldn't believe I'd just admitted that.

But then Dex cupped my chin and tilted my head up. I knew I looked as pathetic as I felt. But he didn't suddenly grimace and walk away. Instead, in a voice barely above a whisper, he said, "I'm sorry. I didn't deserve you back then. And I'm sorry I hurt you."

Who was this person?

"Thank you," I said, trying to figure out how to fill the silence. But then Dex looked at my mouth and a tingle started low in my belly.

The moment stretched tighter.

Was he going to kiss me?

Did I want him to?

I was saved from having to decide by the sound of an engine, followed by the flash of reflected light zipping across the wall announcing the arrival of a car.

For once I was popular, apparently.

Dex and I both stilled. I was the first one to sit back, to look in the direction of the door. "Someone's here," I said unnecessarily, getting to my feet. Dex got up to follow me.

Matt's truck glinted in the sunlight. I caught a glimpse of sandy-brown hair shimmering under the sun before he passed out of sight into the alcove at the front door. I was already turning the handle when he knocked. For a moment I had déjà vu. Except this time it was Matt who stood in the doorway, hands in his pockets, face expressionless.

"How are you feeling this morning?" he said quietly. "I figured you'd want a ride."

A ride? Oh, crap . . . The art room. I was due there . . . now.

"Are you ready?" Matt asked, the words clipped.

"Almost," I lied. "I just . . ."

Then Matt looked over my shoulder and his jaw dropped.

"Dex?" he asked, disbelieving.

Dex put a hand on my shoulder. "Mike, right?"

"It's Matt, actually," Matt ground out.

"Matt. Right. Sorry." Dex didn't sound sorry.

Matt's brow creased.

"Dex is back," I said lamely. "He came to see me."

"No kidding."

There was an awkward moment of silence where the guys glared at each other while I examined the wallpaper and tried to figure out what to do. In the end, I pulled the door wide, stepping back.

"Come in," I said to Matt. "It'll only take me a second to

get ready." I turned to Dex, trying to be subtle about pulling out of his grip. "I have to go to the art room. I'm . . . I'm entering a competition and I have so much work to get done before the deadline . . ."

Dex's face went blank for a second, then he smiled. "Oh, right, your art thing. I can give you a ride if you want. I don't mind hanging out while you get ready. I'm going past there anyway."

I glanced at Matt. He was still frowning.

"Um . . . sure. That would be great," I said, then looked at Matt. "Then you don't have to wait for me."

Matt looked at me, then tugged on my sleeve. "Can I talk to you alone for a second?"

I swallowed. "Can't we talk at school? I'll be there in a few minutes."

Matt glanced at Dex, then shook his head. "I'll leave you to it, then."

"Matt, don't—"

But he was already turning the handle. "Later, Dex. Try not to disappear again before you get her to the art room."

"Matt!"

Dex just glared at Matt's back.

As soon as Matt disappeared behind the door, I turned back to Dex with an apologetic smile. "Sorry about that. He's just protective. Like a big brother."

"Brother?" Dex cocked a brow, then turned to look out the window. Outside, a car door slammed, then an engine roared, whining as it pulled away too fast. "So, you guys are just friends?"

"Yeah." *Whether I want it that way or not.*

But Dex grinned. "Good."

CHAPTER TWELVE

DOC FROWNS. "DEX?"

"My ex-boyfriend. Kind of." I still struggle to categorize Dex that way.

Doc waits for an explanation. I pretend it's no big deal.

"Dex and I dated sophomore year. At least, that's what he called it later. But at the time I wasn't sure. It was never . . . defined."

"Why not?"

I shift my weight, wincing when one of my scars pinches. "Dex was a year older. He and I had different friends." *Meaning he had* some *friends.* "But during the summer between freshman and sophomore year, I decided I wanted to learn to skate. Dex and his friends were the local skaters. They helped me out. We got to talking . . . Things didn't get, you know, *personal* between us until we were almost back at school."

"So, you two were dating."

Were we? I suppose. "Yes."

"And?"

"And we had this weird relationship for almost a year."

"Weird how?"

I open my hands, uncertain how to let Doc know this is no big deal.

"Ashley?"

"I don't *know*, he was just hard to read, you know? He was all over me when we were alone, but wouldn't even hold my hand in front of his friends. He said he hated PDA, but he didn't mind groping me in a movie theater . . . I just never felt . . . sure of him. Turns out he was an addict, which explained a lot."

Doc's frowning at his notebook and scribbling furiously. It makes me nervous. Then his hand stops skittering across the paper. "I assume you would have been happy for people to know you were dating Dex?"

"Yeah. I guess. It wasn't like it was a secret. We were just . . . low key."

"So he hid you. From your peers."

"No! He just liked hanging out with his guy friends. And he had a lot going on."

Doc's lips flatten and I scowl. "It isn't a big deal. We were fifteen," I say.

"Yes. Yet most of your peers were very overt about their relationships, weren't they?"

I snort. "Dex was an outcast, too." It was part of what I liked about him. People hated him, too, but it never seemed to get to him.

"An outcast cautious about letting his peers know he was attracted to you."

"Thanks for putting it that way."

Doc shifts in his seat. "Ashley, I'm sorry he did that to you."

Having prepared myself to defend against a lecture on respecting myself, I'm off balance. I don't answer.

"It concerns me, though, that you were willing to accept such a vaguely defined relationship. It says a lot about how you gauge your own value."

Yeah, yeah. "Past history, Doc. Dex wouldn't get within fifty feet of me now."

"By your choice, or his?"

Probably both. "Mine. Look, I know you're going deep here, but this is old news now. It doesn't have anything to do with what happened."

"Perhaps not directly, but I think your perspective on yourself has a lot to do with the very drastic situation you found yourself in."

Oh, for Pete's sake. "With all due respect—"

"What if it was Matt?"

"What?" I'm taken off guard. I swallow.

Doc's gaze is piercing. "What if Matt were the one offering a relationship without any kind of public commitment . . . would you do it?"

Totally. "No." *I'd have hair implants and call myself a cat if it meant Matt would stroke me one more time.*

Doc stares at me, and there's a disconcerting second when I'm sure he knows what I'm thinking. But he just writes something on his pad. "So, Dex left," he says quietly. I'm waiting for the punch line, but it doesn't come. I nod. "Then he returned. And did Matt have any opinions about Dex's resurfacing?"

"You could say that," I mutter.

* * *

As it happened, I didn't get to talk to Matt right away. Mrs. D was in the art room all morning, banging around with the senior sculpture projects. So we worked quietly, then decided to walk the three blocks to a hot dog cart on the corner.

I sat at the picnic table next to the cart's awning, tipping my face to the sun. Matt ordered for us both, smiling when the vendor teased him about not wanting onions. Matt's shoulders were so wide, they took up almost the whole window as he reached over the glass to pick up three little cardboard boxes, each with a dog and some chips. He was still smiling—until he started toward me and our eyes met.

He dropped two of the boxes on his side of the picnic table, then slid the other box across the table in front of me. He straddled the bench, sitting side-on, and forced a grin. "Enjoy."

"Thanks."

We ate silently for a minute. It took Matt about four bites to get his first hot dog down, his cheek bulging as he chewed. Then he swallowed and glanced at me.

"So . . . Dex is back."

"Subtle," I said dryly.

Matt grinned, but it fell off his face quickly. He watched an old guy in a baggy white T-shirt walk to the window and order. Then, finally, he turned to meet my gaze. His face was serious. "You okay?"

"I'm fine. Why?"

His eyebrows rose. "Oh, I don't know. The guy who screwed with your head and then disappeared has just showed up again."

I shrugged. "I was surprised. But we talked and he seems okay now."

"Huh. So, he *seems* okay," Matt murmured. His voice was soft, but there was an edge to his expression that I knew well.

I frowned. "What are you annoyed about?"

A squirrel skittered up a nearby tree. Someone a few streets over honked their horn. Matt ate a couple of chips before answering. "I'm not annoyed. I just don't want to see you get hurt again. The guy's a jackass."

"I wouldn't argue with that." I took a bite of my hot dog and stared at the table.

"So, what are you doing talking to him?" Matt asked.

I gave him a look. "What, I should just kick him out of my house when he comes to apologize?"

"Sounds like a plan to me."

I scowled. "Why are you being so harsh?"

"Why are you defending him?" Matt swallowed the last of his hot dog and brushed his hands together.

"I'm not defending him! I just . . ." I took a deep breath. "I didn't think I should just cut him off. He's been in rehab."

Matt's eyebrows shot up. *"Really?"*

"That's what he said. And he looks really different." I remembered the open-faced apologies and Dex's wincing admission to acting like a jerk. "He was acting different too."

"Just be careful," Matt said quietly. "Don't do anything stupid."

"Oh, thanks. I'll get right on that."

He gave me a pointed look. "You know what I mean. Sometimes people aren't as good as they look. Just because you want to believe they care doesn't mean they actually do."

Images of Finn and Karyn flashed through my head. I could feel the weight and shape of the words in my mouth.

She's cheating on you.

He's betraying you.

But what I actually said was, "Thanks. I'll be fine."

Matt shook his head, staring off into the distance.

"What?" I asked.

"I don't know. Girls are just . . . weird," Matt grumbled. "You're ready to forgive Dex at the drop of the hat, but you're pissy with me because I don't want you to get hurt. Karyn's annoyed because I took you home last night, even though she told me to. And Mom's mad because I'm not talking to Dad. But you all smile and tell me everything's fine. What is it with you? Why are you mad all the time and pretending you aren't?"

I swallowed. "I don't know about your mom, but Karyn's probably acting weird because she's afraid I'm going to try to break you guys up." I bit my lip to stop myself from saying more on *that*. "And I'm glad you're looking out for me. I'm not mad."

"Wait, Karyn thinks *you'll* break us up?" He looked half worried, half amused. "Did I just walk into a reality show or something?"

I threw a chip at him and he ducked, chuckling.

"Mock me all you want. Girls get jealous. They don't really believe we can hang out without . . . you know . . ."

Matt frowned. "But—"

"C'mon, you know I'm right. Remember Olivia?"

"Bad example. Olivia was insecure about *everything*," he said, stacking his now-empty boxes together. "But I know what you mean. Sometimes I think they're right."

"Who's right about what?"

"About how guys and girls can't ever *really* be just friends. I mean, how many times do I make friends with girls just to see if I want to date them?"

His words placed a strange mix of hope and panic in my chest. "Then I guess you can't blame Karyn for getting upset," I said uncertainly.

Matt blinked, then turned to look at me. "Except for you," he said, hastily. "I mean, I wasn't just . . . we got that sorted out years ago—"

"I know," I said, kicking myself, remembering that day in eighth grade when Matt had asked me to a dance at his middle school. I'd said no. Because I had a crush on *Finn*. Oh, the irony.

"That wasn't what I meant, though," I said, keeping my voice light. "Your girlfriends think that way about me because they know guys think that way about *them*."

Matt thought about that for a minute. Then he shrugged. "Maybe."

He stood, extricated himself from the picnic table, and offered me a hand. I took it gratefully, feeling a pang when he dropped it as soon as I had both feet on the grass.

As we walked toward the sidewalk and back to the art room, inwardly I recoiled from the uncomfortable truth:

I had become such a *friend* to Matt that he didn't even see me as a *girl* anymore.

That night, Older Me paced on the other side of the mirror, arms folded, mouth turned down. To me it looked like she was pacing the floor of my room.

"Rehab, huh?" she murmured, surprised.

I sat on my bed, picking at a loose thread in the quilt. "I almost fell over when he showed up at the door."

She stopped pacing and turned, biting her lip, but she was nodding. "And Dex acted . . . possessive?"

I snorted. "When Matt showed up, Dex practically pissed on my leg."

She grinned, but her heart didn't really seem in it. "Well, I guess . . . I mean, you need to be careful, because he was a complete—"

"Yeah, yeah. I've already had the lecture from Matt. Don't you start in too."

Older Me shook her head. "I'm not. I'm just saying, be on guard. But maybe . . . maybe this is a good thing, you know? Maybe it's a good way to move on from Matt since . . . well, you know." I glanced at her, and her hands came up. "Don't get me wrong—it's nice that Matt's looking out for you."

"It'd be nicer if he'd notice the truth about his own *friends*," I muttered.

Older Me sagged. "Yeah . . . that . . ."

"Will he figure it out?" I asked, my voice so low it was almost a whisper. "Or should I . . . ?"

She ran a hand through her greasy hair. "I don't know, Ashley. I really don't."

I slumped back on my pillows, groaning. "Why does everything have to be so complicated?"

Older Me had stopped pacing, but she stood in profile to me, staring into the middle distance. "You should be grateful," she said absently. "It could be a lot worse."

"Worse how?" I muttered, not expecting her to actually answer.

But she did.

"You can't control how other people hurt you, Ashley. But you can control how you hurt yourself." She turned then, her blue eyes fixing on me. Piercing. "You're doing a lot better on that score than I ever did."

I blinked. "What do you mean?"

The smile she offered was watery and clenched my stomach. She opened her mouth and every muscle in my body went rigid. Was she going to tell me about my future? Her past?

"Look, I know this is going to sound abstract, but I've always had this big gap inside, and I know you do, too. A place that nothing seems to touch and nothing can fill. And I used to think if I was popular, or if Matt loved me . . . that would do it. I would feel whole. But no matter how I tried, no one ever loved me enough to fill the hole up. Not even *him*. In fact, the harder I tried, the less he had to offer . . ." She trailed off miserably. "I'm just telling you that there has to be more to your life than Matt."

I was struck dumb. For a moment her words echoed, vibrating in my skin . . . *I used to think if I was popular, or if Matt loved me . . . that would do it. I thought it would close me up so I could feel whole . . .*

I knew *exactly* what she meant. And that scared me. The sadness on her face scared me. And made me feel bad for her. I swallowed. Hard.

"I have to go," she murmured, with a glance over her shoulder. "But just remember, you're better than the rest of them, Ashley. Trust your instincts. Don't fight fire with fire." She turned away.

"Wait!"

"I'll see you later."

"Older Me, *please.*"

She stopped midstep, her shoulders rigid. "What?" she whispered. "I'm serious, Ashley, I have to go."

"What did you mean, 'Don't fight fire with fire'?"

Her head tipped to the side and she sighed. "I mean . . . You'll never beat them at their own game." She swallowed. "Trust me on that."

CHAPTER THIRTEEN

DOC LACES HIS fingers together. "So, your older self encouraged you to give Dex a chance?"

"I wouldn't go that far. It's more that she didn't *discourage* me."

"Did she ever admit to having a relationship with Dex in her . . . lifetime?"

I have to think for a moment. "You know, Doc, I really don't know. I don't think she ever talked about it. I'm not sure I ever asked her."

I'm surprised by the discomfort I feel when this occurs to me.

Doc must see something on my face, because he leans forward. "That bothers you," he says.

I nod. "I guess I spent so much time trying to figure out what was wrong with me, I forgot to be there for her."

Doc nods. "That would make sense."

I shake my head. "It's very self-involved."

He leans his temple on one hand and smiles at me, which he hasn't really done since we've been here. "I think you've just had what we like to call a 'moment,' Ashley," he says. "So, let's pursue this. If you were, indeed, a little fixated on yourself during those years, how did you cope with that? Obviously, you had a lot of disdain for yourself during this time. So what did all that self-analysis lead to?"

I shrug. "Honestly, I think it was mainly about wishing I could escape the people around me."

"And how did you express that?" he asks, pen poised over his notebook.

"Through my art."

Doc nods, and I know what he's thinking: That all things considered, maybe I should have found another outlet.

Monday at school, walking the halls was like flipping channels on TV—if all the channels were playing gossip talk shows. And all the talk shows featured Dex.

". . . heard his father threatened to sue the school if they didn't let him back in . . ."

". . . He's in my chemistry class. I sat right behind him. He looks even better with the jacket *off*. . ."

". . . wonder if it was one of those places where they make you go to church and stuff. He has that spiritual quality . . ."

". . . Dad said his parents make him see a psychiatrist for his repressed rage . . ."

". . . Coach says he's got a great arm. He's letting him train with the squad . . ."

And when I wasn't hearing about Dex, I was thinking about him—and what Older Me had said. Was he a way to move on from Matt? Had he really changed?

I zoned out all through social sciences while the teacher

talked about ape family circles. She'd closed the curtains and pulled down the screen over the whiteboard, using the projector to show us images of apes in various family groups, eating leaves, playing, hunting.

Yawn.

At least, until the darkness flashed and a picture of an orangutan—belly protruding and lips distended toward a handful of leaves—came onto the screen.

"Isn't that your freshman photo, Ashley?" Finn yelled. Everyone laughed. I tried to make myself invisible, and hunched over my desk until the hour was over.

I spent fourth period ignoring Matt's pointed looks while Mrs. D yammered about the impressionistic masters. Then I made excuses to him about lunch and decided to stay in the art room to work.

After everyone—including Matt—left, I pulled my workbook and folders out of my cubby and sat down. My workbook opened right to the sketches I'd done in bed that night after the dance.

Karyn was there. So were Finn and Matt. Even though they were hurried, there was something in them that felt real.

People were my "thing." Mrs. Driley encouraged me to use the human form in my portfolio as much as possible, because I was good at it. But I felt most vulnerable when I drew people I knew. Sure, I could get the curve of Matt's dark lashes right, the shape of his cheekbone . . . but how could I communicate the warmth of his skin? I flipped back to the image of Finn and considered turning the idea into a painting—using a spatula for hard lines to depict the sharpness of his features, heavy thick paint for his rhinoceros skin, fat brush strokes for his brows, like caterpillars on his face, his long mouth a venomous red slash.

For Karyn I'd use glossy pastels—waxy crayons that shone on the paper. I could layer red, white, beige, and cream to make her cheeks blush. Then, when everything was done, use a tool to scrape her eyes out of the heavy wax, holes in a poisonous blanket.

As her face came to life in my mind, I pulled out the crayons. My hand moved quickly, inspired. A snapshot of possibilities sprang up on the paper in minutes—a shiny, plastic face that hid the darkness beneath. I'd run a candle flame along the edge of her paper so it'd burn unevenly.

I turned to a new page and Mom emerged in pencil, smudged across the paper, most of her face turned away. Dad could be the opposing panel, his face an empty shell, just a few simple strokes without features. I tried Mrs. Driley next, but her graying waves ended up looking drab instead of unruly, and I couldn't quite make her eyes twinkle. She'd need paint—her lined cheeks highlighted with blues and greens. Every color of the rainbow in her face—outshining even the gypsy-clothes she wore. She'd be the only one with color in the background. I gave Dex a stab, but couldn't quite figure out what to do with him. The figure that emerged could have been any good-looking teenage guy. A cartoon.

Starting on Matt felt natural, but as soon as I'd outlined his face, I dropped my pencil. I couldn't do it. Drawing him this way would be like cracking my ribs open and revealing my heart. It was too much to take all of him in at once. With a shaking hand, I looked back through the workbook to the sketches I'd done of him. They were rough, piecemeal snapshots, but I had almost all his features from the shoulders up. Only his mouth was left unfinished.

Intrigued, I pulled the paper from the book and ripped around the edges of each sketch until I had seven scraps, each with a disproportionate body part on it. Taken together, they looked like Picasso's shot at realism—one eye open and from the front, the other downcast in profile. His nose was too big and his jaw took up the space where his shoulders should have been. Yet Matt—all mutilated and betwixt—stared at me from the paper.

"Gracious, Ashley. This is genius! When did you do these?"

I started. Mrs. Driley stood to my right, staring openmouthed at my sketches.

"I . . . uh . . . I was just fooling around . . ." I trailed off.

She nodded. "That's when I do my best work, too. But even in these fast strokes you've captured . . ." She blinked, turning to look at me, understanding dawning on her face. "Has anyone else seen these?" she asked, hushed.

I shook my head. "Of course not."

She turned back to the table, looking from picture to picture, smiling with delight when she landed on the one of her. She gathered the pictures together like a stack of cards, pulling each from the top to the bottom and examining them individually, making small approving noises in her throat.

"Ashley, these are breathtaking. You should use these for your portfolio."

Even though it felt kind of like she was reading my diary without asking, a blush spread through me in the face of her approval. "But it's due in just a few weeks," I reminded her.

She tapped the table. "Yes. But if you've done these in just a few minutes . . . Ashley, if you work hard and get a dozen of these complete, fitting them into the assignments, I really think you've got a shot at a scholarship."

I frowned. It had taken a year to get this far with my portfolio. Then again, each piece had been like pulling fingernails because they weren't *real*. But these? These were real. To make portraits depicting not what each person looked like, but *who* they were to me. To tell the judges about my predators—and my saviors. They wouldn't know who these people were. They would judge only the artistic impression.

Mrs. D stopped leafing through the drawings and looked at me. "Are you brave enough? Because these are very . . . revealing. If any of your classmates see them, they'll understand what you're saying."

I sighed. "I know. It's risky."

Mrs. D nodded. "You could keep some of them at home."

I glanced at the picture of Mom in her hands. "I can't do all of them at home."

Mrs. D thought for a moment. "How about this—I'll let you use the art room on Sundays, too, for the next month, if you go ahead with this concept. You'll have to use every spare minute because you'll have to completely rebuild your workbook. But you've already got that nude, which would work alongside these. And it looks like those pieces of Matt might make up another."

"Thank you," I said, calculating. I could do all the planning in my breaks and lunches, then use the weekends to draw and paint. I was a lot faster with a pen than a brush. I could use acrylics, colored pencil, graphite pencil. It would be harder to impress with them, but if I could deliver something special, the simple tools would only make the work stand out.

Mrs. D clapped her hands. "Good. Then go into the easel room and get started right now. I'll get you excused from your afternoon classes, just this once—let inspiration take you while you have it. By the end of the day, I want to see at least half a dozen developed sketches, canvas sizes, and material lists for each."

My heart thumped. "Sure, but I thought most of them would be pencil, charcoal, crayon. You know? That way I can cut and scrape—"

Mrs. D looked back at the sketches. "You'll have to paint at least two of them—and there's got to be a multimedia." She frowned. "Oh, dear, maybe this is too much—"

"No! No, I can do it. I'll get the others done first and finish with the paintings when I know how much time I have."

"You'll have to make the self-portrait exceptional. In the face of these illuminating pieces, your self-portrait would have to be the central work."

I balked. "What? Why? I thought the Matt concept . . ."

She shook her head. "You're telling a story with these, Ashley. You're opening yourself up to the world. It's what true artists do. But if you hold back, it will give everything else the sense of, I don't know, *plastic*. Each of these is telling a story about you. So *you* have to be the central piece that the others orbit." She glanced at me from the side.

I swallowed. It was hard enough to imagine someone seeing the drawings of Finn or Matt. But one of *me*?

"I'll tell you what," Mrs. D said. "Let's not make a decision now. You spend this afternoon figuring this out. You're going to have to be really organized if you're going to get this done in time. So sort out what you'd do and how you'd put it together. Then we'll see if it's even worth pursuing, okay?"

I took a deep breath and nodded.

Mrs. Driley patted my shoulder. "Good girl. The bell's going to ring in a minute. Get yourself into the easel room before my class arrives. I'll check on you later."

Right on cue, the bell clanged and the door flew open. A couple of seniors frowned when they saw me. I gathered my sketches hastily, then hustled into the easel room, praying I could convince Mrs. Driley to let me go easy on the self-portrait. I'd do something awesome with the Matt one. Knock her socks off. Then she'd forget about me.

CHAPTER FOURTEEN

"THAT WAS A bold move," Doc says, sitting back in his chair. There's the hint of a smile on his face.

"The portfolio?" I say. When he nods, I wave a hand. "Not really. It just felt right."

"Certainly," he says. "But the risk was great—both of being discovered by someone who might take exception to your work, and of forcing yourself to work under an extremely tight deadline."

I nod.

Doc opens a hand toward me. "See? Brave."

I shake my head. He isn't the first to have said this. But I still don't agree.

"Ashley," he starts to say, in his patronizing voice. But I cut him off.

"Can I ask you something?"

"Of course."

I lean forward. "What makes a decision *brave*, Doc? Serious question. I mean, is it just the fact that it's something someone else wouldn't do? Or what?"

His eyebrows descend behind his glasses. He shifts in his seat, watching me. "Well, there's probably an element of the subjective. But . . . I suppose I would define someone—or a decision they made—as brave when they choose a path that could have either serious gains or extreme consequences. When they're choosing that path not out of recklessness, but out of hope. For something better."

"So, choosing to do a new portfolio at the last minute is courageous rather than reckless because of the possible upside?"

He clicks his pen. "Because the gains are actually within your power. For instance, if someone told me they'd spent their life savings on lottery tickets, I would think them reckless. The potential gains were out of their control. In your situation, there were great risks, but you *knew* you had what it took to make the reward a definite possibility."

"Not so sure that's true," I say slowly.

Doc tips his head. "You seem dismissive of the decision you made."

"Not exactly," I say, running a finger along a scar on my forearm. "I just know I wasn't necessarily thinking about *all* the risks."

"Do any of us?" he says, almost smiling again. When I don't respond, he taps his finger on the notepad in his lap. "Ashley, it's a philosophical question, but perhaps it isn't best answered in hindsight. After all, when things work out, would any of us go back and change them if we could? I suspect if you were in that moment again, you'd do the same thing."

"About my portfolio?"

He nods. "Yes. Was there another risky decision at the time?"

I frown, because in hindsight, *yes*. But it all seemed so harmless at the time . . .

On Tuesday, fourth period was a special assembly for the junior class. Someone was visiting to tell us why we shouldn't do drugs. As I wandered down the hallway, I had to grin. Another of those REFUSE TO BE ROADKILL posters had been tacked to the wall. Just like in the rec room, someone had changed it. This one read REFUSE TO ~~BE~~ *eat* ROADKILL—*The hair sticks in your teeth.*

I was still smiling as I walked up the aisle, looking for an out-of-the-way seat in the theater, where the smaller assemblies were always held. I was still considering which row when someone touched my shoulder. I whirled.

Dex took a step back. "Whoa, sorry. I didn't mean to scare you."

Heart pounding, I nodded, feeling sheepish. "Sorry. I thought you were someone else."

After a long beat, Dex nodded toward a row of seats behind me. "Want to sit together?"

I scanned the row. There didn't seem to be anyone who hated me nearby. "Sure. I guess," I replied, trying to ignore the butterflies in my stomach.

I flipped the seat down and settled in, putting my elbows on the armrests. Dex sat down next to me, nodding once at a greeting from Liam—a guy on the baseball team. I'd heard Dex was training with them. Liam sat three rows down, his blue baseball cap turned backward on his head so his nearly white hair peeked out from underneath it. Three or four other guys sat with him, all in letterman's jackets. Liam was motioning for Dex to come down, to join them.

"You can go down there if you want," I offered.

Dex glanced at me, then shook his head. "Nah, I'm good."

We sat in silence as the rows around us filled. The lights were just dropping when three people inched down the row in front of us. I cursed under my breath when I recognized Finn's sharp chin and long body. That made the perky ponytail next to him mostly likely Karyn, and the broad shoulders next to her . . . Matt.

My nerves jangled as they sat directly in front of us.

"I think these are the same guys who came to my rehab . . . Ashley. Ashley?" Fingers snapped in front of my face.

I blinked. Dex leaned toward my chair, his shoulder brushing against mine.

"Earth to Ashley?" he teased.

At the sound of my name, Matt jerked his head around, frowning when he saw Dex next to me.

"Sorry," I murmured, forcing myself to look away from Matt and toward Dex. "What were you saying?"

"I said, I think these guys are from the organization that came to my rehab and ran a group session. They're pretty good."

Dex was right. The group was good. Entertaining and challenging. They even had some high schoolers who talked about their addictions and experiences. Dex spent a lot of time nodding. His jaw got pretty tense at one point, when they talked about hurting people. I patted his hand and smiled at him when he looked down at me.

He smiled back and turned his hand so it was palm up to mine, twining our fingers together on the armrest. It took me by surprise, but the warmth of his skin and the pressure of his shoulder against mine felt good. Reassuring.

And it didn't hurt that Matt looked back once, his gaze lingering on our clasped hands.

When the assembly was over and we'd all murmured our agreement to try to stay clean (*A Healthy Me Is Drug Free!*), I looked at Dex. He still held my hand, but he was staring into the middle distance.

I nudged his shoulder with mine and smiled when he looked at me. "Are you okay?"

He blinked foggily, then shook his head, as if coming back to himself. "Yeah. I am. You?"

I nodded, biting my lip, suddenly unsure if we were still talking about Dex's former drug habit.

He let go of my hand to hoist his bag over his shoulder, and I was surprised by how keenly I felt the loss. But he grabbed it again to pull me through the crowd pushing its way to the cafeteria.

"What're you doing for lunch?" Dex asked casually when we reached the hallway.

"I'm actually headed to the art room," I said. "I've just got so much work to do, I'm spending every break and lunch in there, just about."

"Could you maybe skip one? Have lunch with me?"

Before I could answer, a body hit me from behind and I pitched forward into his chest.

He caught me, held me tight. Didn't let go immediately. "Watch where you're going, Brooke," he snapped. Laughter was the only response.

I pulled away, blushing, and turned to head down the hall. When I glanced back, I realized he'd come to a halt. He was frowning and looking over my shoulder.

"Dex, if you're staring at my ass, you're going to need to be a little more subtle," I said.

But Dex just cursed and swiped at my back.

"Dex, what are you—"

His expression hard, he examined a piece of notepaper fluttering off the end of a large strip of masking tape.

SINGLE WHITE FEMALE SEEKS PROM DATE. WILL PAY HOURLY RATE AND GIVE HEAD. ONLY PICKUP DRIVERS NEED APPLY DUE TO WIDE LOAD.

There was an arrow pointing down. Presumably at my ass.

My face went hot. I shoved my bag strap back up on one shoulder and started down the hall, almost running.

"Ash. Ashley! Wait!" Dex called after me, catching up with me before I'd gone half a dozen feet. He fell in step with me, and I cursed at him because I was trying not to cry and that was going to be harder if he started pitying me.

"Don't let them get to you, babe."

Babe. He called me babe. He used to do that all the time.

"I'm not." I swallowed tears and ran a hand through my hair. Dex gave me a look, but kept walking, glancing around. A few seconds later, he spoke again.

"I forgot how much this school sucks. Everyone here thinks they're better than us." His Adam's apple bobbed. "And that . . .

that used to just kill me, okay? It was part of why I was always high."

"It was?" I'd thought he was untouchable.

"Yeah." He leaned into my ear and whispered, "But if it's any consolation, I always thought your wide load was sexy."

Horrified, my jaw dropped, and I snapped my head around to look at him.

He held up his hands in surrender. But he was grinning. "Too soon?"

I couldn't help it. I laughed. Then Dex laughed. Then when we were finished laughing, I agreed to skip the art room and have lunch with him. And for the first time in a long time, I could breathe.

And if I neglected to mention that lunch to Matt when he asked me later, it was just because I was still thinking about how to handle Dex's . . . friendship. And if Matt had a problem with that, well, frankly, he could kiss my wide load.

CHAPTER FIFTEEN

DOC TAPS HIS lips, which makes him look very thoughtful and makes me feel nervous. But when he opens his mouth, he isn't pulling the carpet out from under me.

"It sounds like Dex was attempting to reignite your former relationship?"

"Yeah. Well, I thought so at the time, anyway."

"And were you supported in your decision to explore that?"

I try to laugh but it comes out dry. "C'mon, Doc. You must've realized by now it could never be that easy."

That Friday night, Dex called me and we talked for two hours. About nothing. It was great. By midnight, we were both getting sleepy, but neither of us wanted to get off the phone.

"Have you got your art thing tomorrow?" Dex asked, his voice gravelly with tiredness.

"Yeah, tomorrow and Sunday." I groaned.

Dex grunted. "How about I take you out for breakfast in the

morning, then?" he said, then yawned. "I can drop you off at the art room after."

I agreed, which is how I ended up walking into the art room fifteen minutes late on Saturday morning. With Dex.

I stopped just inside the door, inhaling the smell of turpentine and wet paper. Dex gave me a hug. "I'll call you later, okay?"

"Okay," I said, and waved as he left, my insides trilling.

"Morning!" I chirped to Matt, who sat on the other side of the tables, hunched over a large cream-colored sketchpad.

"Morning," he replied tightly.

"So, what are you working on?" I asked, laying out my workbook and pencils.

"Just a drawing."

I waited, but he didn't say more, so I settled into the chair next to him and got to work on a study for my portrait of Mrs. D.

A minute later, the skin on my neck prickled. From the corner of my eye, I could see Matt sitting back in his chair, staring. At first I thought he was looking at my drawing. But when I turned, his gaze was on me.

"What's up?" I asked.

The corners of his mouth tipped down and he glanced at the door Dex had just exited through. "I . . . um . . . So, you and Dex are back on, then?" I'm not sure if he realized he'd started tapping his pencil against the tabletop.

"I wouldn't say that." I ducked my head to hide my smile behind my hair. There was no doubt Dex was acting *interested*, but I wasn't about to admit it. What if I was wrong?

Tap, tap, tap, tap. "He was holding your hand in the assembly.

Guys don't really do that stuff unless they're, you know, hoping for more," Matt said.

I felt a stab of pain somewhere in the region of my heart. "Thanks for implying he just wants sex. Tell me how you really feel."

"That isn't what I meant." He flushed. *Tap, tap, tap.* "I just meant . . . I guess I'm surprised. It seems like you guys are taking it kind of fast."

I gave him a look. "You're kidding, right? You do remember the whole 'dating for almost a year' thing, don't you? We hold hands in assembly after a week and we're being *'fast'*?"

Matt's brow creased. "Isn't he just out of rehab? Aren't they supposed to, like, not date for a year or something?"

I rolled my eyes. "You've been watching too many movies. And anyway, he's been clean that long," I said, feeling a little bit like I was sharing Dex's secrets. But I knew I could trust Matt.

Couldn't I? That pencil was speeding up.

Tap, tap, tap, tap, tap.

"I'm just surprised, like I said." *Tap, tap, tap, tap, tap.*

I dropped my own pencil and clapped my hand down over Matt's. He froze, staring at my hand on his. His Adam's apple bobbed.

"You're acting weird," I said flatly. "What's going on?"

He looked up at me, face blank. "I'm just thinking I should be asking you that question."

"What are you talking about? Nothing is going on with me and Dex—not yet, anyway. And I would tell you if it was. So . . . what?" I realized I still had my hand on his, and pulled it back.

Matt frowned. "Has he kissed you?"

"What the *hell*?" I felt my face go up in flames, *whoosh*. "That is *so* none of your business!"

"How do you figure? I'm your best friend. I'm watching out for you."

I laughed. "Great, then you now owe me years' worth of juicy details. But we can start with Karyn—have you rounded third yet?" As soon as the words were out of my mouth, I regretted them. I didn't want to know what he'd been doing with Karyn. Well, I did. But I didn't want to be able to *picture* it.

When he opened his mouth I put my hands up. "No. Wait. Forget I asked. I don't want to know."

"No, no. Fair's fair." Matt grinned. "I'll show you mine if you show me yours."

The reference took me so off guard I couldn't help but laugh. "I can't believe you brought that up!"

Matt chuckled and puffed out his chest. "I'm sorta proud of it, actually. The first time I got naked with a girl, and I was seven!"

"Ugh! Stop!" It was completely innocent, of course. We'd stood across my room and pulled our shorts up and down so fast we barely saw more than pink skin, then giggled and shushed each other. "It was your idea. Pervert."

Matt grinned. "You could have said no."

I smacked my forehead dramatically. "Why didn't I think of that? Thank you! Now I know what to do next time you ask me to get naked."

In my head it had sounded like a joke. Taunting. But as soon as the words were out of my mouth, all I could see was Matt and me back in my bedroom. Except we weren't young and innocent anymore.

And Matt must have seen it, too, because his laughter died right next to mine.

Our eyes latched and my pulse thumped in my ears. I wanted to make light of it, laugh it off. But there was shock in his half-open mouth. And the look on his face . . . it made my hands shake. He had no right to look at me like that.

But he did. He kept staring and I kept imagining him standing in front of me, his hand lifting to touch my face, fingers trailing down my neck to the top button of my blouse. I was close enough to see the tiny pinpricks of stubble in a line on his jaw where he'd shaved too fast. I imagined running my lips along it.

"Ash?"

"Yeah?"

"The other day, when you were holding hands with Dex . . ."

I groaned. *Damn! Why did he have to bring that up?* "It was just . . . I mean it wasn't . . ."

He grimaced. "No, listen . . ." He leaned closer.

"What?" My heart beat too fast. But he just kept staring at my mouth. "What?" I said, a little harder, because I knew what it looked like when a guy thought about kissing you. But Matt wouldn't be thinking about that. Would he? *Oh, God, please let Matt be thinking about that.*

Matt swallowed, but didn't look away. "It made me mad," he said softly.

I waited, but there wasn't any more. Just him, sitting too close, staring at my lips.

He couldn't be doing this. Was he implying that he thought about an "us"? Him and me?

Then he leaned in. I stopped breathing.

Just do it, Ashley. Just close the gap and kiss him. Just do it.

I sucked in a breath and started tipping toward him when the door to the art room shuddered and thumped, then flew open with a bang.

"Don't worry kids, it's just me," Mrs. Driley sang from behind a tall stack of boxes in her arms. "Just got a delivery!"

I whipped around, back to my sketch, tried to get my hands busy drawing the outline. But my fingers trembled. I was desperately aware of Matt beside me. My arm goose-bumped under his gaze.

But a minute later, amid the bumps and swallowed curses echoing from the storage room, Matt pushed to his feet and walked around the tables, disappearing into the easel room.

I grit my teeth and swore under my breath.

An hour later, music drifted out of the easel room, along with more banging and thumps from the storage space. I was still in my seat. I'd retrieved a little mirror from Mrs. D and was whispering at Older Me while I pretended to work.

"I swear! He was going to kiss me! If Mrs. Driley hadn't come in . . ." I trailed off, dabbing at what was supposed to be Mrs. D's hair. So far I had an outline with a hint of shadow on the shoulder.

I didn't need to see the mirror to know Older Me had her arms crossed, and her forehead was creased with lines. "I think it's good that he didn't get the chance—if that's what he was going to do," she said carefully.

"Thanks for the vote of confidence," I muttered. "It was crazy. The only thing I can't figure out is, if he was jealous of Dex and he wanted to kiss me, why is he avoiding me now?"

"Because he's smart. Don't do this, Ashley. Don't be like Finn and Karyn. Don't get pulled into these kinds of games. You're not a cheater. Don't become one."

"Of course I'm not a cheater," I whisper-snapped. "But *she* is. She doesn't deserve any loyalty from me."

"But Matt does," she said. "If anything ever happens between you two it's going to be complicated enough without throwing cheating into the mix. Don't do it, Ashley. Don't risk it. If he wants you, he'll want you enough to break up with whoever."

"Right." I snorted and jabbed my brush at the canvas again. "Matt Gray breaking up with someone like Karyn for me. Right."

"Stranger things have happened, Ashley," she said, a wistful note in her voice.

"Not in my lifetime."

"What was that, dear?" Out of nowhere, Mrs. Driley appeared on the other side of my table. I yelped and dropped my paintbrush.

"N-nothing!" I sang. "Just talking to myself . . . trying to figure out this painting, ha ha ha ha."

Mrs. D flapped a hand at me. "It's okay, Ashley, I get it," she said. "I do that too. Trust me, it isn't until your Self starts talking back that you've got a problem!" She brayed out a laugh and turned for the door, her footsteps fading a lot faster than the snorts and cackles.

I turned back to Older Me, uncertain whether to find the exchange ironically funny, or frighteningly close to home. But just as I opened my mouth, a thump sounded on Older Me's side of the mirror. She gasped and was gone. And frustrating as that was, I almost didn't want to talk to her anymore because the things she was saying rang true. And what if she said something that meant no future for me and Matt?

That thought kept me out of the easel room.

It sucked.

And so did Matt. Because he didn't talk to me again all day.

CHAPTER SIXTEEN

"**SO, MATT ALMOST** kissed you?" Doc asks, sitting back in his chair.

Even now, uncertainty remains. "I think so . . . I mean, it was the first time Matt had ever shown any interest in me. And at the time, I wasn't entirely sure it was even happening."

"How so?" Doc asks, making another note on the pad. I briefly wonder what would if happen if I asked for a page to doodle on. I always feel calmer when my hands are busy. Instead, I trace the outline of a rose on my forearm.

"When you want something so badly, sometimes you over-analyze, see things that aren't there." I shrug. "Besides, it's not like he did anything about it."

"Did *you* do anything about it?"

"No!" I look up, horrified. "He had a girlfriend. The ball was in his court."

"You didn't believe Matt cared enough about you to break up with his girlfriend?" Doc asks casually.

"No. Not that way, at least," I say.

Doc makes a *hmmm* sound. "Did you believe anyone could be attracted to you in that way?"

"Not back then." My voice feels painfully small and pathetic, even to me.

Doc's eyebrows slide up. "At which point did you believe it?"

I hesitate as the truth sinks in. "You know, Doc, I'm not sure. Even when things with Dex happened . . ."

"What things?"

I look up with a wry smile. "Well, you know."

"Not really. Why don't you tell me?"

"Well, there was that whole prom thing . . ."

After several days without a hint of any more weird behavior from Matt, I convinced myself I'd been imagining the almost-kiss. Dex held my hand again a couple of times, but didn't try anything more. I was starting to wonder if I was destined to be every guy's best friend.

Then the prom posters started appearing.

If it hadn't been a really good distraction for my tormentors, I would have cursed the timing. But on Monday, only one person shoved me, and on Tuesday, even Eli's hissed request for "math tutoring" seemed halfhearted. Everyone was too busy strategizing how to score the perfect prom date.

And then there was me . . . the girl who'd famously gotten stood up the year before.

That Thursday, I gathered the courage to visit my locker before lunch. I'd been spending most breaks and lunches in the art room, but that morning I *had* to pick up my chemistry textbook for an open-book test.

As soon as I got within five feet of my locker, I knew something was wrong. The corner of a piece of paper stuck out from between the vents in the door, and a circle of freshman girls stood directly across the hall, watching me intently. I didn't know any of them by name, but their wide, excited expressions were easy to recognize.

Something was up.

I considered skipping my locker and the textbook after all, but I couldn't afford to go without the book for the test. I wrestled with the lock, then jiggled the handle until the door popped open with a clang. I took a deep breath and peered cautiously inside.

A piece of paper was taped to the top shelf, fluttering in the sudden breeze.

Ashley Watson, I think you have the hottest ass in this school.
Will you go to prom with me? DEX

My hand flew to my mouth. For a moment I couldn't even breathe. Then I noticed a large, clear plastic container behind the letter. With trembling hands I reached for it and pulled out a delicate but beautiful corsage of cream-colored roses tinged with yellow and red at the edges of the petals.

My first thought was: *It's a trick.*

But then Dex's voice sounded in my ear. "Do you like it?"

I looked up, startled at his soundless arrival. His smile was stiff and his eyes kept darting anxiously between the flowers and my face. And then I realized: He was afraid I'd say no.

"Are you serious?" I whispered, because what he was doing

was uncharacteristically romantic. And if I said yes and we didn't go after *this* . . .

His brow creased. "Of course," he said softly. And I could have kissed him.

"Then I'd love to," I said.

A smile broke like sunrise on his face. He cracked open the corsage cover and took out the gorgeous bloom.

"May I?" he asked.

I nodded. Heat flared in his eyes as his finger traced down my forearm and wrist to my hand. Then he very gently took my fingers and slipped the corsage over my wrist. As soon as he stopped touching me, I lifted the flowers for a closer look. They smelled amazing.

But Dex wasn't finished. While I was still staring at the flowers he took my hand and placed an envelope in it. Inside were two tickets to the prom. He'd already bought them. I stared down at them for a second, fighting against the rising hope and excitement, reminding myself what had happened the year before.

"I'm going to do it right this time," he whispered, still holding his hands over mine, as if to press the tickets into my skin.

My throat tightened. But for the first time I could ever remember . . . it was with *happy* tears. Suddenly, it seemed like the most natural thing in the world to pull my hand from his grip and cup his face and pull him down. To lay my lips on his, softly.

I took him by surprise. He stiffened for a moment and a bolt of pure embarrassment shot from my heart to my toes. I was about to pull away, when he came alive under my hands, pressing me back into the wall and tilting my chin to deepen the kiss. And

I was so caught up in the moment, I completely forgot where we were, until someone wolf-whistled from the hallway.

I pushed Dex back quickly, but he never stopped staring at me, and I knew I was blushing to my hairline. As the bell jangled through the hall and the passing students picked up their pace, I swallowed and straightened myself. Dex took my hand and pulled me back into the hallway, grinning like he'd just won a prize.

I shook my head slightly, hardly daring to believe that anyone could look that happy to be with me.

CHAPTER SEVENTEEN

DOC SCRATCHES HIS beard and frowns at his notes. "Tell me why you decided to go to prom with Dex, even when, at your own admission, you still had feelings for Matt?" Doc puts his analytical *I'm listening to you* face on and leans on his crossed knees.

"Geez, Doc." I cross my arms over my chest. "You make it sound like it was a big deal. I was seventeen and I wanted to go to prom. Every girl did."

Doc narrows his eyes. "I think there's more to it than that, Ashley."

"No, there isn't. I wasn't thinking that deeply back then—"

"Ashley, I know this is hard, but if we're going to get through this, you have to be honest with me."

"I *am* being honest." Even I'm not convinced by my breathy voice. "I told you about who I see in the mirror."

"Yet you're reluctant to discuss the decisions you made with her. I know we're approaching some difficult events. But if you're serious about your release, you have to be willing to talk things over, even if they're painful."

"Going to prom with Dex wasn't painful! At least, not the way you mean it."

"Ashley—"

"No! I'm sick of this. I'm sick of everyone deciding they know what's going on in my head. Some things *aren't* deep!"

"Yet those very things can have incredibly deep consequences."

I growl in frustration. Then I catch sight of the clock. It's already 11:34.

My tension ratchets higher.

Fine. Let's do this.

"Are you completely nuts?" Matt hissed in my ear after the final bell rang that Thursday.

We stood at my locker. I smiled because I was going to prom and Matt had heard about it from someone else.

For once everyone was gossiping about me in a *good* way.

"What?" I pretended innocence. Slamming my locker door shut and clicking the lock into place, I started down the hall, smiling at my feet.

Matt leaned in. "Ashley, you can't go to Finn's after prom!"

"Wait, what?" I stopped midstride and turned to face him.

Matt's jaw was set, and worry lines creased his brow. "It's always trouble when you and Finn are near each other. You can't go to his house *overnight*."

"Matt, what are you talking about?"

He frowned. "Aren't you going to prom with Dex? Which is, by the way, just about the *worst* idea known to man."

"Yes. But what does that have to do with Finn?"

Matt shook his head. "Dex is training with the baseball team now, remember?"

I nodded. "So?"

"So, Dex is making friends, Ash. Finn invited him to the after-party at his parents' vacation home in Seaside. He said he's coming. Which, if you're going with him, means you're coming, too."

I hadn't even thought about the afterparties. Could I risk another night like the one at Finn's just for a date for the prom? "We haven't talked about it," I said warily. "I'll have to think about it."

"Are you crazy, Ash? You won't be able to just bail and walk home. You won't even be able to have your own room. Finn's only inviting couples. You do know what that means, right? Or do you not care?"

My mouth dropped open. Ignoring an urge to slap his self-righteous face, I turned on my heel and stormed down the hall. Matt followed right alongside.

"I didn't mean it like that," he said. "But you're asking for trouble. This is Finn's house. Are you hearing me?"

"Yes," I said through gritted teeth.

We turned the corner into the main hall just as the bell screamed overhead.

"Ashley, stop!" Matt grasped my arm and pulled me around. He looked scared.

"What is your problem?" I jerked my arm out of his grip. "It's up to me to decide if I'm going, okay? And if I do, I'll stay out of Finn's way."

"And what about Dex? It's an *overnighter*, Ash." He let the implication hang.

I met his worried frown with a glare and stuck my chin out. "Are you going?"

He blinked. "Yes, but—"

"Are you taking Karyn *overnight*?"

His eyebrows shot up. "That's not . . . I mean . . . ," he spluttered.

A little part inside me died because I wanted him to say no. But I could see the double standard clicking into place behind his eyes, so I started walking again.

The next morning before school, I heard my name echoing down the hallway behind me.

"I tried calling you last night, but the line was busy for hours." Dex elbowed me lightly and grinned. "Busy talking to your other prom date?"

I shifted awkwardly on my feet. "Um, my mom was talking to an old friend." It was a lie; I'd knocked the phone off the receiver after she'd gone to bed. I was worried Dex or Matt was going to call, and I wasn't ready to talk about Finn's party or in the mood for another lecture.

The only person I wanted to talk to was Older Me. I'd stayed up until four a.m., hoping she would show up with some timely advice. When she hadn't, I'd had to make the decision on my own. There was no way around it: I simply couldn't go to that party. If Dex didn't want to go the dance with me because I couldn't go to this stupid party, then . . . then I was just going to have to live with that.

Dex rubbed his hands together eagerly. "So, my mom's letting me use the nice car for prom night, *and* I already booked my tux."

"Sweet," I said, glancing at the flow of everyone passing by. "Look, I heard about the party. At Finn's?"

Dex nodded. "It's going to be awesome. I just found out about it yesterday at lunch. And we're invited." His grin turned sly. "The girls are telling their parents that it's a girls-only thing."

"Oh." I squared my shoulders. "Dex, you know Finn hates me, right?" I began. Fear churned in my stomach as his smile faltered.

He scratched the back of his neck. "Don't worry about it. They all used to hate me, too. They're just—"

I put a hand on his arm. "No, you don't understand, Dex. Finn *hates* me. Like, makes vomit noises every time he sees me, hates me. I don't think . . . I don't think I can go."

He glanced around, then took my hand and pulled me through the flow of bodies to an alcove. "Look, I get it, okay?" He laced his fingers through mine. "But wouldn't it be fun? For us, I mean?"

"Yeah," I agreed uncertainly. "But—"

"How about this?" he said, and the gleam was back in his eye. "You talk to your mom and see if it's even an option, and I'll deal with Finn. Okay?"

A pang forced my mouth into a smile. I couldn't resist. I put my free hand flat on his chest and felt the firm muscles there. "I'm just . . . I don't think it's that simple."

"Of course it is!" he said, hushed. "I know how to handle it. I'll make Finn behave. I promise. Trust me."

His eyes hooked mine and then he leaned down to kiss me. For a second, all thoughts of Matt or Karyn or Finn just disappeared.

When he pulled away, he smiled softly. "Deal?"

I nodded, hoping I wouldn't regret this. "Deal."

CHAPTER EIGHTEEN

"YOU FELT ABLE to accept help from Dex, yet not from Matt?" Doc plucks at the material of his pants, frowning. "Why?"

I squirm. "It wasn't like that. The thing with Dex . . . it kind of snuck up on me. And he'd been in my shoes before—unaccepted. He knew how it felt and what he was risking by sticking up for me. Matt always seemed to just believe things would magically work out even when all the evidence suggested otherwise."

Doc folds his hands in his lap, watching me shift in my seat. "Is it possible Matt was optimistic because he wasn't aware of 'all the evidence,' as you put it?"

"Sure."

"Don't be flippant, Ashley. I'm asking you to examine something. Do you think if you'd told Matt what life in that school was really like for you—from the beginning—do you think he might have worked harder to make it easier on you? Or helped find a solution?"

"I don't think there was a solution," I snap.

Doc tips his head like I've said something interesting. "Do you really believe that? Even now?"

"Yes, I do." I meet him stare for stare because I'm not letting up on this.

"Is it possible, then, that your decisions contributed to the problem?"

My eyes narrow. "How do you figure?"

Doc opens a hand toward me. "If you didn't believe your problem was solvable, then the decisions you made—any actions you took—were predicated on that belief. You didn't take steps to solve the issue. You took steps to marginalize it. Correct?"

"Well . . . I mean . . . ," I splutter.

Doc raises a hand to stop me. "I don't mean that as a criticism. I'm just trying to help you peel back the layers of this. Are you able to see that your decision making was, many times, somewhat flawed?"

I exhale sharply. "Yes."

Doc nods like I'm a good child. "So, I'd like you to think about the fact that if you'd first, believed enough in your relationship with Matt to be honest with him, then second, allowed yourself to hope for a solution to your problems, you might have made different decisions. And, ergo, some of what you experienced might not have happened."

"Are you saying I brought this on myself?" I splutter.

"No," he says, emphatic. "I'm saying that what you believe to be true impacts what you do. So, in some ways, your conflicts with others were . . . self-fulfilling prophecy. All completely subconscious, of course."

I am suddenly humming with nervous tension.

He can't be right, can he?

I swallow. "Can I walk?"

He gives a short nod. "Certainly. Whatever makes you comfortable."

I push to my feet, past the big coffee table, past the lamps, to the other side of the room, near the broad, heavy desk, the floor-to-ceiling bookshelves, and the ugly wallpaper.

I stop in front of a fake fireplace in the corner. There's a huge picture of one of those old-fashioned sailing ships with a dozen square sails hung over it, and I've been wondering whether it's real.

A lot of people don't understand the difference between a real painting and a print. They figure, you get a picture to look at either way, so what's the big deal? Right? They don't understand. Artists don't just work with color and shape. They work with texture. With material. With light. You can't get that from a print of a painting any more than you understand the taste of rain from a photograph.

Anyone can fake in two dimensions.

Either Doc has taste, or he got lucky. The painting over his fake fireplace is real.

It's an oil painting. Realism. A near photographic reproduction. A boat is lurching out of the white-topped, green-gray waves, the clouds behind her deep and ominous.

It's not my style, but it's beautifully done. I can feel the wind chasing her. Feel her deck pressing on the feet of the sailors as it crests the wave. Like the way you feel when an elevator takes off too fast—

"Ashley?"

I jump. "Yes? Sorry, what were we . . . ?"

"We were talking about whether it was a good decision to attend the afterparty."

Oh. That.

"Overnight?" Mom chewed on the word. She stood at the kitchen counter, stirring pasta sauce into noodles. Her dark hair hung in layers around her shoulders, and she wore heels even though there was no one other than me around to admire them.

I picked at my thumbnail. "Yes."

"With boys?" She pursed her lips. For a second I wondered how this conversation would go with another mom.

"Yes." To hide my blush, I grabbed two glasses out of the cabinet and filled them with water, getting ready to set the table.

"And you're supposedly going with Dex again?"

I flinched. "Yes."

"Will Matt be there?"

"Yes, Mom." I groaned. My nerves shrilled because I was suddenly sure she'd say yes. I couldn't decide how I felt about that. Thinking about the kiss with Dex that morning made me melt inside. But also . . . this was an overnighter.

Was I ready for that?

Then Mom put the wooden spoon on the counter, the red pasta sauce pooling around it like blood. "I guess . . . I mean, I went overnight with my date after my prom. I can't see why . . ."

Oh, Lord, she's going to say yes. I opened the silverware door and pulled out some forks and knives.

"But, Ashley, you're going to have to promise me you'll be careful." She grabbed a sponge and wiped up the mess of sauce.

I pressed the tines of a fork into my finger until it turned white. "I will be."

"I'm not joking, Ashley," she said, pointing the sponge at me.

"I'm not laughing."

She picked up the spoon and started stirring again—a little faster this time. Then she smiled. "Can I help you get ready?" she asked, almost shyly.

"Oh, um, sure," I said, caught off guard.

"Great!" Mom picked a piece of pasta out of the bowl and chewed it. "Try to find a dark-colored dress," she said, pulling plates out of the cupboard over her head. "It'll be more slimming."

After a dinner during which I simmered and Mom was quieter than usual, I headed to my room. I'd intended to work on my portfolio, but as soon as I passed the mirror, Older Me appeared.

"So . . . you're definitely going?" she whispered. She looked at me and I couldn't tell if she was afraid of what I would say, or sad about it.

I nodded. "It's weird. I'm nervous, but . . . I don't want to miss it."

Older Me nodded, too, but she didn't smile. Little white lines of tension framed her mouth.

Then her head snapped around and she muttered something I didn't catch. She just kept glancing behind her. "Look, I have to—"

"Again?" She hardly ever showed up anymore, and when she did, she'd been running off almost every time we did get a chance to talk. I knew she had to be careful. Her roommates had heard her talking to me a lot lately.

"I'm sorry. But . . . I have to go."

That was when I realized she looked different. A little more put together than usual. She was in black slacks with a simple, collared button-up over the top. Her hair had been blown out. She had some makeup on.

"Where are you going?"

She jerked to look at me. "Nowhere. I mean, just . . . work stuff."

"Since when do you work?"

"I'll talk to you later, okay? Or maybe tomorrow. Just, whatever you do . . . just remember, no one's perfect. But you want to be able to look at yourself in the mirror the next morning. No regrets. Better to make the *right* choice than to hate yourself the next day. You know?"

"I guess . . . ?"

She ran a hand through her hair, and for once it tumbled onto her shoulders prettily. "Look, don't do anything Karyn would do. Okay?"

And with that totally random piece of advice, she walked out of the frame.

I was left sitting on my carpet, staring at my own open mouth, wondering what I had missed.

CHAPTER NINETEEN

DOC TAPS HIS pen against his pad. "You keep mentioning abrupt ends to these conversations. What was happening to keep the two of you apart?"

I try not to sneer, try to keep the cynicism off my face. "People like you," I say under my breath.

Doc looks surprised. "Excuse me?"

I drop my head back against the chair. "Doc, you aren't the first person to think I talk to *myself* when I look in the mirror. Sometimes . . . sometimes I think both of us were just trying to get through. Trying not to draw too much attention to ourselves. Sometimes keeping our relationship a secret seemed more important than the relationship itself." I grind my teeth as soon as the words come out of my mouth, because I know they're true. "It shouldn't have been that way," I mutter. "People you love should always be more important than people who judge you."

Doc nods. "Is that an adage you've always lived by?"

Will wonders never cease. "No. Clearly. Otherwise I wouldn't be *here*." I flip my hand, indicating the room.

"Do *you* think you need to be here?" Doc asks. "Because some important people in your life think you do. Like your mother."

"Yeah, because my mother's such a paradigm of mental health," I say sarcastically.

Doc's lips twitch, as if he's trying not to smile. "So I take it getting ready for prom wasn't your favorite mother-daughter activity?"

I smirk. "How did you guess?"

A couple of weeks later I stood in my room, just in front of the mirror. The floor was scattered with hair tongs and curling irons, cords snaking across the floor to the socket in the wall, and bags of Mom's makeup were strewn everywhere. I'd worked on my portfolio right up to the minute Mom insisted I get in the shower, and all my paintbrushes and pencils were piled around an unfinished sketch on my desk.

She immediately started reminding me of Dex's no-show the year before and making comments like ". . . such a pity. You'd be *so* pretty if you just lost a little weight."

By the time we got to the eye shadow, I was ready to become an emancipated minor.

Older Me appeared, silently watching the proceedings while Mom put my hair in massive curlers. When Mom turned to find a new roller, I glared at Older Me.

She gave me an innocent look. "What?"

I gritted my teeth. With Mom there, I couldn't ask Older Me where she'd been recently—since she certainly hadn't been in the mirror. In fact, apart from showing up twice to remind me to be careful tonight, then disappearing before I could ask her why, I hadn't seen her in almost two weeks.

Finally, Mom let the rollers out and my hair fell just past my shoulders in big, loose curls. My bangs were wrangled into a stylish swoosh that cut just over one eye and made me look two years older.

"You look pretty," Older Me murmured.

My stomach swooped.

Matt was going to freak.

I meant, Dex. *Dex* was going to freak.

"Something just isn't right." Mom sighed dramatically and dug into her makeup bag again. "Oh!" she exclaimed, pulling yet another bottle out of her bag. "I do still have the glitter! That would look great on your arms—"

"Glitter?" Older Me and I cried simultaneously.

Mom's head snapped up. "Well, not *glitter*, but shimmer—"

"No! No, that's it. I'm done." I put my hands up to wave off whatever it was she was pulling out of her bag. "This is fine. This is all I need, Mom. Thank you," I finished, working hard not to let the sarcasm into my tone.

Mom stared at me for a long moment. "Then there's only one more thing I need to give you," she said quietly, and in a tone I'd never heard before. It was stilted. Almost wistful. And she kept looking at the carpet when she lifted her hand out of the bag, clutching a small, shiny packet.

I frowned, uncertain, until I realized that pinched between her fingers was a thin, foil-wrapped square.

"A condom, Mom? *Really*?" I didn't know whether to laugh or cry. "You can't be—"

"I'm very serious," she said, tucking a strand of hair behind her ear.

Behind me, Older Me made a choking noise.

"Ashley, I know this is your first overnight party . . . and you probably don't really know what to expect. I wish we'd had time to sort of . . . grow you into this. But the fact is, your school friends are getting up to all kinds of things, and they have been for years," she said. "And I don't want you going into that kind of thing unprepared."

"Take it," Older Me said in a strange voice. "Just take it and—"

What the *hell*?

"I'm not taking that!" I snapped at both of them. "I'm not having sex with Dex!" The idiocy of the rhyme struck me. I swallowed a laugh that hurt going down.

"You might not be *planning* to—" Mom said carefully.

"I'm not planning to because I'm not *going* to," I cut her off.

"We all think that when we're standing in the light of day. But when you're with a boy and he's excited and you want him to be happy . . ." She trailed off with a meaningful look.

My mouth dropped open.

"Just take it," Older Me said, tugging on the strings of her hoodie. "It doesn't mean you have to use it. It will end the conversation sooner."

"I can't believe we're having this conversation at all," I muttered.

"This is *Mom*," Older Me said. "Ignore her. Pretend she's telling you to wait for love and . . . and not to undervalue yourself. That your self-respect is worth more than Dex's—than *anyone's*—hard-on."

Mom twitched under my glare. "There are plenty of parents

who wouldn't allow you to go tonight, Ashley. And I'm sure they'd all mean well. But if a girl like you wants to keep a guy's interest—"

"Are you seriously telling me to use sex to keep a guy interested?"

Her lips thinned. "I'm telling you I would understand if you did."

Older Me dropped her head into one hand. "She is terrible! The *worst!*"

I was quivering. Absolutely seething. My skin felt like fire. "Is that what you did, Mom?" I snapped. "'Cause it looks like it worked out *great* for you."

Mom's head whipped back as if I'd hit her. But years' worth of anger at her was curling into rage. Older Me's voice broke through. "Don't make her mad—"

"Listen . . . ," Mom hissed. She leaned in, waving the condom in my face. "I don't know what possessed that boy to invite you tonight, but he did. And I'm telling you, this is your chance for something like a normal high school experience. I'm *helping* you—"

"So I should take advice from you?" I laughed, but even to my ears it sounded forced and brittle. "I may be a hopeless social leper, *Mother*, but you're still a woman whose husband left her for a younger woman, and who hasn't been on a date in two years. But maybe I've got it all wrong. Maybe you don't bother with the dating part. Maybe you just jump into bed—"

I didn't even see her hand move, just felt the ringing slap on my cheek, saw a crack of lightning across my vision.

Older Me swore. "Oh, Ash . . ."

My mother and I stood toe-to-toe in front of the mirror. Her breath sucked in and out as if she'd been running. Mine was locked inside. Until it all came out in a shaky rush on the words, "Better do the other side, too. Otherwise my blush will be uneven."

This time I saw it coming. I closed my eyes and let it happen. Now both my cheeks stung.

"Are you finished?" Mom held my gaze, her jaw hard, hands clenched at her sides now.

I waited. Her chest rose and fell too fast. Mine too slowly.

But she just stared, her nostrils flared. "Most of the girls in your class would *kill* to have a mother like me."

"Too bad I'm not one of them."

Her cheeks sucked in and her knuckles turned white. For a second, the fury on her face made my courage falter.

But then the sound of the doorbell rang through the house.

Dex was here to pick me up.

Mom shoved the condom into my hand, then brushed past me without another word, slamming my door behind her.

A minute later the sound of footsteps down the hallway broke through everything else. Mom had sent Dex to my room?

"Ashley?" Dex said quietly. The door started to open. With a little yelp, I dove for my purse, shoving the condom deep inside, then stepping back to face the mirror, playing with my hair as if I was trying to get it to lay right.

"*Hey*, you look great!" Dex said from the now-open doorway.

I tried to smile, smoothed the front of my royal blue skirt. The neckline of my dress was deep and round, offering a hint of my cleavage without being too revealing. And it showed off my

141

shoulders, while the tiny sleeves capped the thickest part of my arm. I'd felt *pretty* when I tried it on, and given the way Dex was looking at me now, it seemed like he thought so, too.

"Thanks," I said, relieved that my voice sounded normal, if somewhat subdued.

I turned away to grab my purse from the bed and suddenly his hands were on my arms. He turned me around.

"Are you okay?" Dex's voice sounded gentle.

I shrugged. "Just nervous, I guess."

One of his hands rose to touch under my chin, force it up, force me to look at him. Dex fixed me with a dark, penetrating stare. He frowned. I took in the perfectly cut suit jacket that hugged his massive shoulders, tapering to his trim waist. The way the trim-cut pants slouched over his shoes.

He looked sleek and sexy. And he was looking at me like he *cared*.

"This is our night, Ash. The night we should have had a year ago. We'll get through it together." Something deepened in his gaze.

He tipped his forehead to mine. "Are you ready for this?" he asked, his voice a little hoarse.

"Not even close," I said honestly.

Dex chuckled, grabbed my hand, and pulled me to the door. I slung my bag over my free shoulder and followed, wobbling a little in my new heels, half afraid and half excited about what was to come.

CHAPTER TWENTY

DOC'S EXPRESSION IS halfway between concerned and amused. I glare at him.

"So your mother . . ."

"Encouraged me to act like a whore. Yes," I say darkly.

He frowns. "From what you're describing, that wasn't her goal."

"Really? Then let me describe it again, so I get it right this time."

"Ashley—"

I flap a hand at him. "I know what you mean. It just . . . bugs me."

"The condom?"

I shake my head. "No, that was probably smart. But it was the reasoning behind it. She wasn't trying to help me be careful, or whatever. She just assumed I'd give myself up for Dex—for any guy who gave me that kind of attention."

"You did ask to go away overnight. With a date."

"Yes, I did. But you'd think that would have spurred a little motherly advice, right? Something about caution, maybe?"

Doc shifts his weight and his notes start sliding off his lap. He grabs for them, straightening them as he talks. "So, did she do anything right that night?"

I looked past him to the hideous wallpaper. I don't want to give Mom credit for anything—after she shoved me in here. But in hindsight . . . "I think she understood the situation better than I did," I admit reluctantly. "That's why she offered me the means to protect myself."

"From sex?"

I shiver, and the weight of all of it presses me into my chair. "Yes. But also from guys who only think about themselves."

"Dex?"

"Everyone."

I was at prom.

I was at prom.

I swayed on the dance floor in the arms of a good-looking baseball player. And no one pointed or laughed. Not even Finn, who was dancing with some blond sophomore who looked like a carbon copy of Karyn.

Dex wrapped his arms around my waist. He'd taken off his jacket and pulled his tie loose to dangle on his chest. I played with it while we danced, my fingers following it up his chest, to his neck, where his shirt lay open to reveal that triangle of skin at his throat. When I touched it, his breath caught.

I lay my head against his chest. His heart thumped and pulsed fast and I smiled wider. Dex leaned down and his lips touched the skin under my ear, sending jolts across my skin and down my arm. I turned my chin to meet him halfway and stopped breathing when he kissed me.

His lips slid softly across mine, and I sank into the sensation of it, letting myself feel the tingle in my belly, and the goose bumps prickling my skin. When we pulled apart. I ducked my chin and snuggled into his chest, barely moving to the music.

"Are you thirsty?" he asked a few songs later.

"Sure," I said, fanning myself with my hand. I stood at the edge of the dance floor, watching his back as he walked toward the drinks table. I swallowed hard. He looked *really* good.

"Enjoying yourself?"

I turned to find Matt standing next to me, hair slicked back like some fifties gangster, jacket off, tie already gone. He looked amazing.

Except for the twitching muscle at the back of his jaw.

"Apparently more than you are," I said. "What's up? Where's Karyn?"

"Can we talk?" He nodded toward the exit.

Confused, I followed him through swinging fire doors into a deserted hallway. When we were a few feet from the door, I put a hand on his arm. "What's going on?"

Matt whirled on me. "You told someone, didn't you?"

I jerked back a step. "Told someone what?"

"About the afterparty. That the boys would be there, too."

Inside the dance, the DJ changed to a fast song. The crowd cheered. I stared at Matt. "What are you talking about?"

Matt leaned in. "*Someone* told Terese's mom the truth. She's picking Terese up right after the dance, and threatening to tell the other parents the truth, too. If they all find out, the party's ruined."

I frowned. "What's that got to do with me?"

He raked a hand through his hair. "Everyone *else* is really excited for tonight," he said pointedly.

"Wait. You think *I* told?" I rubbed my hands up and down my arms, suddenly freezing. "I wouldn't *do* that, Matt. How could you even—" I gasped, realization dawning. "Karyn said it was me, didn't she!"

For the first time, Matt looked uncertain. Then he fixed me with a hard look. "Ash, this wasn't the time to get revenge, or whatever. You might not just ruin it for Karyn. You might ruin it for all of us."

"I didn't ruin anything!" I wanted to grab his shirt and shake him.

"Then who told?" he demanded.

"I don't know!" Though I had a strong suspicion. *Finn.* No doubt he was jealous of Karyn sleeping with Matt, and he was just selfish enough to ruin the party to keep it from happening. Not that I could tell Matt that. So far, Finn had held up his end of the bargain. I had to hold up mine.

The door to the hallway opened again, and a giggling couple emerged. The guy pressed his date against the wall and began making out with her. Matt sighed in exasperation and pulled me farther down the corridor.

"I can't believe you'd listen to *her* over me!" I said.

"Why not?" He was strung tighter than a coiled spring. "You aren't listening to me anymore. You won't come anywhere when I invite you, but Dex snaps his fingers and suddenly you're there."

He pointed a finger at me. "You've changed, Ash. I don't know what's going on with you anymore. For all I know, you and Dex did this together. Maybe you've forgiven him, but I remember what he used to be like."

At that, something inside me snapped. Anger coursed through my veins. I shoved Matt in the chest so he stumbled back a step. "No! You don't get to treat me like they do! You're my best friend. You're the only one who . . ." I closed my eyes, struggled for control.

Matt's mouth dropped open. I moved to shove him again, unable to find any other way to express how *pissed off* I felt, but he caught my hands at the wrist, his face softening just when I needed him to be angry so I could be angrier back.

"Ash—"

"No!" I fumed. "I didn't do it, and you know it. I can't believe you're siding with them!"

He frowned. "I'm not *siding*, it just makes sense—"

"To *who*?" I looked at him, pleading. Confusion flittered across his face. His grip on my wrists tightened and for a second I thought he would pull me closer. But then he swallowed and his gaze dropped to our hands.

"I just can't think of anyone else who'd want to," he said softly. "It seemed like . . . maybe you didn't want me and Karyn to . . ."

A blush rose in my cheeks. He thought I'd done this so he couldn't sleep with Karyn. Yanking my hands out of his grip, I took a step back. Then another. I took in the guy who I thought was my best friend. In that moment, I barely even recognized him.

Matt's brow furrowed. "Ash—"

"I didn't do it. And even though I'd love to see those girls get a taste of their own medicine, I never would have done it because it would have hurt *you*," I admitted in a voice barely above a whisper. "And you, of all people, should know that."

Matt's face dropped in surprise. But then he swallowed. "I—I'm sorry . . . I just—"

I turned and fled. Because the truth was, even though I hadn't told, there was a part of me that hoped all their nights *were* ruined.

They all deserved it.

Maybe even Matt.

CHAPTER TWENTY-ONE

DOC LOOKS SURPRISED. "So you finally stood up to Matt. Did you call him out for ruining your prom?"

"Doc, that fight was just the tip of the iceberg." The bitterness in my voice is plain, even to me.

Doc's gaze sharpens. "So what happened next?"

I press my toes into the carpet to stop the feeling of vertigo. "What *didn't*?"

After I stormed away from Matt, I spent ten minutes in one of the bathroom's handicap stalls, pulling myself together. I knew I couldn't go back to the dance with bloodshot eyes. But every time I thought of Matt's tight jaw, of his hands so hard on my wrists, the tears sprang up again and I had to start over, breathing away the urge to cry.

When I had myself in check, and the mirror revealed clear eyes, I took a deep breath. "Are you there?" I said cautiously to the surface. I waited, but she never showed. Finally, I left the bathroom and walked down the hall, toward the auditorium. Toward whatever the rest of the night held.

I found Dex at a corner table. Eli sat next to him, his date on his lap as they made out.

Dex stood up, beaming, and hugged me to his chest. "There you are!"

"Yeah, sorry," I said into his shirt. "I had to call my mom and—"

"Don' worry 'bout it," Dex said, tipping my chin up. "I missed you." He lowered his lips to mine. At first I welcomed the contact, needing comfort after my confrontation with Matt. But then Dex deepened the kiss. His tongue slipped across my bottom lip, and I tasted the sweet, sickly tang of alcohol.

I tried to pull back, but he followed me, his lips never losing contact. When I turned my head away, he kissed his way down my jaw and neck.

"Dex . . ." I gave him a gentle shove.

"You're so hot, Ashley," he whispered, grabbing my butt.

I gripped his shirt, taken off guard. Then I pushed him back for real. His face was slack and his temples were sweaty.

I felt chilled. "Have you been drinking?" I asked quietly.

His brows pinched in over his nose. "Barely." He looked around us, smiled nervously at someone, then pulled me closer again.

I let him, but didn't lift my chin for another kiss. I swallowed hard. "Is that okay? I mean, aren't you just out of rehab?" I asked carefully.

Dex shook his head, muttering something I didn't catch. "I'm a drug addict, Ashley. Not an alcoholic." He said it like I should have known better. Liked I'd pissed him off.

I considered calling him on it, but I didn't want to ruin the night. And if he had a couple of shots for courage, well, I could understand that. Pushing away the uneasy feeling in the pit of my stomach, I let my hands slide up his chest and locked my fingers at the back of his neck. When he kissed me again, I tried to get into it. Tried to ignore the pungent tang on his breath. I should have been ecstatic. But I was uncomfortable and awkward. And embarrassingly close to tears.

Dex didn't seem to notice when I turned my face away. His fingers stayed at my neck and he dragged his lips across my cheek to whisper in my ear, "I can't wait to see you without that dress."

I froze. Everything inside me resisted the idea. I opened my mouth to say it, but Liam stepped up to Dex's shoulder and patted his shoulder.

"Dude, we have to get out of here. Some of the girls' parents are starting to call—they heard about the party."

Dex grabbed my hand and pulled me along in Liam's wake. Around us, everyone was grabbing jackets and purses and hurrying away from the table, headed in the same direction.

I didn't want to go to the party, but I had to. I'd already been accused of ruining everyone else's night. If I left now, left Dex, they'd all think I was the rat.

No *way* was I letting Finn pin that on me.

"I think you better let me drive tonight," I said in a low voice as we trotted down the cement steps outside.

Dex frowned. "I'm fine, Ash," he muttered. "Your mom said you could go tonight, right? She isn't going to show up?"

"All the more reason to get there safe, right?" I said carefully, holding out my hand.

I saw him brace and for a second I was afraid we'd really argue and the night would be ruined after all. But then he shook his head.

"Okay, sure. But you'll owe me," he said, winking.

I forced a laugh and tried not to snatch the keys when he held them out.

It was a long drive, well over an hour. Dex seemed to sober up a little as we went. Perhaps if he didn't drink any more we could still salvage the night, I thought. I glanced to the side, examining Dex's profile in the constantly moving light of traffic on the freeway.

He caught me looking and smiled, laid a hand on my knee and squeezed. "You having fun?"

I swallowed and kept driving. "Yeah, of course."

The beach house glimmered on the edge of sand dunes. It was a massive, two-story square with a wraparound porch and gabled windows in the roof. I pulled the car off the wide driveway to a grassy spot under a tree and turned it off. Without the engine noise, all I could hear was the sound of breaking waves.

I grabbed Dex's hand and smiled when he looked at me. "Let's go for a walk on the beach."

"Let's take our bags and stuff inside first, though, okay?" Dex said, eyeing the house. I nodded and he grabbed both our bags, throwing them effortlessly over one shoulder. Then, hand in hand, we crossed the driveway.

Music drifted out of every window and open door. Light spilled across the deck and onto the grassy dunes below. A guy leaned against the railing of the porch, nursing a beer.

"Hey, Eli. When'd you get here?"

Eli, the bead necklace visible in the open neck of his shirt, turned and grinned back.

"Dex! You made it!" He grinned when he looked at me and stood straight, giving Dex two thumbs-up. "And you got another girl through the parental barricade. Good work."

Dex nodded. "Where's Lanie?"

Eli's eyes widened, like he'd suddenly remembered his date. Then he looked around. "Um, she's here somewhere . . ."

It wasn't until Dex had tugged me past and we were walking into the house that I realized that Eli hadn't insulted me.

The French doors opened into a long living room, where Liam sat slumped on a leather couch, his arm around Layla. "Do we just find a room?" Dex asked.

Liam winked. "First come, first served." They both laughed but it took me a second to get the double meaning. I pulled Dex away.

He came willingly, moving past to tug me up the stairs to a wide hallway with a carpet runner and round brass light fixtures. He opened a couple of doors until he found an empty one. "Here we go!"

The room had a closet and a tiny en suite bathroom to the left. A fluffy comforter covered the queen-size bed. Dex dropped our bags at the end of the bed, then took my chin in one hand and made me look at him.

"Tonight is going to be so much fun," he said.

"Yeah, sure." I said.

It had become my pat answer to everything.

Wanna go to prom, Ashley? Yeah, sure.

Wanna go to Finn's beach house for a party? Yeah, sure.

Wanna become the slut everyone already thinks you are?

Yeah . . . sure . . .

Dex dropped his mouth to mine and kissed me. Deeply. Then nudged me toward the bed. I tensed. My hands came up to his chest and he pulled me in tighter, kissing my neck as one hand drifted up my side to my ribcage.

"Dex," I gasped. "I can't . . ."

"Don't worry," he whispered against my neck. "We'll fool around for a while first."

"That's not what I meant." I pushed at his shoulders, but he just twisted a little and took my lips again.

"Relax."

I pulled back. "Dex! I'm not kidding."

"Neither am I," he said, voice husky. "We're good together, Ash."

He palmed my breast through my dress. I shoved him away, hard, and he stumbled back at the same time I stepped away from him, toward the door. He ended up next to the bed, panting. When he'd regained his balance, he glared at me.

"What the hell's your problem?" Dex growled.

I smoothed down my dress. "This is too fast. I'm not . . . You're acting like it's just a done deal. And it's not. *I'm* not. I mean . . . I won't do it. Not tonight. I'm sorry if you thought—"

His jaw dropped. "I asked you to come with me *overnight*, Ash. What did you think I was asking?"

I clenched my teeth. "I thought you wanted to take me to prom."

Dex pushed up his shirt cuffs. "I did everything you wanted.

I made a big deal out of asking you. I got you flowers and did the stupid pictures. I danced with you—"

"Groped me on the dance floor, you mean," I shot back.

"You want me to apologize for finding you attractive?"

I threw my arms in the air. "No, I want you to care more about how I feel than you do about feeling me up!"

He ran a hand through his hair. "You're unbelievable."

"Why? Because I won't drop my panties the second you snap your fingers?"

"No," he answered. "Because you make this big deal about not being like *them*, then you use me just to get you here tonight."

"What?" I gasped.

Dex gave me a wry look. "Oh, don't play stupid with me, Ash. I know you're in love with Matt. Everyone does. It's obvious."

"Whatever." I turned to look at a pen and ink drawing of tern on the wall so he wouldn't see me blush.

He put his hand on my shoulder. "But I *thought* we had something. I *thought* maybe you'd see that he's not interested, and you'd give us a shot."

I whirled back around. "I gave you a shot last year. Look where that got me."

"And I apologized!"

"Oh, you're right, Dex. That makes it all better!" Tears welled up in my eyes and I swiped them away with the back of my hand. "Let's go sleep together now!"

Dex shook his head. His hands clenched to fists at his sides, and his jaw tightened. "I can't believe I wasted this night on you."

The blow landed. I took a step back. "You're just as bad as they are."

"Yeah, well, so are you. Find yourself a ride tomorrow," he snapped, pushing past me. "We're done."

After he slammed the door, I stood there trembling, staring at it. I replayed the entire conversation, trying to figure out exactly where everything had gone wrong, and my stomach sank.

Was he right? Had I used him? I squirmed. Maybe. Probably. I'd wanted to go to prom so badly . . . it almost didn't matter with whom. And he'd done all those romantic things—asking me out at school, buying me a corsage, borrowing his mom's car. He'd even performed the miracle of all miracles: He'd gotten Finn off my back for an entire night.

I stood and started pacing the room, filled with doubt. Maybe I'd overreacted. Maybe if I'd been honest with him up front he would have agreed to keep it PG-13 tonight. Or, I could have just slowed things down. Maybe I should apologize. Let him see that I hadn't meant to reject him.

Before I could chicken out, I yanked the door open, padded along the hall and down the stairs. Laughter and voices traveled up from the living room, drifting over the music and the deep bass that thumped in the old floorboards.

But just as I got downstairs, Dex's voice rose from right around the corner, stopping me in my tracks.

". . . don't think she'd do it. Seriously. She's trying way too hard to get in with everyone."

The high-pitched cackle that followed that comment raised the hairs on the back of my neck. *Brooke.* "She's such a loser. Why are you even here with her?"

"*Shhhhh*, keep it down. I don't know where she is." He sounded loose, like he'd found another shot or two.

"Who, Ashley?" she said, too loudly.

He shushed her again. "Stop it!" But there was a smile in his voice. Then Brooke squeaked and shuffled footsteps rose over the music.

"Stop it! That tickles!" Brooke giggled. A shiver rode down my spine.

Dex laughed. More shuffling, and a thump. Then there was nothing but the music.

In fact, they were quiet for so long, I figured maybe they'd moved into the next room. But just as I was about to peer around the side to check, Brooke spoke again, in a strangely anxious tone.

"I'm serious, Dex. Why'd you bring *her*?" The disdain in her tone was no surprise. But it still hurt.

"Well, *someone* told me I didn't stand a chance. I didn't want to be alone tonight, so . . . ," Dex said in a suggestive tone.

"And you believed me?" she asked.

Dex was quiet.

"Okay, fine," she said. "My bad. But you've gotta get some game, Dex. You can't believe *everything* a girl tells you. I mean, you know . . ."

Her voice dropped so I couldn't hear. Then she laughed and Dex whined, "Aw, man. I can't believe I wasted my time getting Finn and everyone to be nice to her!" Both their voices faded into the music.

I backed away, but my feet felt like cement, my legs blocks of wood. Dex liked *Brooke*. He wasn't nice because he liked me. He truly only brought me here for sex. And somehow he'd made Finn be nice so I wouldn't say no.

With a sob, I whirled, stumbled down the hall, past more doors and an alcove. I reached an open doorway on my right. The room beyond was dark, but another door led out to the back porch. I clapped a hand over my mouth to stifle my cries, slipped outside and ran across the porch and onto the sand.

At first I stumbled blindly through the dunes, but occasional shouts and whoops said my *friends* had spilled out of the house and onto the beach. I wasn't going to be safe just wandering around.

So I turned for the patchy trees that lined the dunes behind the house and the deepest shadows between them, trying to keep my tearful hiccups quiet. I hadn't gone ten feet before I realized the darkest shadow was actually behind the house—and solid enough to be some kind of building.

It was a tiny A-frame with a wide, rickety door that wasn't locked. Barely bigger than my bedroom, it had rails on the ground that suggested it had once been a boathouse. But the moonlight seeping in through the now-open door cast blue light on a bunch of boxes lining one wall, and some kind of couch in the corner.

Beggars can't be choosers. Praying there weren't any deadly species of sand-beetles in Oregon, I wrenched the door shut behind me, cursing and embarrassing myself with more tears when I immediately tripped on one of the rails and fell to my knees.

Gritty sand covered the floorboards, and I distinctly heard scuttling in the corner.

Gasping, I launched myself onto the couch and huddled down.

Ten points for pathetic desperation, Ashley.

Tears slid down my cheeks and I dropped my face into my hands. I had to get out of there. But how? I'd come in Dex's car. Mom wasn't going to drive all the way out here . . . I tried to find an easier solution, but no matter how I looked at it, there was only one option.

Matt.

If I told him what I'd heard, he'd take me home.

But I didn't know where he was. And wherever he was, I'd no doubt find Karyn, too. What if they were upstairs right now?

I sucked in deep breaths of sea air and told myself to get it together.

I could do this. I could figure this out. Even if it meant hiding all night and commandeering Matt's car in the morning . . . I could do this.

But, man, I wished I didn't have to.

CHAPTER TWENTY-TWO

"SO DEX WAS just hoping to sleep with you," Doc sums up, somewhat redundantly.

"Yeah. In fairness, I should have known," I said.

Doc leans back in his chair. "Let's explore that a little bit. Do you feel you should've known because your older self should have told you? Or because Matt warned you?"

"Neither." I shook my head. "Dex was an eighteen-year-old boy. Even I knew that sex was beyond important—it was imperative for most guys. Even for Matt. Matt talked big about being a good guy, but the reality was, sex blinded him. If he was attracted to a girl, he wasn't really thinking about anything else. And he was one of the *nice* ones."

"That's a pretty bleak view of men," Doc pointed out. "But I can see how, after prom, you would feel that way." Doc's voice is quiet, sympathetic. "I am sorry you had to go through that."

I squirm. "I don't know. I mean, it sucked. But oddly, the night wasn't all bad. There was one part when I was really happy. I don't get to feel that way very often."

* * *

I have no idea how long I sat out there. Over time, my tears sub-sided and my eyes adjusted. I could make out lines of moonlight on the floor where it peeked between boards in the rotten door, and a hole in the wall that no doubt let in the inhabitants that gave my hideout its uniquely flavorful smell. Dust rose to mingle with the sea air every time I moved. But I couldn't find the cour-age to move back toward the house.

The night got darker and the party got louder. At some point several voices raised in argument inside the house, someone shriek-ing, another cursing. Then came the slam of car doors and a roaring engine. I wondered who had left, then decided I didn't care.

The party got quieter after that.

I listened to the waves crashing onto the sand and decided I couldn't risk walking in on Matt and Karyn *together*—it might finally send me over the edge. I'd wait. Try to get some sleep. Find Matt in the morning, preferably after he was dressed.

An old blanket had been draped over the back of the couch. I tugged it off and shook it out, coughing with all the dust and blinking sand out of my already dry eyes. Then I laid it over the couch and sat down on top of it, loathe to cover my beautiful new dress in the scratchy, dirty cloth.

I'd just pulled my knees up and eyed a suspicious shadow in the corner when voices rose again, this time from out on the sand.

A minute later, a deep voice called, "*Aaaaashley!*" Between the slats in the door, a shadow of a guy rose from the dunes a few feet away.

He stopped near the trees, peering between them, and shouted *"Ash?"*

161

It was Matt.

I gasped and he whirled around, stumbling through the dune-grass toward me. "Ash?"

When he reached the door, he wrenched it open.

"Ash? Are you okay?" He paused in the doorway, then rushed toward me, his feet making hollow thumps on the floorboards, before sliding to his knees beside the couch. I shushed him, uncertain whether to be dismayed or elated that he'd found me.

"Seriously, Ash, everyone's looking for you. What happened?" He searched my face in the dark, one hand on my shoulder. "What are you doing out here? What's wrong?"

"I—I had to get away from *Dex* . . ." My voice was breathy and broken.

Matt's fingers dug into my shoulder. "What did he do?" he asked, his voice deep and stilted.

I looked up and found him there, *caring*—and I cracked, spilling out the whole stupid story. Matt didn't move or speak the whole time, though his fingers tightened when I talked about maybe sleeping with Dex.

When I finished, he let out a huge breath. The tension fell off him. He got to his feet and dropped to sit next to me.

"C'mere," he whispered, mouth twisted into a grimace. Then he gathered me close and stroked my back. I buried my face in his shoulder and gripped him tight.

"I'm sorry," he said, so close his lips brushed my ear. "I wondered, but he didn't talk about you in front of me. And Finn didn't tell me . . . Man, he sucks."

I didn't know if he meant Finn or Dex, but I nodded against

his chest. For the first time since I'd walked into this hellhole, I felt safe.

Matt held me. He wasn't doing that thing guys do when a girl cries, where they put an awkward arm around her and wish they were *anywhere* else. Matt *held* me—and muttered curses at the people who'd hurt me.

"Ashley, look at me." Matt squeezed my shoulders. Then he moved to tip my chin, forcing my head up. "Look at me."

My chest tightened with the urgency in his voice. I met his eyes with tears blurring my own. I could smell the sweet after-breath of beer over his cologne.

"Have you been drinking?" I hiccupped.

One side of Matt's mouth slid toward a smile. "Barely. I got a little distracted when we realized you were gone."

I swallowed. "Well, I'm sorry for ruining your night. You should probably go. Karyn will have a cow if you disappear, too."

"Karyn's not here." He frowned. "We had a fight. Didn't you hear?"

Oh. "I didn't realize that was you." I pushed my lips together so I wouldn't smile.

"Half the girls got called home by their parents before they even got here. The rest joined forces with Karyn when she stormed out an hour ago and went to a motel. Including Brooke." He grinned. "Only you would miss that."

"Wait, there are no other girls here now?"

Matt shook his head and I groaned, burying my face in my hands.

Stories would go around school about how I'd been the only

girl left. I could only *imagine* what Karyn and her friends would do with that.

"Hey, hey. Don't worry." Matt's arms closed around me again, but I could hear the smile in his voice. "We'll hang out tonight, stay out of everyone's way, and I'll drive you home in the morning, okay? Relax. It's fine."

I looked up at him then. His grin broadened to a smile and he reached forward to brush a tear from my cheek. Then the thumb traced my cheek again.

"Please stop crying," he murmured and there was a new note in his voice that made me shiver.

"Okay," was the only thing I could think to say.

Matt grinned, but only for a second. His eyes latched on mine and his thumb traced my cheekbone again, fingers coming to rest under my ear.

"You look beautiful tonight. You know that?"

"Sure. Puffy eyes and all—"

His other hand cupped my face and he stared at me. "I'm serious."

I was frozen in that look.

Matt ran his thumb across my bottom lip. "Ash?" he whispered.

"Yes," I said. And it was an answer to anything. Everything.

Then, slowly, he tilted his head toward me.

And for a second, when his lips closed on mine, I felt like I was watching it happen to someone else. But then . . . so softly, but so sure, I fell into his kiss. Matt was kissing me.

Matt was *kissing* me.

Matt was kissing *me*.

CHAPTER TWENTY-THREE

MATT HELD MY face so I couldn't move away. His breath mingled with mine, and the hot, sweet smell of alcohol didn't even matter. He kissed me like he *wanted* to, and I could have stayed there for hours. I didn't care that we were in a creaky shack, or about the rush of air chilling my ankles. I grabbed at his shoulders and didn't care what happened. I wanted to spend the rest of my life in that moment.

Matt's breath thundered in my ear as his fingers laced behind my neck and he kissed his way down my jaw to my throat, my collarbone.

"I've been waiting to do that," he breathed against the skin of my neck, his lips brushing the words away. "Every time I saw you tonight, I wanted to grab you and leave."

My head spun. Was this possible?

"I always feel that way," I whispered.

He pulled back to meet my eyes. His hair was mussed, standing up in places. He cleared his throat, but I could hear his rapid breath. His lips parted and I ached to have them back. We stared at each other in the dark.

"Why didn't you say something?" Then he pulled me close again and kissed away my reply.

The collar of his shirt twisted between my fingers. His kiss took mine and reflected it back. I let my hands drift down to his waist. I pulled his shirt out of his belt in rapid tugs, sliding my hands under it. The muscles of his abdomen clenched under my touch. My own tightened in response.

Matt groaned and the sound echoed in my chest, sending electric currents through my insides. Our kiss deepened.

When he pulled away, his fingers ran slow circuits on my upper arms.

"Every time Dex touched you, I wanted to punch him," he said softly.

"Next time he does, you have my permission," I said. Matt chuckled, then we were both quiet. His hand slid up my arm, leaving a delicious, tingling trail behind.

I let my hands explore his neck and hair, marveling in the freedom to touch him. As his breath came faster and he pulled me closer, my hands slid under his arms and down his back. My fingers slipped under his loose shirt and traveled the curves and ridges of his back. He kissed my neck, his breath hot in my ear. With a start, I realized his hands were shaking and I smiled because he was nervous.

Of course, he wasn't the only one. Especially after he sat up and tugged his shirt off from the back. I sucked in a breath as he balled it up and shoved it over the crack between the couch arm and the seat. He lowered me slowly so my head rested on his shirt, and the smell of the boathouse faded underneath the clean, crisp scent of his cologne.

Matt covered me with his body, and the weight of him was delicious. I wrapped my arms around him while he took all his weight on one arm as the other hand slid down my chest and stomach, down, under the hem of my skirt and back up, tickling the outside of my thigh with his gentle touch. I gasped and pulled him closer, *wanting* him. He kissed a line from my ear to my shoulder.

"Have you got . . . I mean . . ." I panted, sure of what I wanted, but horrified by the idea of saying it.

"Don't worry," he breathed in my ear. "We'll be safe."

I smiled. I did feel safe. I was with Matt. I was going to *be* with Matt.

Suddenly, Older Me's voice rang in my head as clearly as if she were standing right there.

"Don't be like Finn and Karyn . . . You want to be able to look at yourself in the mirror the next morning . . . Better to make the right choice than to hate yourself the next day. You know?"

Karyn was Matt's girlfriend.

She was a lying, cheating sack of pus.

And she was also the reason he'd come *prepared*.

"Wait! Stop!"

I pushed at Matt, and he sprang away as if he'd been burned, landing on his side between me and the seat back.

"What? Did I hurt you?" he gasped, one hand on my stomach, his head strained up awkwardly to examine me in the dark.

I sat up, lightheaded. My clothes were askew and I was panting. I pulled my skirt down over my knees.

"You're prepared?" My voice wavered.

Matt exhaled and dropped his head to my shoulder. "Yes,"

he breathed, sounding relieved. "Don't worry." One hand drifted across my stomach and onto my waist, his fingertips following the line from my ribs to my hip, up and down.

I pushed away his hand, hating myself for doing it. "That's not what I meant." I swallowed hard. "You came here prepared. You came here with *Karyn* and you came *prepared*. This—us—it's only happening because you guys fought."

Matt drew away and propped himself up on one elbow. "You came here with Dex. You said you were *prepared*, too."

I shook my head. "I didn't . . . I didn't actually want to. And as soon as I realized he just wanted . . . It isn't the same. This—you—this is something else."

Matt ran a hand through his hair, puffing a long, slow breath between his lips. Then he sat up, cocking a knee to lean on it. "What are you worried about?"

What was I worried about? Everything. I was afraid that he'd look at me in the light of day and regret what we'd done. That, even if we slept together, he'd choose Karyn, the girl who was beautiful. Popular. Accepted.

"You have a girlfriend, Matt," I reminded him. "A girlfriend who *hates* me. And you came here ready to . . . to sleep with her. I'm second best. I'm only here because I'm second best. Only here with you because she left."

Matt frowned. "That isn't . . . I mean . . ."

"What would happen, Matt? If she found out?"

He was silent. Did he hear the question I hadn't asked? Would he feel good about this in the morning? Would he still want me tomorrow?

"This is stupid. You're stressing about something that isn't . . .

I mean, we can't know what's going to happen in two hours, let alone tomorrow. Do we have to figure it out now?"

But he was wrong. I *could* know what would happen tomorrow. And all of the sudden, I *had* to know. I had to ask Older Me. Was this a drunken mistake? Were we going to do this, then Matt would go running back to Karyn tomorrow? Or wish he could?

"Ash?" His voice was little more than a whisper.

He reached for me, but I was on my feet before I could change my mind. Matt called after me as I ran across the creaking boards, out onto the sand, and back into the house, but I knew if I let him touch me or talk to me I wouldn't be able to stop. If I let him have me and he threw me away, I wouldn't recover. I would smash into a million pieces, too small for anyone to glue back together. It was that simple. I couldn't handle having Matt tonight and losing him tomorrow.

CHAPTER TWENTY-FOUR

DOC'S STARING AT me, his fingers rigid on his pen. I stare at them so I don't have to think about what happened that night. For the first time I notice the wrinkles on his fingers. The way the hair on the back of his hand is faded and his skin has dark splotches. His hands look older than he does.

Doc starts tapping the clicker on his pen against the notebook in his lap. I sigh. I don't know if he realizes he's doing it in time to the clock on the wall, ticking away the minutes left until none of this is going to matter anymore.

"This was the first time you and Matt had had any kind of physical relationship?"

I nod miserably as the memory comes rushing back.

"And?" Doc asks softly.

I meet his piercing stare and it's like he's at the end of a tunnel. I can't see anything else. My breath is short, and my skin hums.

"And while it was happening, it was amazing," I say honestly. "But after . . ."

Doc lifts his eyebrows.

I swallow. "Afterward, it was a disaster."

Inside the beach house, music pumped a heavy rhythm through the old walls. I shouldered past Liam and Eli as I raced up the stairs, but neither of them said anything.

I was vaguely aware that the voices drifting up from the living room stopped when my feet pounded on the stairs, but that just made me run faster. I topped the stairs and paused at the end of the carpet runner. My eyes fell on the door of the room Dex had claimed and I decided I didn't have any other options.

Slamming the door behind me, I patted the wall until I found a light switch and flipped it on, then made straight for the closet-size half-bath.

"Are you there?" I peered into the round mirror over the basin sink. "I need to talk to you. It's an emergency!" My hands shook while I found the light, closed the door, and locked it.

Footsteps sounded on the other side of the door. "Ashhhh-ley?" It was Dex. Drunk. A gentle knock rattled the old door and I dropped my head into my hands. "Ash, come out."

"Please, please, I need you," I whispered, ignoring him. "I don't know what to do."

More footsteps sounded.

"Is she in there?" Eli asked.

"Ugh, she's probably puking. Leave her to it." Finn.

"She's just being dramatic."

Then a comment I didn't catch and laughter from the hallway outside the room.

"Shuddup!" Dex again.

Then Older Me appeared, standing in the mirror, arms wrapped around herself.

We stared at each other. "I can only stay a minute," she whispered, glancing over her shoulder. "I have to go back . . ."

I forced myself to keep my voice down. "I'm sorry, but this is an emergency!"

She swallowed, nodded. "What is it?"

A knock sounded on the door and Dex's voice came through, hushed and smothered like he had his lips right up against the crack in the door.

"What'd you say, Ash? I couldn't hear you. Come talk to me, babe. I don care if you're drunk. Ish okay."

Older Me's head whipped back to face me, alarmed as I told her what happened with Dex.

She gave me a small smile. "So you didn't—?"

I shook my head. "No. I ran away and hid. But Matt found me and . . . I have to ask you . . ."

"Ash?" Dex said softly.

"Leave me alone!" I screamed at him. "I don't want to talk to you."

I turned back to Older Me just as she jerked to look at something behind her and went pale with horror. She whispered a frantic "No!"

"What—?"

I broke off as a man, tall and broad, stepped into the frame. Older Me backed away. She tried to run, but he held her in place.

His words were hushed, shoved between his teeth. "What happened? Why did you leave? They're almost done and now they're waiting for *you*."

The voice. Oh . . . My . . .

"Matt?" I gasped.

Older Me covered her face with her hands, while Older Matt stepped closer, his voice growing more ragged, more angry, as he kept asking her what was wrong. Then he looked directly into the mirror and his lips pressed in tight.

I was so stunned that for a moment I thought his tight, angry look was for me.

He jerked back to look at Older Me and scowled. "Again? You're doing this *now*? Those people are trying to help us—help you! You know this is our last chance, right? Without this . . . I can't keep going, Ashley. Not like this."

"Matt is . . . You're with *Matt*?" I hissed.

Older Me wouldn't look at me.

"Just give me five minutes," she hissed to Older Matt. "It's group therapy. Having a crisis at some point is practically a requirement."

"This is out of control. You said you were getting past it—"

"Go, Matt! Before I raise my voice so they can hear me! Wouldn't *that* be embarrassing?"

"You need help," he said quietly. Coldly. Then he turned on his heel and stormed out. A second later the door creaked again. She flinched when it was followed by the slightly-too-loud bang of it closing.

I glared at her half-turned back, heart thumping in my ears. "You're dating *Matt*?"

Her reddened eyes met mine and her next words cut through skin and bone. "Ashley, Matt and I have been together for years. He thinks I'm crazy. He's had me committed. Twice."

"What?" I couldn't have heard her right. It couldn't be possible. Images whipped through my head, snatches of conversation with Older Me. I catalogued everything I knew about her life . . . and realized it was next to nothing.

"You told me you had roommates!"

"Matt and I were roommates. In college. Later in college. He transferred before junior year. We . . . reconnected . . ."

My mouth wouldn't work. I couldn't get the questions out. Couldn't think straight. Couldn't decide if I was furious or in heaven.

"I could have had him tonight," I said through gritted teeth. "But I thought . . . I left him because of what you said. How *could* you?"

She hugged herself tightly, rocking slightly. "I'm so sorry. I'm so sorry. But he isn't . . . he isn't the one, Ashley. Believe me. Please. You can't let yourself love him like that. He'll hurt you. *So* bad . . ." Her words dissolved into sobs.

"I can't believe this," I said, shaking my head.

"It will be okay. We'll make it okay," she whispered, whether to herself or me, I wasn't sure.

"No. It won't be okay." Suddenly, my anger morphed into despair. Certainty. "It's all ruined. It's all ruined because you lied to me. You didn't tell me. And now I've ruined *everything*."

Older Me snapped to attention. "What did you do?"

"I wrote a letter. To Matt." It was pointless to hide it from her any longer. Might as well light every last fuse and let everything blow.

She frowned. "I did too. I wondered if you had."

I held up a hand. "But I didn't give it to him. Finn—"

174

"—stole it," she finished with a sigh. "I know. But why didn't you just tell me? I went through that, too. And really, it wasn't so bad. It was embarrassing, but people already guessed how I felt about Matt."

Hope rose in a wave. "So he was fine when he heard about, you know, *us*?"

"Yes, I—wait, *what*?" Older Me leapt to her feet and came to the surface of the mirror until her nose almost met the glass. "What do you mean *us*?"

I took a step back, stammering. "I—I didn't . . . I mean, it isn't as bad as you think—"

"Tell me what you wrote!"

She looked possessed, her eyes so wide the whites showed all the way around.

"Stop yelling! I didn't tell him about *you*, exactly," I lied, "I just said that I . . . I had a secret . . . that I talked to myself all the time. Because . . . well, I talk to *myself*."

"Oh man. Oh man oh man oh man . . ." Her voice trailed off, but her lips kept moving. She paced back and forth in front of the mirror, tears spilling over.

"The mirror. Did you mention the mirror?"

"I . . ." I slumped. "Yes."

"Oh, no. Oh, *no*."

"Why are you—?"

"I told you never to tell anyone, Ashley. I told you we couldn't ever tell anyone, *especially* Matt. Why didn't you listen to me?"

"I told you, I didn't explain it in detail. Not really."

"It doesn't matter." She breathed, one hand raking through her hair. "He'll know. He'll know. He'll put it together and . . .

oh, Ashley. Finally, *finally* you break the pattern and it had to be *this*?" Her hands flew to her face. "Why did it have to be this?"

I stared at her, uncomprehending. "I don't understand. Pattern? What are you—"

Her hands fisted in her hair. "I had an Older Me, Ash. Now I *am* Older Me. I wanted you to take a different path. To be free of all this! I couldn't let you think Matt was your future because if I could go back and change it, I would. Ashley, you know what he's like. He just . . . he keeps trying to *fix* me. Trying to convince me that I need help. And he's so *angry* when I refuse . . ." She trailed off.

I couldn't breathe. It was all coming together in my head. No matter her motives, or what she thought she was doing, she'd been lying. About all of it. I stumbled away from her, but came up against the wall. There was no space to think. No space to breathe. "How could you lie to me? How could you leave me in the dark? How *could* you?"

"Ashley, please, believe me—"

I stopped cold. Then turned on her. The closer I got to the mirror, the farther she backed away.

"Believe you? Why should I believe a single word that comes out of your mouth?"

"You have to let me explain. We have to figure out—"

I met her eye. "I hate you."

Her cries cut off as if she'd been shot. "Don't say that. You can't—"

"I do. I hate you." Since the day those words had become a weapon against me, I'd never used them toward another human being. But they were true.

"You can't hate me! I'm you!" she pled.

I leaned in until I was two inches away. Let her see the truth in my face. "Exactly."

Her mouth dropped open.

"You've been so busy lying and hiding, you couldn't see what you were doing to me. You've taken everything. Everything I want. Everything I *need*. You're worse than Mom."

Her head jerked back like I'd slapped her.

A hand thumped on the door again. "Ash?" Dex slurred again.

"Dude, leave her alone," a deep voice snapped.

"Mind your own business, Matt."

Oh, no. Matt was there. My Matt. Outside the door . . .

I wanted to throw myself out there and into his arms. I wanted to run so I'd never have to see his face again.

Older Me swallowed hard, her gaze flickering from my face to her own hands. "You . . . you don't understand," she whispered. "You will. I promise. I had to do it. For you. Right now it feels like—"

"Right now everything is ruined!" I screamed.

All voices, on both sides of the mirror, went silent. I could almost hear everyone in the room behind me holding their breath.

"He isn't perfect, Ashley." Her words came out fast, clipped. "You've got him up on this pedestal and . . . When you get close to someone, you find out they aren't quite the person you thought they were—"

"Ashley? Ashley, come out. We'll talk." It was Matt. He sounded worried.

Older Me stepped forward again. "You said you could have . . . that Matt would have slept with you. Why'd you stop?"

"Because . . . because he has a girlfriend. And I didn't want to be a cheater like she is . . ."

"Good." Her eyes closed and her chin dropped. "You only get one shot at this, Ashley. Don't do anything until it's right. Until you *know* it's right. If Matt wants to be with you, he'll still want it tomorrow. He'll break up with Karyn. He'll *be there* the way you need him. He'll wait."

"Who're you talking to, Ash? Open the door. Please!"

"Get lost, jerk, she's my date."

I looked at Older Me and she looked back me.

"I love you," she whispered. "I do. And one of these days that will mean something."

A big bang sounded on the door and I jumped.

"Back off, Dex!"

"Guys, guys, we're talking about *Watson* here. Seriously, let's go drink. She'll crawl out eventually."

Matt snapped "Shut *up*, Finn."

"Ashley, please—" Older Me began.

But I turned my back on her, flipped open the lock, and let the chaos in.

CHAPTER TWENTY-FIVE

DOC SHIFTS IN his seat. "Seems like a lot of people let you down that night," he says.

I sigh. "It wasn't over yet."

When I pulled open the bathroom door, Finn was leaning against the wall, smirking. Dex stood a couple of feet away, swaying. And Matt was in profile to me, looking over his shoulder. For a split second, the image of him in later years—slightly heavier, still devastatingly handsome—was superimposed over his averted face. I wanted to rush into his arms and tell him everything. But when he stepped forward with a gentle "Ash?" it wasn't the hush of tamped desire, but a careful, wary whisper. "Who were you talking to?"

My stomach tightened. "Oh, um, I called my mom."

Matt glanced at my empty hands before I could think to hold them behind my back. He cleared his throat. "Look, we need to talk."

Here it comes. I nodded miserably. "Just give me one second."

Then, with a grim smile, I stepped over to Dex and slapped him, putting my weight behind it. The crack echoed against the vaulted ceiling.

Matt's and Finn's jaws dropped. All conversation in the hallway ceased.

Dex glared at me, swaying, rubbing his cheek. "What was *that* for?"

"You should have taken your chances with Brooke," I said. "Because you've got zero chance with me."

Dex's mouth dropped open. But instead of waiting for a response, I walked over to Finn, whose face was wide with amusement.

"I find it really interesting that it was Terese's mom who called all the other parents tonight. I mean, who called her?"

Finn's eyes narrowed, and his expression turned icy cold. "You."

I pretended to think about it. "Problem with that is, it couldn't be me. 'Cause Terese's numbers are all private—I know, because my caller ID can't pick it up when she texts me about how fat I am. So I don't actually know her number—couldn't even find it when I tried to get it blocked."

Finn's face went blank.

"Do you have her number, Finn? Don't your moms play tennis, or something?"

There was a flash of alarm on his face, but he covered it well. Instead of responding, he folded his arms and moved aside, tipped his head at the door. "If you aren't putting out, there's no reason for you to be here. So leave."

"Hey!" Matt sprang forward, but I put a hand up to stop him and turned back to Finn.

"You didn't answer the question."

Finn leaned into my face until we were almost nose to nose. "This is *my* party. Why would I want to ruin it? Oh, wait, I already did—by letting you show up."

Ignoring his jab, I shook my head. "I know why," I said quietly.

"Why?" Matt snapped.

Finn looked at Matt, then back to me. "Careful," he breathed through unmoving lips, quiet enough that only I could hear. "I'm not the only one with secrets."

I pushed past him, livid with myself for letting him get his hands on that letter.

Matt's feet thumped on the stairs behind me.

"Wh—"

"I have to get out of here, Matt. Can I have your car, please? Finn will give you a ride home tomorrow."

We'd reached the bottom floor. Bumps and shouts rose overhead, but there were no feet on the stairs. Music still pounded out of the empty living room. I took a right at the bottom of the stairs and headed for the kitchen.

"Ashley, stop!" Matt grabbed my arm again. I stopped, whirled on him. "Stay. We'll talk, figure this out."

I shook my head. "It's better if I leave. No one will be able to say we were cheating . . ."

Matt stiffened. "Ash— Tonight . . . You weren't the one cheating."

"Story of my life." I snorted to cover the tears. "Look, forget about it, okay? I'm done. This is one of the worst nights of my life. I just want to get out of here and forget it ever happened."

Matt frowned. In the dark his brows pressed together like a couple fists. "All of it?"

I shook my head. "Of . . . of course not. But you have a girlfriend."

I was giving him an opening, a chance to tell me he didn't care about Karyn, or what his friends thought. Images of him leaning in to kiss me, his hands cupping my face, the delicious sensations of his touch, bombarded me. I wanted him to pull me to him, to promise he was going to call Karyn right then and break up with her. To promise that it would be different for us. Different from what he'd done to Older Me.

But he just stood there, staring.

Hope shriveled in my chest. I stepped back. "Those guys aren't ever going to let this go. I have to leave. You know that. Can I have your car? Please?"

Matt nodded and reached into his pocket for his keys. He held them out, placing them carefully into my outstretched hand. I took them and turned, walking slowly enough that if he came after me, tried to stop me, he wouldn't have had any trouble catching me.

But he didn't.

When I reached the car and locked myself inside, I realized Older Me had been right about one thing: Matt Gray, the love of my life and the most amazing kisser in the world, wasn't perfect.

He wasn't even close.

CHAPTER TWENTY-SIX

DOC'S MAKING NOTES again. I stop talking. When he's finished writing, he looks up, peers at me over his glasses. "It seems like this was the first night you ever realized that Matt was . . . flawed."

I nod. "I realize now, of course, that we all are. That I'm never going to find a guy who won't hurt me sometimes, or do stuff I can't respect. But at the time . . ."

"Matt wasn't living up to your ideals," Doc says quietly, making another note on his paper.

I shake my head. "It's more than that. It wasn't just that he fell short of some stupid fantasy . . . It was that he turned out to be exactly the kind of person I thought he *wasn't*."

Doc stops writing and looks up to frown at me. "And what kind of person is that?"

I swallow. "A coward, just like the rest of them. The kind of person who makes the easy choice rather than the right one. The kind who knows that what he's doing is hurting someone but does it anyway."

The kind who hurt me.

* * *

The art room on Sunday morning after prom was a sanctuary of silence. I could be truly alone.

The silence hollowed me out, left me thinking of Matt. What would he tell Karyn?

What would he tell *himself*?

I pushed all those thoughts away. I had to work. There was no time to cry about Matt now. No time to hate on Dex. I had a portfolio to finish.

Now, more than ever, I had to get out of this town. The competition was my ticket.

The massive black tri-boards for my art portfolio had finally arrived. I had three days to get them ready and approved by Mrs. D for submission. By the middle of the afternoon, I had two-thirds of them covered. Mom and Dad were up there as the diptych. Mrs. Driley, Karyn, Finn, and Dex, too. I threw in a couple of older paintings I'd done where faces weren't the main focus, just to show my range. I was left with two big blank spaces and one small one. Matt's portrait had to fill one of the big ones. I'd throw something together for the small one. But it was the big, central gap that was chilling me. Mrs. Driley insisted that it be my self-portrait. But who wanted to look at a picture just of *me*?

I put on some music and pulled out the pieces of Matt's portrait. Then I grabbed a canvas board out of the easel room and took it to my table, pulling all the sketches, drawings, and scratchings of Matt's features from the folder. I found myself sitting in front of a table full of his eyes and his smile and his jaw, and it almost killed me. There was only one sketch of his hand— holding a pencil while he drew something. I'd gotten the fingers just right: The heavy knuckles and long digits. The nails short and rounded off, but clean. The tendons that ran from the back of each finger to his wrist. Now, all I could see when I looked at it was those fingers touching my skin. That thumb tracing along my cheekbone. That hand reaching to pull me back when I ran . . .

I turned it over, took a breath, and then started filtering the images.

Those eyes were too narrow. That nose a fraction too big. That ear was angular. On and on, until I had only one or two pictures left of each feature. Except his mouth.

Without letting myself think too deeply about it, I pulled a heavy cartridge paper pad onto my lap and started drawing. There was a slight indentation at the middle of his bottom lip—a plane of soft, unmarred skin that stretched when he smiled and wrinkled when he stopped. His upper lip was slightly thinner than his lower, but both were long and pulled into sharp corners. I drew them in less than ten minutes, and they were perfect. Well, as perfect as I was capable of, anyway.

With that done, I took the canvas board into the easel room and set it up, pulled another stool up to put my pictures on it, and started playing with the pieces. An hour later, Matt stared at me from the canvas. He looked like he was turned to look at me, holding a pencil as if he were about to use it.

All his pieces were there, and I wanted to kiss him again.

Turning the easel around to the natural light from the window, I stepped a few feet back to take in the full effect. But from that distance, something was missing. The use of different media to draw the pieces meant certain parts of his face drew the eye immediately, while others faded into the background. It was exactly the effect I wanted, but it was pulling my attention to the wrong piece first.

Without my planning it, I'd drawn his eyes and mouth in flat pencil. With his hair and nose in the heavy acrylic crayon and his jaw a dusty charcoal, the lips looked framed. They were perfect and my eye went right to them. But I wanted the viewer to look at Matt's eyes and see what I saw. Should I go back to some of the other sketches? Find a nose that wasn't so dramatic so the eyes would pop more?

"You need to paint them in oil."

I yelped and whirled around.

Matt stood in the door of the easel room, hands in his pockets. There were dark circles under his eyes and heavy stubble on his chin and jaw. He looked terrible.

He looked fantastic.

He stared at the picture I'd made of him. It was like I'd opened my chest, pulled my heart out, and handed it to him. He knew me too well not to understand what I was trying to achieve with the picture.

Trying not to look flustered, I reached for the easel and angled it away. "It isn't finished," I said to my own feet.

"I haven't seen that before," he said. "Is that why you didn't tell me you were coming in here all those times by yourself?"

"I would have shown you when it was done," I lied. "I—I just wasn't expecting you today. I thought you'd be . . . getting some rest."

"I need it," he said. He didn't smile. "Last night the guys got pretty drunk. Noisy. And Dex kept trying to fight me."

"I'm sorry."

Our eyes locked and the heat that had sizzled last night snapped between us again, a tangible frisson in the air.

I got brave. Took a slow step closer. Matt was more confident, apparently. He closed the distance, but his hands were still balled at his sides.

I touched his chest with trembling fingers. "Last night, when you said—"

"Well, this looks *cozy*."

My head whipped up. Matt tensed but didn't turn around.

Karyn stood inside the door, arms folded, perfect golden hair swaying around her shoulders. The look on her face was pure fury.

Matt grimaced, but still didn't turn around. "It's not a good time, Kar. Just give us a few minutes, would you?"

Her eyes about popped out of her head.

"I don't care if it's a good *time*," she hissed.

"Look, after you left last night, Ashley had to deal with some real crap, so just back off, okay?" Matt's voice got harder, angrier.

Karyn scoffed and started toward us. Matt huffed and turned to meet her. But she was coming for me. I braced as she tried to step past Matt, but he grabbed her arm.

"Hey!" she spat.

"Get out of here, Karyn."

"You're sticking up for *her*? I'm your *girlfriend*!"

"Get *out*!" Matt roared and even I jumped. I couldn't take my eyes off him.

Karyn's mouth dropped open and she yanked her arm out of his grip. I was willing to bet she'd never seen him truly angry before. When she spoke, her voice was strong. "It's always about her in the end, isn't it? You're always spouting this 'just friends'

BS, but every time she makes an ass out of herself, you've got to be there. Why don't you admit she's the one you want to be with? Oh, wait, that's right—because you don't want everyone to hate you, too."

Matt grabbed her arm again, but she didn't come closer, just pointed at me and sneered. "He hates it, you know. He hates that everyone else hates you. He laughs about you when you're not there—"

Her words pelted me like stones, leaving bruises. "That's not true!" Matt snapped.

She slapped at his hands. "You're such a pussy, Matt! And you!" She whirled on me. "I know you were there last night with all those guys. You think *that's* going to make people like you?"

It only took three steps to get close enough to shove her. Karyn smirked.

Matt put one hand on my shoulder. "Let me handle this."

But I just spoke past him. "You two-faced cow!" I wanted to throttle her. "You don't deserve Matt and he definitely doesn't deserve to be with a backstabber like you. You let everyone think you're a little princess, but you're a total snake. You lie! You cheat! You're—"

Karyn gasped. "Oh my—"

But I didn't let her finish. "Tell Matt about all those times your friends cornered me and you just stood back and laughed. Tell him about how you dumped me as a friend when you realized I wasn't popular enough! Tell him *all* about your little 'meetings' in the library!"

Karyn's eyes widened and her teeth pulled back from her lips. "Finn told you what would happen if—" She clapped her hands over her mouth and immediately looked at Matt.

My breath came too fast and my hands shook. "I never said a name," I hissed. "You did."

Matt stared between us. But all he said was "Finn?"

Karyn's mouth dropped open. She stared at me. But then, slowly, she turned from me to Matt and her eyes got all liquid and pleading. "It wasn't . . . I mean . . ."

A silence fell heavy over the room.

"Matt, I—" She reached for him, but he flinched and she stopped.

Matt's shoulders were hunched and rigid. He glanced back and forth and I could see him making connections, asking himself questions, *seeing* things differently. Then he looked at me for confirmation of his fears. I nodded.

His face went blank. With a jaw like stone, he got up in Karyn's face and growled, "What's going on with *Finn?*"

Whatever spell Karyn was under broke. Her crystal facade returned. She shoved her nose in the air, folded her arms, and huffed out a shaky breath. "Nothing!" She made a big show of tipping her head at me. "*She* wants you to break up with me for her. You're so gullible!" But she never looked at me. She stared at Matt a minute and he glared back, then she swore and stormed out of the room.

Matt tensed when the door slammed, but he didn't go after her.

"Matt?" I said softly.

His face was expressionless.

"Matt?" I touched his arm. "Are you okay?" His head snapped down, looking at where we touched.

"Just . . . give me a minute," he said through clenched teeth, peeling my fingers off his arm.

I bit my lip and stepped back. Matt gave a cold chuckle. "Don't worry," he said. "It's not you I'm mad at."

Small relief. I wanted to reach for him again. I wanted to put my arms around him and bury my face in his chest and rub his back. I wanted to comfort him.

"Not much, anyway," he said in a flat voice.

"Well, that's reassuring."

A minute later, Matt blew out a breath, then turned to face me again. The hardness still clung to his jaw and shoulders, but he ran a hand through his hair and shook his head.

"Finn?" he said.

I swallowed, still holding my insides together. "I caught them kissing."

He frowned. "When?"

"A few weeks ago."

Disbelief and anger pinched his face. "A few *weeks*? And you didn't tell me? You just let me stay with her, like an idiot? Why?"

"Because I had no proof. And you always believe them when they tell you things."

Matt's jaw dropped. "You really think I'd believe them over you?" His voice went up sharply at the end.

"Of course I do. You've been doing it for years!"

"I have not!"

"Matt, you choose them every time. You believed them when they accused me of calling Terese's mom. You hang out with them at school even though they make my life hell. You go out with girls who *hate* me—then believe them when they tell you they don't."

Matt grimaced and ran a hand through his hair. "That's not true. I don't understand why you would think that."

And that was all it took. "You don't *understand*? Seriously?"

He must have heard the shift in my tone, because he answered warily. "Yes."

I took a step closer. "Fine, then I'll explain it. Let's start with Karyn. Last month, she and her friends threw my jeans in the sink during PE. I told the teacher, so they told everyone else I wet my pants. Someone left a pack of bladder control pads on top of my locker."

His head jerked back. "Why didn't you—"

"A couple of weeks ago, Brooke drew a picture of me giving the math teacher a blowjob and passed it around class. I've been getting cracks about 'math tutoring' ever since!"

Matt looked away, but I was on a roll now.

"Finn humiliates me and tells me he hates me pretty much every time he sees me. He makes sure his friends tell me that, too. Do you have any idea how it feels to have people look you in the face and tell you they wish you were dead, and *mean* it?"

Matt blew out a breath, but he was staring at the carpet. "I'm sorry. I didn't know it was so—"

"You didn't want to know. I embarrass you," I said quietly. "I get it."

He shook his head. "*No.* I am *not* embarrassed by you."

"Then what was Karyn talking about?"

"Grow up, Ash." His voice kept rising. "She's jealous because I'm always there for you. Do you realize that—that I'm *always* there for you? Even when you're a total idiot, I stick up for you! You should know you can trust me by now."

That felt like a slap. "Me? It's your friends who are the idiots—"

"Oh, come *on*! You could get away from them if you wanted to. You keep throwing yourself in front of them, then crying when they make fun of you."

"I do not!"

"Really?" Matt's face got hard and he leaned in. "You really want to have this conversation? How about that party at Finn's house, where you got drunk and started crying over a fight with Finn that *you* started?"

"I didn't start it, and I *wasn't* drunk!"

"And what about last night?" he yelled. "I get that you were upset, but instead of finding someone—finding me!—and asking for help like a normal person, you disappear. *Everyone* looked for you—even Finn. Did you know that? They thought something had happened to you! Then it turned out you're just crying in a corner. People don't like drama. And you make drama all the time."

Matt's words were knives on my skin, cutting to the bone. Couldn't he see that drama just happened because of who they thought I was? I couldn't change that.

Could I?

"I couldn't have confronted them last night. Finn would have crucified me. It isn't a petty fight with him. He . . . he . . ."

"What? What did he *do*, Ash? If he's *so* awful, why did you agree to go to his house? *Twice*?"

Matt leaned down in my face, angry but wanting answers. I wanted to tell him. I wanted to tell him the whole story and give him the letter and have him fold me in those strong arms like he had a few hours earlier. I wanted to feel his fingers twined with mine again.

192

Then I remembered Finn's face—the wicked grin he got when he talked about the letter.

Could I trust Matt to stick around if he knew the truth about what I saw when I looked in the mirror? Finn didn't think so. Neither did Older Me.

I stepped back, shaking my head.

"Oh, for—!"

The tears were back, sheets of tears. "Stop yelling at me!" I hugged myself and backed away from him.

Matt groaned through gritted teeth, then whirled. "Fine. Forget about it. Forget everything." He stalked toward the door, shoving the pile of easels leaned against the wall as he passed, sending them clattering to the floor with a crash. I jumped and the tears came harder.

"Matt!"

The door slammed and he was gone. I waited a minute, holding my breath, praying for him to come back. But the longer I stood there, the more certain I was that he wasn't coming back.

My heart thumped against my ribs and my breath came too fast. I should have picked up the easels Matt knocked over, but my arms felt like jelly. Then my knees shook and I sank to the floor.

I teetered on the edge for a long time before I could breathe without wheezing. Until the shivers stopped running up and down my spine. I stayed on the floor, wrapped around the pain, forcing the cracks inside to hold. Until I could breathe. But with oxygen came a weird kind of clarity.

This. I had to capture *this.*

I rolled onto my hands and knees, waiting to make sure my

head would stay in one place. When it did, I pushed to my feet and used my trembling hands to pull around the easel I'd been using.

Tearing the pieces of Matt off the canvas, I picked up a pencil and started sketching—very light so the lead wouldn't show through later brushstrokes. Then I thumbed through the brushes until I found a tiny, thin one suitable for drawing in paint.

I painted me. Surrounded by nothing. Zero. Alone. Just my face and my shoulders, chin in my hand, and blank, blank space beside and behind me. I drew my eyes and outlined my forehead and turned my hair into something resembling a nice cut.

The world became a very small place. Just me and the painting.

Once the basics were in place, I pulled a huge, full-length mirror out of the storage area and propped it up against the wall so I could study myself. It was weird to have a mirror out and not call Older Me, but it was hard enough looking at myself. Every time I did, I heard my own voice.

He doesn't want you. You're too much drama.

I spent hours sketching and mixing colors, working the details. But every time I stepped back to take in the effect, something was missing. I went back to my workbook and tried sketching the same form on a piece of paper and messing with watercolors over the top. I even drew glasses, like Mom's, to see if a different line balance would light it up. But it didn't help. In frustration, I tore the sketch in half and stormed back into the easel room.

I turned around, looking for inspiration, but instead I found the window. Somehow it had already grown dark outside. With a sigh, I packed everything up and cleaned my brushes. My painting was finished, sort of. But it was a flat, blank image. Nothing surprising. Nothing revealing. I knew Mrs. D would hate it.

I certainly did. But it was all I had left.

CHAPTER TWENTY-SEVEN

THE CLOCK ON the wall says 1:16. I bite my lip. When I turn back to Doc, he glances at the clock, then back to me.

"Are you in a hurry, Ashley?" he asks.

Yes. In a hurry to get out of this place. To be out of here before all hell breaks loose. To be free of this junk they call therapy.

But I say, "Wouldn't you be, if you thought after six months you might get free of this place?"

Doc doesn't respond immediately. When he does, there's a sharpness in his face that's mirrored in his tone. "Is that it? Or is it that we're getting close to your incident? When I read your file, it was obvious there's been a pattern in your past sessions: Whenever your therapists start to analyze that day—to ask you to confront everything that happened—you get tense. Clam up. Or get so upset they're forced to abandon the topic *and* your session."

I blink. Did I?

"It isn't easy to talk about," I say. My voice sounds like I haven't used it for a day or so.

Doc nods quickly. "I can imagine that's true."

The problem with imagining is that it's got nothing on the reality.

"I have a theory," Doc says.

Peachy.

He clears his throat. "I believe that human beings have a tendency to live up to expectations: what we expect of ourselves, what we believe others expect of us. I believe we *all* fit our lives to those patterns. And I wonder if that hasn't been part of your problem. You make choices based on how you perceive others expect you to behave. You—perhaps subconsciously—draw their attention to your flaws."

I roll my eyes. "Man, you're just as bad as the rest of them."

"The rest of who?" he asks, coolly.

"*Them.* Parents. Teachers. *Shrinks.* Whoever. Anyone who hasn't had to walk down a hall and fear for their life on a daily basis."

"You feel they are—were—all against you?"

"Not against me, exactly. But they didn't understand."

Doc leans forward slightly. "Understand what?"

I consider not answering. But hell, I'm kind of curious to hear what he'll say.

"Okay . . . In high school, *they* told me just to stay out of the way of the people who hated me. But it didn't matter what I did—ignore them, fight back, walk away—they'd just find me. Again and again."

He touches a finger to his lips. His face looks pinched. "Go on."

"So, given your theory, I brought it all on myself? I pushed people to the point where they *couldn't* walk away? To a state so aggravated, they *had* to seek me out?"

"And if the answer is yes?"

Anger flares, burning up my ribs. I swallow it down. "I wasn't the one doing the pushing. That's what *they* did to *me*."

"Pushed you?"

"To the point that I was ready to snap."

He glances at his notes. "And your incident?"

I glare. He fixes me with an impassive expression and waits.

"I *know* I didn't invite that," I mutter. "I know because I wasn't looking for them. They came looking for me. In fact, it seemed like, those last few months, it was always that way. They looked for me. And when they found me . . ." I trail off.

He knows.

Monday morning, I waited until fifteen minutes before the bell was due to ring, but Matt didn't show up to give me a ride. At the last second, I threw on my shoes and ran the mile or so to school. When I was a block away, close enough to hear the sounds of people laughing and shouting, the events of the entire weekend came home to me and I realized I was shaking.

I tried not to think as I stepped through the gates, just scanned the buildings and told myself there was only one week of real school left before finals, when I could just show up for my tests, then leave.

"Hey! It's Ashley! Ohmigosh! Someone call a doctor!" Brooke cackled when she saw me crossing the parking lot.

What? I turned my head away and pushed forward faster, but a curl of dread started in my chest. What was going on?

I shoved inside a side entrance and walked down the short hallway from the door to the main hall.

"Oh! Ashley! Where's your better half?" Layla called.

Oh, God. Was she talking about Dex . . . or Matt? What rumors were circulating?

I turned the corner. Only three classroom doors between me and my locker. I could do that. I could walk past three classes.

A snorting noise sounded right behind me and someone stood on the back of my shoe. A round of laughter was quickly followed by the thump of a body bracing against mine, shoving me into the wall.

"Crazy slut," Eli muttered as he stalked on.

I bounced off the wall and scrambled for my bag as it slipped off my shoulder. Tears welled in my eyes and I hissed a curse, determined to stay mad so I wouldn't give in.

Only two more classroom doors.

Then one.

Then I got to my locker and saw a piece of paper taped to the front.

My dread sputtered, then morphed into outright terror.

I held my breath and read the first line of my own handwriting.

Dear Matt,

Things have been a little strange lately, but I want you to know I understand . . .

The letter.

Oh, no. Oh, no no *no*.

I panicked. My mind went blank. Then flooded with every

one of my fears. How many people had seen it? Had *Matt* seen it? I snatched it off my locker door and scrunched it into the tiniest ball possible, then shoved that deep in my pocket.

"Oh, Matt, *I* understand . . ." a voice cooed from behind me, followed by a cloud of laughter. Mortification fizzed through every nerve ending in my skin. My locker blurred in front of me and I dashed the tears away. I needed to get out of here. Now. I'd go straight to the nurse, tell her I was sick, make her sign me out of class. Yes. Good plan.

But before I could move, a group of my classmates, led by Terese, trooped past.

"How was Friday, Ashley? Did you find anyone drunk enough to hook up with you?"

"Or crazy enough?" someone else added.

"Hey, does your other self give you sex tips? Or does everyone run screaming from her, too?"

"Ohmigosh, why doesn't she just die already?"

I flinched. Their taunts and laughter echoed in my ears as they sauntered down the hallway. It wasn't until someone else bumped my shoulder that I could snap myself into action. I whirled, and walked smack into a broad chest. Firm, familiar hands took hold of my upper arms.

Matt. "I'm really sorry, I was going to pick you up, but I was running late . . ." He trailed off, gazing at my face. "Hey. What's wrong?"

He clearly hadn't seen—or heard about—the letter yet. My chest squeezed. Should I tell him? Show him myself, so I didn't have to wait to find out what his face was going to look like when he rejected me?

"Seriously, Ashley, you're scaring me." The tone in his voice had changed, like something had just dawned on him. The hallway around us was abnormally quiet, though there were plenty of bodies in my peripheral vision.

They were watching.

Waiting.

I couldn't look away from his chest.

Something brushed my hair and I flinched. Two guys ran past singing "Crazy in Love."

Matt swore at them, then turned back. "What's going on?"

In that moment I decided: I didn't want to be there to see the horror dawn on his face. Suddenly, I was desperate to be somewhere else. *Someone* else. I didn't need to be popular, or even accepted. I would have been happy with invisible. To be able to wander the halls without having to watch out. To do *anything* and not have someone tell me to kill myself.

I stumbled away from him because it hurt too much to be that close.

Matt grabbed my sleeve. "Where are you going?"

"The nurse. I'm sick," I croaked. I tugged out of his grip and marched down the hall, watching my shoes. Over our heads the bell clanged. This hall led to the main lobby at the front of the school. I was already shaking. Pale. The nurse would believe I was sick.

Matt took my hand and pushed ahead. When we reached the lobby, he gasped and halted. The bell had run, but the lobby was full of people. Everyone pressed in on the notice board wall, peering over one another's shoulders, laughing, pointing, gasping, whispering . . .

"Is that her?"

"Oh my g—"

"Go kill yourself, you freak!"

"Hey!" Matt lunged at some girl, but I pulled him back.

"What is it now?" My voice broke.

Before he could respond, Mrs. Driley walked into the lobby. "What is going on here?" When her gaze landed on the notice board, her hands flew to her mouth. Then she looked right at me, and the pity on her face made me wish I'd never been born.

"All of you! Leave! Now!" Mrs. Driley demanded.

I gritted my teeth and pushed forward as everyone else pressed back. Matt shook his head and tried to pull me away, but it only made me more determined to see.

"Stop her, Matt!" Mrs. Driley shrilled.

"Ashley, don't!" He grabbed for me again, but I dodged. Bodies pummeled me as I tried to push between the last two guys. Then, my foot landed on something slick. My leg slid forward and I almost fell. Matt caught my arm and steadied me. We both looked down.

There was paint on the floor.

A mixing cup lay on its side on the linoleum, crudely mixed white and red paint spilling from inside it. Slick, shoe-width lines said more than one person had slipped in it already.

I looked up and my heart stopped. There it was.

There *I* was.

Someone had tacked my self-portrait to the notice board. Except it wasn't my painting anymore. When I'd left the easel room the day before, the nearly square canvas showed a flat, accurately painted representation of me. Nothing special. Nothing spectacularly bad. That painting was still there, but now there was a crudely drawn penis pointing right at my mouth.

Matt swore. "I can't believe . . ." He trailed off. "Ash, I'm so sorry. I'll help you fix it." He reached for it, but I grabbed his arm. I had to see it all.

Diagonally across the top, in jagged capital letters, the words CRAZY ASHLEY LOVES DICK screamed out from the canvas.

On either side of the canvas, two copies of the letter were pinned to the notice board.

No, no, no, no, no, no. "Matt, please leave. Now." It came out in a breath. I don't think he heard me, because he just squinted and leaned forward, his lips moving silently as he read the awful words in the letter. He turned slowly to look at me, openmouthed shock in every line of his gorgeous face. He reached for one of them, but my hand slapped his away and I tore it off first. But I couldn't ignore the way he jerked back, put half a step between us. Pain roared, then I was numb.

Suddenly it felt as though I were outside my body, like a silent observer just watching my life crumble. My hand lifted, tore the second letter off the wall and shoved it into my pocket. Then I took hold of the canvas on the corner where it was dry, then grabbed the other corner. I struggled for a moment to pull it off. But it finally gave and I turned away from the wall.

Mrs. Driley's lips moved, but I couldn't hear her.

Matt got in my face, but I couldn't hear him anymore, either.

There was a short circuit somewhere and all I could do was hold on to the painting so no one else could see it. I was terrified. I was exhausted. I needed to go home.

I'm not sure if I said that, or they just figured it out, because

Matt let go of my arm and Mrs. Driley—looking on the verge of tears—nodded and headed for the door ahead of me.

I was a few steps into the lobby before I realized there was still a crowd of people there. I tried to ignore the smiles and the whispers, the too-bright eyes and the shaking heads. Right then, right there, I wanted to be dead. Nothing. Untouchable.

Someone said my name. It bubbled toward me like air through water. But I didn't want to hear it. Pretty soon I was running and since I was crying, everything passed in a literal blur. I hit the bar on the double doors and ran down the stairs and out, across the parking lot, wondering why my name kept bouncing off the air behind me. But I didn't have any answers. I had to be alone. And maybe I did need to kill myself, because if it could get worse than this, I didn't have it in me to survive anyway.

CHAPTER TWENTY-EIGHT

DOC HAS HIS head tipped down. If it weren't for the pained expression on his face, I'd think he was praying.

Then he inhales and his eyes tip up to meet mine. "They told you to kill yourself?"

I almost bark a laugh. If I wasn't strung tighter than a guitar string right now, I would have. *That's* what's got him all quiet and careful?

"They used to say stuff like that all the time," I said incredulously. "If I'd done everything someone else told me to do, I wouldn't have made it through high school." I try to crack a smile, but it doesn't really work. "Seriously, Doc, *that's* not why we're here."

He gestures for me to keep going, but I can't help noticing that he hasn't agreed with me.

I don't remember the walk home, or how I got into the house with the painting in my hands. I don't remember anything except seeing that it wasn't even nine o'clock in the morning and already

I wished I'd never been born. I walked into my room and found Older Me in the mirror, her face pinched with worry.

"What happened? What's wrong?"

For a second, I considered ignoring her completely. But then I dragged the chair from my desk into the space in front of the mirror and placed the painting on it. All the color drained from her face. She froze in the beam of it. "Finn and Karyn . . ." She trailed off.

I nodded, then drew the curtains, got in bed, and pulled the quilt over my head.

A minute later she cleared her throat. Spoke softly. "It's okay, Ashley. You're—"

"Shut up!" I screamed at the cotton over my face. "I can't do this anymore! I'm done!" My whole body shook. My breath came in jagged gasps.

Her breath was audible. "Ashley . . . I didn't—"

"Shut *up*! Just. Shut. UP!"

There was a massive *bang!* and for a split second, I thought Older Me had come through the mirror. That somehow she was alive and here with me.

But when I threw the blankets back and sat up, it was Mom in the doorway, in her pajamas, panting, hair twisted and wild. She had one of her long-necked vases in her hand, brandishing it like a club.

What was she doing there?

Oh, crud. It was Monday. Her sleep-in day.

"Who are you yelling at?" Mom barked, still frantically scanning the room. "Who's here?"

"No one," I breathed.

"Ashley Watson, *who is in this room with you?*" Mom ran to the closet and threw the door open. Older Me swore as the mirror—with her in it—swung out of sight.

Mom then proceeded to search my room. She checked behind the curtains, even though they were only halfway down the wall. She even opened some drawers and got on the floor to look under my bed. The whole time, she had that dripping vase clasped so hard in her hand, her knuckles turned white. Then she got up from the floor and stood over me, face red and twisted with rage.

"Who were you yelling at? Where are they, Ashley? Why aren't you at school?"

"There's no one—"

She slammed the vase down on my desk. "You were yelling *at* someone!"

"Leave me alone!" I yelled, pulling the covers back up over my head.

"You skip class to come home to sulk and yell at yourself in the mirror?"

"It isn't like that!" My voice came out muffled.

"Ashley, if any of the neighbors heard you, they'd think you were being murdered. For a second *I* thought you were being murdered! *What the hell is going on in your head?*"

Struck speechless, I just huddled up in the blankets, hating her. Hating how worthless she made me feel. Well, I'd kept the worst from her before, but now I'd show her. Maybe if I embarrassed her enough she'd give up and leave me alone. Scooting out of bed, I skirted around her to the chair she'd shoved out of her way on her rampage across the room.

"Don't walk away when I'm talking to you!"

I grabbed the chair and swiveled it around so the painting faced her.

She opened her mouth to chastise me again, then saw the painting and stopped. She took one step closer. Then another. She clapped a hand over her mouth, but I could see her lips moving behind it, reading the words. Finally she looked at me and dropped her hand.

"Did someone else do this?"

My jaw dropped. "Do you think *I'd* do it?"

She stared at the painting again, shaking her head. "Ashley . . . why do they hate you so much? What did you do?"

I blanked.

She thought it was *my* fault?

A few months ago, Mom had hit a bump in the road and her windscreen cracked. Nothing major, just a tiny little line that started at the bottom of the glass.

She drove home, parked the car in the garage, and made an appointment to take it to the shop the next day.

Except, when we pulled the car out the next morning, that tiny line had turned into a jagged crack a foot long. And as we drove, it moved—never when you were watching—sliding farther, branching off, until a third of the glass was marred by the lines.

When we got it to the mechanic, he whistled and said we were lucky. He said that crack was under so much pressure that the tiniest bump from the wrong direction could have broken it into a million pieces and showered us with shards of glass.

Now, as Mom put her hands to her face and shook her head, I felt like that windscreen.

Crack, crack, crack.

A fracture started behind my navel, the brittle pieces shivering, on the edge of letting go. I hunched forward, pain exploding through my body.

"I can't believe this. You're a . . . a mess. A laughingstock. No wonder the other mothers act so awkward when they come in to the store . . ."

". . . I do everything I can to help you, and you just screw *everything* up . . ."

". . . I don't know what to do anymore. I don't know how to fix you . . ."

". . . have you ever thought about how embarrassing it is for me to have a daughter who's so . . . so . . ."

"Ashley . . . just breathe through it," Older Me called. "I know this is awful but we'll get through this, okay? I . . . I can help. I promise."

Awful didn't cover it. Awful didn't even *start* to describe it. I was an embarrassment to my own mother. I was the laughingstock of my school. Matt knew everything . . .

Matt.

That was the last straw. I breathed too hard, then I broke. All the pieces inside snapped apart and fell away, tinkling to the floor of my life and leaving a yawning hole where my heart should have been.

I sucked in a breath, but nothing came.

"Ashley?" Mom stopped her tirade long enough to realize I was imploding.

"Can't . . ."—*wheeze*—"breathe . . ."

"Ashley! Ashley, listen to me—"

209

I shook my head, tumbled forward onto my hands and knees. My fingers clawed into the carpet, twisting until the tiny fibers caught beneath my nails. My balance wavered.

"You have to relax. You have to breathe!"

Black shimmered around my edges, turning my room into a tunnel. Tiny sparks flared and snapped across my vision. I couldn't tell if it was Mom or Older Me calling to me.

"Look at me. Ashley, look at me!"

I swung my head drunkenly, gasping like a fish, certain I was about to suffocate. My heart pounded against my ribs, throbbed in my skin, pulsed in my ears.

I felt like I would die. And frankly, that had a plus side.

Mom dropped to the carpet and hit me hard on the back. My vision blurred, I coughed, and suddenly I could suck in air again—if only to shove it back out in a sob. For a moment, her expression was earnest and desperate in a way I'd never seen before. But then it dissolved as if it had never been there at all. Mom looked at me flatly and muttered, "You need help."

I puddled to the floor. Couldn't she see? She was too late.

CHAPTER TWENTY-NINE

"ALL ROADS LEAD back to Mom," Doc mutters.

I lean my head on my hand and wait for him to explain. When he catches my look, he shrugs. "It's a cliché, but it's true," he says, waving a hand in the air. "Our parents mold us, whether they mean to or not. Your mother convinced you that you were inadequate, that you lacked the necessary value. It's inherent in you. It colors every decision you've ever made."

I sit up straight. "I take responsibility for my choices, Doc. I don't blame her."

"Whether you *blame* her or not is entirely up to you," he says flippantly, pushing his glasses up the bridge of his nose. "But the fact remains that *she* was your first bully. She wrote the script, so to speak, that echoed in your head. When your peers began to deliver the same lines, it was easy for you to believe them, because, let's face it, you'd been hearing it at home for a while."

It is something that niggles at me at times. Would I feel differently about myself if Mom thought differently of me?

There is no way to know. I've never had any other mother, so it seems pointless to speculate. Instead, I flap a hand. "I think it's a good theory," I say. "But who knows?"

"I do," he says emphatically, making another note—this time his pen scratches across the paper, as if he's angry at it. "I do."

I turn away, discomfited by the resolution in his tone. I am angry at my mother, sure. But I can see through her now. She can't manipulate me like she used to.

But can Matt? Does he still have that power over me?

Sunlight from the window hits the mirror and glares in my peripheral vision. Without thinking, I turn to look at it.

When I look back, Doc has an eyebrow raised. "So what did you do next?"

I swallow hard. "What I always did. Art."

After Mom finally left my room, I sat on the carpet in front of my mirror, my entire body rigid. For the longest time, I couldn't move. Eventually, I managed to crawl over and close the closet door so I could see Older Me, though I couldn't miss seeing myself, too. My face was so swollen from tears that it looked like I'd gone two rounds in the boxing ring.

"What am I going to do *now*?" I whispered.

Older Me sat on the floor, hugging her own knees. "They aren't going to beat you, do you hear me?" she choked. Then I realized she was crying.

For me.

"But . . ." And my own tears broke.

"Finn and Karyn aren't going to win." She inhaled sharply. "They won't. In just a few minutes, you're going to wipe your face clean, stand up, and do this. And you'll prove them all wrong."

"D-do what?"

"Win. You're going to win, Ashley. Do you understand? You're going to take the crap they're throwing at you and turn it into something good. Something beautiful. And you'll *win*."

"How? H-*how*?"

She dropped her head for a second. When she raised it again, her eyes were full of tears. "Look at it, Ashley. Really look at it." She looked over my shoulder. I turned, wiping my eyes, chest catching in shuddering breaths I couldn't stop.

She was looking at the painting.

The painting of me that was plain and empty and devoid of life. The one with hate scrawled all over my face.

How apt.

Then I blinked. And sucked in hard.

The painting was still there—a forced, two-dimensional image of me covered by sabotage in bright pink. But this time, I *saw* it. My painting—with their words—had become more real, more representative of *me*, than anything I'd managed on my own. It told the story—the me that didn't look special. That didn't have depth. Nothing to appeal. And their words, their spite, their *hate*, scrawled across it. Then I looked at Older Me's face and realized why she wasn't talking. She wasn't worried, or afraid. She was . . . remembering.

"You—" I cut myself off.

Older Me's breath caught and I knew.

"This happened to you, too," I breathed.

Tears tipped onto her cheeks. She dashed them away with an impatient knuckle. But then she laughed. "Yes," she said. "I mean, it was a little different for me, but they did this to my painting . . . yes."

I swallowed. Awed. Angered. What else had I missed? But there was no time.

"The p-painting. If I use it . . ."

"You will." She nodded.

"Can I do it?" My voice was barely more than a whisper.

"Yes," she said vehemently. "Absolutely. *You* can." She swallowed. "You have to."

"But—"

"Now, Ashley. Don't think. You know this will work. And . . . and it's the way it has to be."

I stared, but no matter what else had happened, I knew she was right. I nodded and scrambled to my feet, holding on to the closet door until I felt like I wasn't going to fall over anymore. Then I turned for the painting, but stopped myself. Turned back.

Older Me still knelt on the ground, a world of pain and determination on her face.

"Hey, are you okay?"

On her side of the mirror, a knock sounded and a muffled voice called, "Ashley, it's time." She glanced over her shoulder, then turned back to me. "I'm so sorry, but I have to go." She smiled wanly. "And don't worry about me. I'm fine, Ashley. I've already been through this. And I know how it has to end."

It seemed an odd way to phrase it and I wanted to ask, but she was already gone. So, ignoring the tightness in my throat that was at complete odds with the sense of emptiness in my chest, I locked my door, set the painting up on my desk, and tried to prepare myself to show the world my monsters.

* * *

That afternoon, sight blurring after focusing on my painting for so many hours, I walked back to school, head down, carrying the painting, in a sick reflection of the way I'd left just hours earlier. I arrived in the middle of fifth period.

My footsteps echoed on the quad. There was no sound except a murmur of voices from a classroom too far away to be dangerous, and the twittering of a few birds still looking for crumbs left by thoughtless students at lunch.

Classes were in. Chances were, people would look out the window and see me crossing the quad. Someone who hated me would hear that I was back.

But the path to New York was through those doors.

When I reached the art room, I didn't slow down. I didn't flinch. I just opened the door and stepped inside.

Empty.

Of course, the seniors were already having their finals. And they had the afternoon block for electives, so the room would stay blessedly clear.

Shaking with relief, I started across the floor, then yelped as I ran into Mrs. D rushing out of the storage cupboard.

"Ashley!" she panted, hand on her ample bosom. "I didn't know you were here . . ."

She trailed off as she saw the painting in my hand. Her jaw dropped slightly. I flinched. But when her gaze cut back up to meet mine, her face was tender. She swallowed. "Are you here to work?"

I nodded, tears in my eyes. She put a hand on my arm, her brow creased. "You're very brave to come back," she said.

I wiped my face on my sleeve. "I am the furthest thing from brave." I was still trembling just from crossing the quad.

"Ashley," she started gently.

I shook my head. "Mrs. D, please don't. I have to draw or I'm just going to . . ." *Die? Kill myself?* ". . . to fall apart."

She frowned, as if she could hear my unspoken words. But if there was one thing Mrs. D didn't question, it was the creative outlet as therapy. She stared at me for a second, then pushed her lips together and nodded.

"The easel room still has the big mirror in it," she said quietly. "And I'll give you as long as I can, but . . . I'm sorry, I will have to make a decision by the end of the day."

"I know," I managed.

Grabbing my paints and brushes, I ducked into the easel room. At first I headed for my usual corner, but something tugged at me. Instead, I took three easels from the stack and set them up facing the light from the window, like Matt always did. I dragged the large, full-length mirror along the wall until it leaned just a couple of feet to my left.

I stacked the three big portfolio boards on easels next to each other, then took my still-drying painting and gently tacked it onto the space I'd left on the middle board.

Ignoring my thumping heart, I picked up a paintbrush and stared at the awful painting, trying to see it as someone else might. But all I could see was that I had put myself out there for the world to see and gotten a penis drawn on my face. I exhaled. Now that I was over the shock, there was a strange kind of relief in looking at the painting. Horrific as the fallout would be, they'd done their worst.

I worked for a few minutes on final touches, but there wasn't a lot more I could do. When I stepped back to take in the overall effect, two things hit me. First, there was still a big hole where the Matt picture was supposed to go on the left. Second, my eyes were sucked to the self-portrait, just like I'd wanted. It stood out, stark against the black and demanding attention. It screamed.

Since Finn had taken his poison to it, I'd only changed three things: The portrait of me now looked down and away, trying not to see the words and pictures Finn had scrawled. I'd cleaned up the edges on all the letters. The unpracticed eye wouldn't notice, but there was the tiniest black outline to give them crispness. They and the other . . . additions cut through the rest of the picture and jumped off the canvas.

It was deeply satisfying and deeply painful. I suddenly felt very vulnerable and sure the judges wouldn't get it at all. But what choice did I have? It was use the painting, or nothing.

I had no idea what had happened to the pieces of the Matt picture I'd torn off the canvas. I rummaged through my cubby until I found my workbook. Sure enough, a large brown envelope fell out, all the pieces of the Matt sketches jumbled inside it. I'd have to remember to thank Mrs. D. Again.

I turned it upside down on the floor and knelt to sort the pictures out. Three were smudged, the forehead had been torn almost in half, and the waxy acrylic on one cheek had a long scrape through it—had I done that? They weren't salvageable, but at least I could copy them. That would make the redo much quicker.

So I grabbed another canvas board from the resource room and tacked it to the panel where Matt should have been, and got busy placing the pieces as I would when they were clean and complete.

Minutes melted into hours until the clock said 1:36. My hands still shook, but I set myself at the picture with a sense of purpose I hadn't felt . . . well, ever. Deep down, I knew this day was the turning point. The moment I'd look back on and say, "That's when my life changed." I needed to forget about how it came about and just use it to my advantage. Use Older Me's betrayal as fuel to keep going. Use Finn's spite to headline my success.

He'd *hate* that.

He'd tried to ruin me. But I wasn't giving up. There was still one door I could walk through. One worthwhile version of my future still waiting for me.

With a deep breath, I picked up a different brush.

And there, in the middle of the dark, yawning hole inside me, a tiny ball of hope sprang to life.

CHAPTER THIRTY

FOR THE FIRST time, Doc looks troubled. I scan back through everything I've just said, trying to figure out which part is bothering him. But then he taps his foot.

"Ashley, I think I should tell you: I saw some of your pictures. Including your self-portrait. Or rather, images of them."

"*What?* How?"

"Given the part your art plays in all this, I contacted your high school and asked to see them when you requested to leave. They had pictures of three or four of them—from the teacher and the yearbook photographer."

"That's not fair! You can't just go snooping around in my life!"

Doc grimaces. "I'm sorry I didn't let you know sooner, but I wasn't even sure I'd be able to get them and didn't want to upset you if it wasn't relevant. Your teacher was right, by the way—they're incredibly revealing."

"Those pictures were *art*, not therapy!"

"Relax, Ashley. I said they were revealing. I didn't say I was concerned about them."

Pause. "You weren't?"

"Heavens, no! I wish all my patients could communicate themselves so articulately. I'm glad you did. They give me a very clear picture of your view of yourself and those around you prior to your incident."

I swallow hard. "They do?"

"Yes. Even more than your recollections of events, I think, because your memories are tainted by your choices to hide things or modify them as you think I want to hear." His expression is kindly, but there's a warning in those words.

"I'm not lying to you."

"And I'm not accusing you of that. But it's clear to me that you're very aware of how others think of you. You modify your word choices, downplay feelings, sugarcoat events. You hide behind these things because you've grown accustomed to being ridiculed simply for being yourself. But that's why I'm so glad I saw your paintings. They tell me a big part of the story."

Gulp. "Like what?"

Behind his glasses, Doc loses the analytical glaze.

"They show me how you were hurt. Deeply. That each wound was unique, but all left you bleeding." I flinch, but he waves a hand. "My apologies, bad choice of word. I meant it figuratively." He crosses his legs again. His eyes won't let me go. "Ashley, your paintings tell me your story is real and regardless of how others may view it, that your pain—even before the incident—was extensive."

Oh crap oh crap oh crap oh crap. My throat aches. My vision blurs. I'm swallowing a lump that keeps bobbing back to the surface.

I can't cry. I can't! If I lose it, he'll think I'm not ready.

I look away. I can't respond to what he's said. I have to move on. Have to change the subject. I let my head rest on the back of my seat and breathe deeply.

"It wasn't all bad," I manage.

"Ashley—"

"Just give me a minute, will you?"

I have to get a grip. I can't afford to let him sideswipe me again. Not with what's coming.

It's 1:48. I have an hour. *An hour.*

I am already strung so tight I feel like if someone touched me, I'd twang.

Doc clears his throat and I jerk my attention back to him.

He's tapping his pen on the arm of his chair. I wonder if that is what has creased the leather there. The metal tip makes a muffled *whump* at each click.

"About that day . . . ," he says carefully. "About your incident." His voice is soft, but his eyes are bullets trained on me.

Every muscle in my body tenses. I take a deep breath, let it out slowly the way a therapist showed me years ago. I imagine water sliding off my head, through my hair, down my back, my chest, my arms—down, down, down, all the way to my toes, letting my muscles unwind with it as it passes.

"Ashley?" There's a note of impatience in his tone.

"Why is everyone so fixated on that day?" I mutter.

Doc tips his head. "It is rather pivotal, don't you think?"

I am immediately tense again. I can't stop jiggling my foot. "No, actually. It's nothing but the . . . the frosting on the cake. All the ingredients, all the time, all the cooking? That had all been going on for years."

Doc drops the pen so it thumps onto the large notepad in his lap. "Well, then, I guess we're interested to see how the culmination of all that affected you. Tell me what happened."

"I'm sure it's in your little file."

"I'd like to hear it in your words, please."

My body is rigid, but I won't be able to relax until I'm out this place. And I'm running out of time.

"Ashley—"

"Fine! I'll tell you!" I think I shout it, but it comes out as barely a whisper. "I was just deciding which of Matt's ears I liked best when the door opened. I thought it was Mrs. Driley, back early, but it wasn't. It was Karyn . . . and Finn. It was a half hour before the final bell rang. There was an end-of-year assembly that day. I'd forgotten that."

My jaw feels like iron. I am sinking back to that place. I don't want to go. Against my will, images of that day come to me in flashes.

Karyn standing behind Finn, arms folded, staring at my portfolio.

Karyn ripping off the little pieces of Matt's eyes. His nose. His ear.

Finn holding my arms as Karyn destroyed it all. Every last piece that should have taken me to New York.

The cold, hard floor where I fell, sobbing.

The laughter and taunts echoing in my ears.

The knowing that everything was gone—Matt, my future, my last chance at a *life*.

What happened after that was . . . not me. It was Someone Else.

Someone Else stumbled upright and put a foot through my father's silhouette.

Someone Else punched a hole in Dex's chest.

Someone Else stomped on my mother's face.

Someone Else grabbed the easel and swung it toward Finn's head.

And when hands closed around my legs, and a voice shouted *STOP!* it didn't matter.

Because the sound that left my mouth wasn't mine. The momentum of the easel left me hurtling toward the wall. Toward the mirror.

I tumbled into that shining surface so fast I barely had time to think, *yes*.

Let it all be over.

Please.

CHAPTER THIRTY-ONE

I TAKE ANOTHER deep breath, squeezing out the last of the tears.

Doc waits. I can hear his breath sliding in and out. When I look up, his face is blank.

"That was a very traumatic day for you," he says quietly.

I nod. Swallow. "Yes. It was."

Doc looks down at his notepad. "You were injured very badly."

I nod, though it's the understatement of the century.

"Ashley . . . did you want to die that day?"

I tip my head against the back of the chair and swallow more tears.

"I wished I was dead," I say quietly. "It's not the same thing."

Doc is quiet for a moment, shuffling papers. "You're right," he says eventually. "But I wonder . . . I wonder if your role was perhaps a little more . . . active than you've suggested?"

I jerk my head up. "What are you saying?"

Doc's expression says he wants me to think he's not enjoying this. "According to the school's report, Finn and Karyn found you in the art room tearing up your own work, crying, babbling incoherently."

"Finn and Karyn lied to cover their own asses," I say through gritted teeth.

Doc nods, but his face doesn't look like he agrees with me. "Your teacher said she knew something was wrong when you showed up that afternoon. That was the reason she left assembly early to come back to the art room. She sensed something in you that made her uneasy. Something . . . destructive?"

I give him an angry look and clench my teeth harder. "Of course I was in bad shape. I'd just been humiliated in front of the entire school and accused of being an embarrassment by my mom!"

"And it was your older self—your future self, whom you see in the mirror—that convinced you to go back?"

Where was he going with this? "I wouldn't say she convinced me. She let me see the potential of what I had. That New York was still possible . . ." I trail off. Because, of course, it wasn't possible. Not after what Karyn and Finn had done to my work.

Doc drops his pen on the notebook and rubs a hand over his face. "Ashley, your story—"

"I didn't try to kill myself," I snap.

He stares, disbelieving, like I am a difficult child. He carefully picks up his notebook and the pen, placing them on the coffee table between us, and leans forward to rest his elbows on his knees. His glasses make his eyes look bigger as he rubs his hands together and fixes me with what I assume is supposed to be a comforting expression.

"I'm going to be completely honest with you, Ashley. I don't think you're ready to leave this facility."

The clock ticks twice before the implications of those words sink in.

"You can't be serious." I spring to my feet.

"I am deadly serious," Doc says calmly, sitting back. "I wanted to hear your account of this because if you'd owned up to what happened that day, told me the truth of it, I could have been sure that *you* see things differently now. But as it stands, I fear for your stability. I fear for what you might do to yourself—or to others—if I were to let you loose."

"Let me *loose*? I'm a human being, not an unlicensed dog!"

He tips his head and gives me a stern look. "Precisely why I am not about to let you go if you might hurt yourself or someone else. I value you, Ashley. Perhaps more than you value yourself."

I bark a laugh. The irony is so thick it is suffocating. "No one—no one!—values *me* more than I value myself, Doc. I wouldn't be here today if I didn't count myself as something precious."

He blinks, hearing the depth of meaning in my words, no doubt. But he won't understand them. Not yet.

I glance at the clock. It says 2:14. He can't do this. Not when I am so close!

Doc follows my gaze, frowns, and turns back to me. "I'm glad to hear you speak so highly of yourself," he says eventually. Dubiously. "I won't be alone in hoping that attitude continues."

Now I can hear something behind his words.

I glare at him, search his blank and passive face. For a moment I hate him. "What do you mean?" I blurt.

His brow creases. The stripes of beard that frame his mouth are bent by his frown. He leans his temple on one fist, examining me. "I'm trying to decide if, under the circumstances, the course of action I'd planned is still worth pursuing," he says quietly.

My heart thrums. "What. Do. You. *Mean?*"

He considers me for a moment, then his mouth opens. Adrenaline floods my system, because somehow I know whatever he's about to say is going to change the game. But he's interrupted by a knock at the door.

Both Doc and I go still. We're staring at each other.

Then it sounds again, slightly faster this time, and I raise a brow at him. Doc hesitates, then murmurs, "Excuse me," and pushes himself out of his plush chair, weaves his way around the glossy coffee table, past his desk, and checks through a tiny peephole in the door. Designed, no doubt, to keep Doc safe in the event that a psychotic ex-patient with a grudge comes knocking.

I'm beginning to see the appeal.

But it's not a psycho, apparently, because Doc reaches for the combination lock and starts pressing numbers.

My head whirls.

He isn't going to sign me out. Should I try to run when the door is open?

I get to my feet and take slow, faltering steps up behind Doc. I'm not going to be able to shove out the door with that duffel on my back. I'll have to leave it.

". . . very sorry about the late notice, but I think we can make it quick. I appreciate you coming," Doc murmurs, pulling the door wider.

I brace, watching the slice of sunlight along the door widen. My hands are clenched into fists so tightly I can feel my nails digging into my palms.

Then I hear *his* voice.

"Ashley?"

The word—it's just a word!—slices me open. I make a tiny noise and slowly look up from the brown leather shoes, to the waist that is thicker than it used to be, but still firm and tight. To the shoulders that I have gripped, and hugged, and cried on for almost six years. Almost. Until the day he threw me at my mom and together they got me committed. My gaze slides up to the hard line of his jaw, the butter-smooth finish of his cheeks, the bright but wary blue of his eyes.

"M-Matt?" I gasp, both hands flying to my mouth.

Matt glances at Doc, then back to me. He wipes his hands on his thighs. "How are you?" The words are stilted. Awkward.

I'm not sure what expression lands on my face, but all I can think is, *Seriously?*

Matt's head jerks back, just a tiny bit. Fear flashes in his eyes.

He is afraid. Of me. I don't know whether to laugh, or cry. I look at Doc, mouth open to ask him what the hell he was thinking, when he answers the question I haven't asked.

"Matt, take a seat. Ashley, I asked Matt to come today because I felt like his perspective on your past, on the events leading up to that day, might help you . . . process."

"Process?"

"I think the problems you've had over the past few years all stem from those days—from the way you feel about yourself as a result of the bullying and cruelty you experienced."

"Cruelty?" When in shock I become a parrot, apparently.

Doc nods. "And I think you need to be honest with your-self about just how dark things got on that day. For you. About how you . . . how your self-destructive tendencies may have . . . peaked."

My mouth opens twice before I'm able to get the words out. "Finn pushed me through that mirror," I finally manage from between my teeth. "I told you that."

A deep sigh rises from the circle of chairs and couches. Matt has settled himself into the chair I was sitting in. He isn't facing us, but he's shaking his head.

"No one asked for your opinion," I snap.

"Actually, I did," Doc says quietly, unapologetic. "Let's take a seat, Ashley. This won't take long."

Doc leads by example, wending his way back to his chair, and sweeping a hand toward the thick seat on the other side of the coffee table. Next to Matt.

I walk behind Matt's chair so I can't feel him watching, and take the seat to his left.

My entire right side tingles with awareness of him, and I hate myself for it.

We are all silent for a moment. Doc shuffles papers. I play with the frayed hem on the sleeve of my hoodie and avoid Matt's eyes. I can see him looking between me and Doc.

"So . . . where are we at?" he says.

Doc finds what he wants, sets it on his knee, and puts the rest of his notes on the coffee table. Then he looks up.

"I have been with Ashley all day," he says, as if this is a gift and we should both be thankful. Strangely, I am not overwhelmed with gratitude in that moment. "I've learned a lot, and she has definitely opened up. However . . . just before you arrived, we met with what I would describe as an obstacle to her recovery."

I snort. "Telling the truth is an obstacle now, is it?"

Doc shoots me a glance, then returns his attention to Matt. "Matt, I told you the reason I wanted you here today was because I believed your perspective on the events of that day could help Ashley see it more clearly."

"I'm seeing fine," I mutter. "I didn't try to kill myself."

Matt's head whips around and his frown has become stern disapproval. "I disagree," he says sharply.

My anger fuels my courage. I meet his gaze with my mouth open to demonstrate how incredulous I am. "You weren't even there."

"Yes, I was. You just don't remember because you were too busy destroying everything."

I shake my head. "If you'd been there, you would have seen Finn tackle me."

"When I walked in, I saw you throwing an easel, then Finn trying to stop you from throwing yourself through the mirror."

I am livid. "I can't believe you're still defending him after all this time!"

"I'm not defending him! I'm telling you what I saw!"

"Great! Then talk about how my art had been completely destroyed! Talk about how Finn told me he wanted me dead! Talk about that!"

Matt's jaw flexes. But it is Doc who responds.

"Ashley, from what you described, Karyn only tore three or four pieces—"

"Just enough to ruin any chance I had of getting a portfolio together for New York," I snap. "You guys are just as blind as they were. Don't you get it? Don't you understand what these people do? They take everything. They roll over you time and time and time again until you don't have any strength left. Then they laugh and do it again, just to make sure you don't have an ounce of self-respect, either. Those two people ruined my life, and now you want me to say that they were trying to help me? I'm not the insane person at this table!" I yell and push to my feet.

"Ashley," Doc says in his most patronizing tone.

I cut him off. "I need to walk."

"Ash," Matt begins.

My hand flexes, wanting to touch him. I curl my fingers into a fist and force myself to walk away, toward the door. Toward freedom.

Matt is staring at my back. I can feel his gaze on the back of my neck.

"Ash," he says again, softer this time. "I've never said they didn't hurt you, or that they were right for . . . for what they did. I'm just worried that you won't admit that you also hurt yourself."

I throw up my hands and keep pacing. My reflection moves in the mirror and I turn my face away because it is too painful. I am failing. I am failing her and she doesn't even know it yet.

I stop, turn on my heel and face the men who've remained in their seats. Doc has removed his glasses and is holding them in one hand as he tips back, legs crossed, to examine me.

Matt sits forward in his chair, as if he might rise. But there is fear on his face and I am reminded that he has never fully believed in me. Never.

Even our good days were underlined with doubt.

Matt opens his mouth and I brace. But Doc raises a hand to stop him.

"Ashley," Doc says, "I believe that on that day, you were so unhappy, so under pressure, that you were capable of making decisions you wouldn't have made any other day in your life. We call it a breaking point. I believe you reached your breaking point that day, and there is no shame in that."

I snort. "I don't feel shame because *I didn't do it.*" *Not intentionally.*

Matt shakes his head. His face drags toward the floor and I feel a pang at his grief. Unable to keep watching him, I turn, begin to pace again. But suddenly the movement in the mirror doesn't match my own and I'm drawn to a stop in front of it, my adrenaline pumping.

Little Me's already in the art room. Of course she is. I told her to go back to school. I told her, and I didn't warn her about what was going to happen.

I thought about what Doc said. About how I only thought about me. My life. All the times I hadn't told Ashley what was coming while hoping it would go differently . . . Was I protecting her? Or myself? Did I need her to experience what I had experienced to validate my own decisions? My own mistakes?

And that's when I realize . . .

For history to change, history will need to repeat.

The clock says 2:30. I glance at the mirror, looming to my right, and swallow again. Could I do it here? If I had to? Even if it means proving Doc right?

My muscles turn to stone in the same moment Little Me catches sight of me in the mirror.

She's in the art room, tightening screws on three easels, which are holding her boards for the competition. She's got most of the pieces already attached, but a couple are stacked neatly against the opposite wall. She stops moving for a moment when she sees me, then turns back to the easel.

"Hello," she says. She is still angry. Still aching from the blow.

I swallow. "Hi," I say through rapidly gathering tears. "Ashley, I know this is going to sound weird, and I know my timing sucks, but I have something to tell you."

Both Matt and Doc gasp. "Who are you talking to, Ashley?" Matt says in a voice two steps too high. I ignore him.

I am fixed now. I know what I have to do. I have failed in freeing myself, but at least I can still free her. "Ashley?" I say.

She sighs, stands straight and turns to face me. "What?"

"You know all those times I refused to tell you the future?" My voice cracks.

She nods.

"I've changed my mind."

CHAPTER THIRTY-TWO

I'M STANDING IN the middle of Doc's floor, staring at the huge mirror he brought in to try and intimidate me, and finally I am grateful. He's given me the opportunity to make this right.

Matt's gaping at me from his chair, while Doc looks professionally disappointed.

Like I care.

I swallow the lump in my throat and meet Little Me's stunned expression.

"What?" she says.

"You have to listen to me, and you have to do exactly what I say if you want to get to New York, okay?"

"Oh-kay." She breaks the word into two doubtful syllables. My hands tighten. I know she's doubting herself. I will her to believe what I'm about to say.

There are whispers behind me, footsteps. Then Matt is at my shoulder. "Ash, honey, what are you doing?"

I don't take my eyes off Little Me. She's standing there, shoulders slumped. I remember the heaviness of that day and I want to cry.

I blink to press the tears back. "I get it, all right? I was there too. It feels like too much. They've won. They've scared Matt off. They've destroyed your self-portrait. And everyone is laughing. Your skin is crawling, you hate yourself, and you hate them. But you're trapped." I have to work hard to keep my voice above a whisper. "You have to get out."

Little Me squirms. Unshed tears shine. "Stop," she says.

I shake my head. "I won't. And I won't leave you alone, okay? I'm going to be here the whole time. And I'm going to help you."

"Help with w-what?" she asks.

"Ash, please . . ." Matt touches my arm and I yank it away without looking at him.

I take a deep breath. "In a few minutes, Finn and Karyn are going to arrive," I tell her softly. Her brow furrows. "Karyn's going to try and destroy your artwork and Finn's going to hold you back so you can't stop her."

Matt inhales sharply.

"It will feel like it's the end of the world. You will want to just walk away from everything. You'll feel trapped and dark and wish you'd never been born."

"I already do," she says in a tiny voice. Her shoulders shake and I am broken for her. I wipe my own tears back with a hurried hand and keep my voice strong. For her.

"You can't give up. You can't let go. No matter how bad it gets, you can't let them win today," I say. "You are better than this. You're better than me. I'm . . . Ashley, I'm proud of you."

Little Me has turned her back on me. She's wiping tears away and she's shaking. But she's walking to the canvases in the corner, picking them up.

"How could you possibly be proud of me?" she says when she returns.

"When I went to prom, I slept with Matt," I say, feeling him tense next to me. "But he just . . . left. He didn't break up with Karyn. He said he was *confused*. Then Monday, with the letter and everything . . ."

"I wasn't confused about my feelings for you," Matt mutters. "I was confused about how to handle the whole thing."

"You were scared to break up with her and go out with me," I snap, glancing at him, but then look back to the mirror.

Little Me blinks. "Is he there? With you?" She peers around me.

I put my hands up. "He is here reluctantly," I say. "And he's not important."

Matt grunts. "This is getting ridiculous. Ashley, stop. If you want to talk to me, talk to me. Don't talk to . . . that."

Doc approaches, and the hair on the back of my neck stands up.

"What do you see there, Ashley?" he asks, like it's no big deal.

I see through his crap but decide to answer him anyway. What do I have to lose? "I see my younger self, at the end of junior year. She's going to fight, and she's going to win," I say, determined for her.

I turn back to the mirror. "Now, listen," I tell her. "I'm not kidding. I get it, okay? I know how hard this is and it's going to get harder. But you can't give up. You can never stop fighting. No matter what they say, no matter how alone or trapped you feel, you keep fighting. Because if you don't, they'll win." My voice cracks again and I have to take a breath. "If you give up on yourself, they'll ride right over you and it will never let you go."

She frowns. "What are you talking about?"

"I'm talking about your future," I tell her as calmly as I can. "*Our* future. You have a chance to make yours different. I gave up, Ash," I say through tears. "I gave up because everyone thought I was worthless. I believed them. I didn't get to New York. I only got Matt by default. And Finn and Karyn . . . they never paid. For this." I grab my hoodie at the hem and pull it up before I can think about it. I'm only wearing a tank top underneath. The scars on my arms and neck and chest glow like iridescent spiderwebs.

Little Me gasps, her hands fly to her mouth.

"Ashley, stop it!" Matt grabs my arm and shakes me, but I claw at his grip until he lets go. Doc raises his voice. But all I can see is her—her face, her fear, her hands twisted together as she takes a step back.

"What . . . how . . . I didn't know." Her tears well, making my own press to the surface again.

I nod. "I didn't want you to know. I didn't want you to be scared. I was trying to . . . hoping you wouldn't have to go through this at all, but . . ." How do I say it? How do I tell her?

"What are they going to do to me?" she asks and her voice is so small it breaks my heart.

I clear my throat. I'll focus on the practicalities. The rest we can deal with later. She can.

"Karyn's going to try and destroy your art. Don't let her. Stay between her and your boards. Keep out of Finn's grip. And stay away from the mirror!"

"But—"

"Just do it, Ashley. I'll be here. I'll help you. I'm not leaving.

We'll get through this," I say through tears. I know they aren't helping. They're just scaring her. But I can't stop. Because I know what I have to do and it terrifies me. But it also gives me hope.

And I haven't had hope in a long time.

"Ashley!" Matt says beside me, his voice tight.

"Older Me?" she says.

"So you really are nuts," an oily voice says from behind Little Me.

I gasped and whirled. Karyn followed Finn into the easel room, immediately looking to my boards. Remembering Older Me's warning, I stepped sideways to put myself between them and my art, my pulse pounding in my ears. A stream of expletives rose from Older Me and the mirror.

"Go away," I said, wishing my voice didn't shake. Knowing they wouldn't.

Finn just cocked an eyebrow and came to stand in front of me, hands on his hips. "You are seriously mental," he said. "I mean, the whole school knows now, so I can see why you might not hide it anymore. Still . . ." He shook his head like a disappointed parent—except for the gleeful light in his eyes.

Karyn looked at the portrait I'd drawn of her, and her face lit like fire. "You pathetic loser," she snapped.

"Hard to face the truth, is it?" I snapped back.

Finn lunged at me and I dodged. Karyn didn't even bother with me, just strode right for my paintings, stopping at the middle easel to examine the pieces of Matt I'd tacked to a canvas board. "Pah-thet-ic," she repeated and yanked at Matt's ear. The paper tore in half.

"No!" I dove at her, but Finn got his arm around my middle and swung me back so I almost lost my feet. I shoved at him, but he just laughed.

"You're like one of those viruses, C," he said. "You just won't go away."

"Don't give in, Ashley!" Older Me called from the mirror.

I tried to punch Finn, but he easily ducked out of the way.

"Nope, C. Sorry. Time to take your medicine, crazy girl."

His arms circled me, pinning my elbows to my sides and stopping me from doing anything except jerking around in his grip. I struggled, but he was so strong. Tears prickled.

"Haven't you done enough?" I grunted, still trying to get free of Finn's grip. "Why can't you just leave me alone?"

"Because if I had my way, you'd crawl into a hole and die," Finn muttered into my hair. "Failing that, I'll be happy with ruining your life."

Karyn tore another piece of Matt's face off the board. Then Finn twisted the skin on my wrist until it burned, and Karyn reached for another piece. Suddenly I understood why Older Me had warned me to keep going, because the urge was there to just . . . sag. I couldn't beat these two . . . could I?

"Keep fighting," Older Me called again, a hitch in her voice. "Please. Don't give up! Don't become me."

"I won't." I gritted my teeth and heaved with everything I had.

CHAPTER THIRTY-THREE

"ASHLEY," MATT SAID, his voice rough and hoarse. "What is going on?"

"She's fighting Finn," I said. "Better than I ever did." There is pride in my voice. Of the two of us, she is better. And I am truly proud of her.

In my peripheral vision, I can see Matt shake his head. His hand remains on my arm. "You can't keep doing this," he breathes and a chill dances down my neck.

"What? Caring about what happens to me? Caring about the wrong people winning?" I snap. "I'm not going to let her go through everything I went through!" I yell, pointing at the mirror.

Matt plows his hands into his hair and turns away. "I give up, doctor. I give up."

"Of course you do," I hiss at him, turning back to the mirror. "You always have."

Little Me is still struggling. She's dragged Finn close enough to the boards that Karyn's had to move out of their way. I take a breath and dare to hope.

"I can't do this anymore," Matt says in a broken voice, and I'm horribly afraid he's about to cry, so I don't look at him.

"She's having a psychotic break," Doc says grimly. "Reliving that day."

"I'm not reliving it!" I shriek. "*She's* living it. For the first time! And I'm going to make sure it turns out differently for her!" For a moment the blackness of that day washes over me. I'm once again in a room with two people who would destroy me. And I once again feel powerless.

But then I look at Little Me, her face all screwed up. Her hair sticking to her temples where she's beginning to sweat from fighting Finn, and I grit my teeth. She's not giving up. And neither am I.

"Fight!" I tell her. I don't even know if she can hear me. She grunts and hauls herself forward, pulling Finn off his feet and onto her back. He shouts, slides sideways and almost falls. They both stumble toward the mirror and I gasp, leap forward, because it's reflex to try and be there. To try and catch her.

As Finn loses his grip on Little Me and she throws herself at Karyn, the voices behind me come into focus.

"Doc?"

"I'm calling the orderlies. We'll sedate her."

"No, you won't," I seethe.

Matt doesn't say anything. Typical.

I turn on my heel and take two steps away from the mirror, toward Doc. Put my finger in his face. "I do not give you permission to medicate me," I say. "So you stay the hell away from me!"

"At times that I deem to be extreme stress or anxiety, I do not need your permission to medicate you, Ashley," he says.

"I'm not anxious," I snap. "I am trying to help *her*." I point back at the mirror where I can hear her screaming at Finn. I have to get back there. It can't be long until he comes. Has she kept them away long enough?

Doc doesn't even glance at the mirror. "There is no *her*, Ashley. *She* does not exist, except in your mind. *She* is the manifestation of *your* grief and fear. *You* cannot save *her* from the suicidal and self-destructive actions you have taken because *she* is *you*."

"You got one part right," I tell him and turn back to the mirror.

Matt hasn't moved, hasn't spoken since he says he gave up. I will pretend he isn't here. It's just one more in a long line of moments he's let me down. I will not cry over him again. I will not. I turn back to the mirror to watch.

I was able to cut loose from Finn for a minute, our struggles turning into a violent game of tag, in which I tried to get Karyn away from my pictures and Finn kept grabbing me, laughing when I dodged.

Then she took the picture of Matt's lips, the ones I drew after he'd kissed me, and yanked them off the board. I screamed "NO!" so loud my voice cracked. And instead of trying to dodge Finn, I stepped forward and shoved him.

I punched at his chest and tried to knee him in the balls. But he was too fast. Soon I was back, pinned inside his embrace, the warmth in my cheeks fading to grief in my chest.

Karyn grabbed the picture of Matt's chin and tore it in half. "Whoops!" she laughed.

"How can you laugh?" I sobbed. "You're ruining my life!"

Finn leaned into my ear and hissed, "Welcome to my wor—"

"What the hell is going on?"

Matt stood in the doorway, feet shoulder-width apart, his hands in fists at his sides. Everyone froze. Karyn stilled, her hand hovering in the air just in front of Matt's picture—or what was left of it. Finn loosened his grip.

"Take. Your hands. Off her," Matt said in a voice so dark even I felt scared.

But instead of releasing me, Finn spoke over my shoulder. "She was going crazy, Matt. Tearing up her art stuff. I'm telling you, she's nuts."

Karyn blinked, then nodded. "It was terrifying."

"No! They're lying!" I cried. "I would never do that!"

Matt looked back and forth between them, then at me. I could see the confusion on his face. The question. I held my breath. Had he been so blinded by that letter that he'd believe them?

But then he stormed over to Finn. "Get your hands off her, Finn," he demanded.

Relief broke over me like a wave.

"It's your funeral, man," he said, slowly letting me go.

I tore away from him, slapping at his hands, then darted across the room to Karyn and pushed her away from my boards. I knelt on the dusty floor to retrieve the pieces of my pictures, to see if any of them could be salvaged.

She just stepped back, arms folded. "Don't listen to her, Matt. I mean—"

Matt shook his head. "Don't speak to me. Don't ever say another word to me. I have nothing to say to you. Ever."

For a moment she just stared at him, then she turned on her heel and flounced off, slamming the door behind her.

"Finn," he said darkly, and the sweet guy I loved had a vein pulsing in his forehead. "I defended you."

"And I helped you. That's what friends do," Finn snapped. "They don't go postal and write love letters and show the whole world how crazy they are."

"I didn't—!"

Matt raised a hand to cut me off, his eyes never leaving Finn's face. "I told her you weren't as bad as she said. I told her to stay out of your way," he spat, pointing at me. "And the whole time, you were torturing her and hooking up with my girlfriend."

"Whatever."

I opened my mouth, but Matt cut me a glare and I snapped it shut again.

"Turns out, she wasn't the only one who saw you guys," he said through gritted teeth, leaning into Finn's face until they were nose to nose. "Turns out, when I started asking, there were a lot of people who knew. But no one had the guts to tell me the truth."

Dropping all pretense, Finn sneered. "Well, I hope you two will be very happy together. Good luck having any kind of social life when you're dating her."

"Ashley is amazing. She's my best friend, and she'd never do to me what you and Karyn did."

Finn scoffed, "She wouldn't have the choice. No one ever wants to be within ten feet of her because she's a complete nut job. But if that's your thing, knock yourself out." He paused and I saw the edge return to his expression. "No wonder Karyn liked screwing me more."

Matt blinked once. Then he plowed a fist right into Finn's face.

Finn staggered, then righted himself. He grunted, launching himself and taking Matt out at the waist. They tumbled together, a tangle of limbs and curses flying toward my feet. I tried to get out of their way and tripped backward, falling into an easel.

We all crashed to the floor.

CHAPTER THIRTY-FOUR

"NO!" I YELL.

I'd thought she'd done it. She'd delayed them long enough to let Matt get there in time to help. But the fight's not over yet. As I watch Matt pound on Finn, tears prick again. I wish he'd had that kind of courage for me.

A hand brushes my arm and I pull it away without looking away from the mirror.

"Ms. Watson? Please come with me." The deep voice is familiar. I turn to find Alex, my favorite orderly, standing over me with a concerned, but firm, look on his face.

I frown. "I'm not leaving yet."

Large hands close on my upper arms. Hands that don't budge when I pull forward. "What are you—?"

"Time to come with us, Ashley," he says, already tugging me backwards.

"What? No!" I twist in his grip and claw at his fingers.

Another orderly with pockmarked cheeks and black hair appears. He and Alex each take an arm. I brace against the carpet.

But they are mountains compared to me. I begin sliding along the floor.

"Stop!" I scream. I can still see the mirror. See Little Me trip as the guys tumble toward her. "Please don't take me, not now!" I plead with Alex. He doesn't even look at me.

They drag me alongside the circle of chairs around the coffee table and I struggle, strain and twist, but they are too strong, and for a minute I want to give up. But I remember how Ashley didn't give up, and I won't, either. So I fight. I kick and heave and scream until dark spots flicker at the edge of my vision. But they keep moving me farther and farther from her. Just when she needs me most.

"Matt! Matt! Don't let them do this!"

He shakes his head and my stomach drops.

"You know I didn't lie to you back then!" I shout. "I'm not lying about the mirror, either! I'm not!"

Without warning, Matt is on his feet, lips curled away from his teeth. He darts between the chairs and storms over until he's in front of our little trio, hands clenched at his sides. "Give up, Ashley!" he roars. "It's over! Give *up*!" Matt points at me. "I almost lost you then, and now I have to sit up at night after you cry, wondering if it's gotten bad enough for you to try again. I have to sneak up to the bathroom door to see if the conversations you're having with yourself are lighthearted, or if you're at risk of going back into that hole. I can't do it anymore, Ashley. It's a mirror! It's only *you*!" He turns to the mirror as he shouts . . . and double takes.

His mouth drops open. The color drains from his face.

Alex and the other guy are starting to turn me, to move me around Matt, who's standing mute and unmoving.

"Please!" I scream, scrabbling at the hands of the orderlies.

"Let her go," Matt commands.

I whip my head around to stare at him, but he's still looking at the mirror. His face hardens.

"Matt?" I question.

"Let. Her. Go," he says again.

Both orderlies look at Doc, who must have given them some kind of signal, because all of a sudden, their hands are off me. I scramble back to the mirror as fast as I can.

I sob with relief. She's still there. Still safe.

Little Me stands in front of her easels, hands out, watching the boys pummel each other. In my lifetime, Matt beat up Finn as soon as the ambulance took me away. Now they roll on the floor, Finn shouting curses as he manages to get on top of Matt for a moment. One of Matt's legs kicks out, taking Little Me in the knee. She yelps and jumps aside.

Closer to the mirror.

"Stop!" I plead with her. "Get away from the mirror!"

"How are you doing this?" Matt says. I startle because he's right behind me, his head almost on my shoulder.

"Doing what?" I ask without looking at him.

"This. Making this show up in the mirror. How are you doing this? Is this some kind of sick joke?"

My heart stops. Literally pauses in my chest. I am so afraid that he didn't say what I think he just said, it takes me several seconds to turn around.

He's staring at the mirror, watching the guys move, wincing when one of them lands a punch.

"You . . . you can see that?" I breathe.

"How are you doing this, Ashley?" he demands. Then he turns to Doc. "Is this a trick? Are you trying to make me crazy, too?"

Doc frowns. "Of course not," he says, his face strangely blank. "What are you seeing, Matt?"

Matt turns back to the mirror without answering. I do, too, but I can't stop glancing at him. Hope rises so high and fast I almost can't stand it. I clasp my hands together to stop them from shaking. "You can see it?" I ask him in a whisper. "You can see them?"

"I see . . . I see us. That day . . . ," he says hoarsely. "I see you, and your art and . . . that's *me* fighting with Finn."

My hands fly to my mouth and I'm crying. "You can see them!"

His expression is something I've never seen before—disbelief, fear, uncertainty all mingle and come out looking like someone's rapped him over the head with a steel bar.

"Matt—"

"How are you doing this, Ashley?" he pleads.

"I'm not," I say, unable to stop smiling because we're in this together now. "I've been telling you the truth."

There's a clatter in the mirror and I turn. Little Matt and Finn have rolled into the easels. Little Me was knocked to the floor. She's hunched in on herself, both arms over her head.

She rocks, breathing hard. "My head," she groans.

"Ashley?" I gasp. "Are you okay?"

I was on my feet, but the entire room swayed every time I took a breath. My head rang. Scuffles and grunts sounded somewhere near the floor. Then there was a shout to my left. I tried to sidestep.

I wasn't sure what direction I ended up moving, but I heard Matt, breathless and hoarse, swearing at Finn.

I tried to look at them, but my neck didn't want to work. I stumbled sideways again.

"Stop, Ashley. Stop! Stay away from the mirror."

I wasn't sure which direction her voice came from. The spinning in my head was disorienting. So I stopped moving, tried to stand still. But it was as if I was on a boat in a rocky sea. I swayed and lurched.

". . . did you do that . . . to her painting? Did you?" Matt growled.

"Your girlfriend helped." Despite the wheeze in his voice, Finn sounded like he was smiling.

"She's not my girlfriend," Matt shoved out.

"Oops . . . forgot." Finn grunted. "You'd rather screw a psycho."

Matt made a noise I'd never heard before. He straddled Finn, one fist cocked back, the other gripping Finn's shirt, pulling Finn so he was half sitting.

"Screw. *You.*" Matt threw a punch that snapped Finn's head back with a sickening *whack*. I gasped. Finn slumped. The room went quiet except for Matt's panting.

I stumbled forward, wincing when each footstep ricocheted in my skull. But I grabbed Matt's arm and helped him stand.

When he was upright, he pulled me to him. With a deep breath, I rested my forehead on his chest and wrapped my arms around his waist. Even the waves of nausea faded into the background. Then his hands came up to bracket my face and I gasped. One of his eyes was already purple and almost swollen shut. He had a fat lip, and blood trickled from his nose.

"You're hurt!" I winced again. My own voice was a razorblade to my temples.

He touched his face, looking over my shoulder into the mirror to examine his wounds.

"It isn't as bad as . . ." He trailed off. "What the—" The flush drained out of his cheeks.

Forgetting my head, I twisted to see what he was looking at and lost my balance. Matt caught me from behind, but he didn't say anything. I blinked several times into the mirror. Older Me was there, tears welling over the hands clasped over her mouth. Older Matt was there, too. And he stared as if he'd just seen God create the world.

"That's me," my Matt said. I felt the rumble in his chest at my back. He sounded awed.

"What—?" I started.

But in the mirror, Older Matt leaned forward. "Wait . . . can he see me?" he asked hoarsely.

"Yes, I think so." Older Me touched Older Matt's chest, then turned to beam at me. "He can see himself, Ashley. He's . . . they're . . ."

"What is this?" Matt says, his hands tightening on my arms. "How did you do this?"

The mirror faded in and out of focus in time with the throbbing in my head, but I could see my Matt, his face pale. He was fixated on the reflected image of his older self, and he was beginning to shake.

"Ash, how are you doing this?" Matt said through his teeth, his hands tightening on my arms, almost the point of pain.

"I don't know," I breathed. "But it's real. I promise."

CHAPTER THIRTY-FIVE

LITTLE ME IS obviously shaken. I turn to Matt, touch his pale, stunned face. He jerks, then turns his head to look at me.

"I know it's scary," I say quietly. "But you'll get used to it. I promise."

He just stares, his head slowly shaking back and forth.

I swallow. "You have to believe me. I'm not crazy. And neither are you."

Matt's gaze never leaves mine. He breathes twice before he speaks. "We're done here."

The hope in me crumbles away. I drop my head into my hands.

"Excuse me?" Doc says, his voice tighter than I've ever heard it.

"I said we're done here. Ashley's done here. You can sign her out, or I can go get her mom to sign her out, but either way, she's not staying here a second longer."

I gasp and look up, straight at Matt. He swallows and glances at the mirror, then back to me.

I throw myself into his chest and the tears come because . . . because . . . oh, my . . . I can't . . . this isn't even possible. Is it? I pull back again and I'm going to tell him how amazing he is, and how happy I am, but everything happens at once.

Doc says, "Ashley will not be leaving. In my professional opinion, she is suffering delusions and psychosis. I will be recommending at least another six months of treatment." Then he tips his head at the orderlies.

But Matt pulls me away, shoves a hand out, places himself between us. There's a flash of movement in the mirror. It's a reflex to turn.

Little Me and Little Matt are staring at each other, worry and hope on both their faces.

And Finn is staggering to his feet behind them.

"Watch out!" I scream.

Matt thinks I'm talking to him and swings around.

The orderlies grab for him.

Finn launches himself at Little Matt's back.

The three of them tumble toward the mirror.

"NO!" I scream, and dive to catch her.

"NO!" both Matts scream, and the entire world echoes.

And for the second time in my life, I see the glass coming. It's worse this time because I know what it's going to feel like.

But it's better, too. Because this time I know I want it.

I need it.

For her.

And so I brace, then dive, hands first into the mirror, reaching to stop her before she hits the shining surface, stretching toward her even when the mirror flashes, then detonates . . .

There's a special kind of pain reserved for dancing with shattered glass. It comes in stages: The initial assault is fear; you see the glass coming and you know it's going to hurt.

Then there's the moment everything explodes and the glass tears at your skin, catching, peeling, shaving you away and you think, *I might die.*

Then the pieces fall and break into new pieces. You're heading to the floor, too, but they beat you there and all the tattered parts of you land on all the shattered parts of it. They are needles in open wounds. Knives on raw flesh.

And then the fire arrives—hot, burning flames that lick the wounds. And every time you move, the tiny pieces that stuck with you cut a little deeper and the flames roar higher.

In short, it sucks.

Even more the second time.

But as my shredded body slumps toward the floor, it doesn't land on thick carpet. My screams aren't muffled by furniture and curtained windows. Instead, my screams become a shrieking, grating sound that crosses time, echoing in my ears.

My hands connect with Ashley's shoulders, pushing her back before she can crash into the mirror. A moment later my knees hit hard on cold and dusty linoleum. But the rest of me lands in soft arms.

Violently trembling arms.

When I stop moving—when I am afraid to move again—my nose is in her hair, and she is holding me.

"Y-you came . . . you're h-here." Her voice is high and thin, wavering.

I try to pull back, to meet her eyes, but my head is too heavy for my neck. I end up lolling around until she pulls back far enough to look at me. Her cheeks shine with tears.

"How?" she asks.

"I caught you," I say weakly. "It was always about catching you. Every time. I just didn't always know how."

Her face crumples, and her hands tighten. She clings to me, blood like a veil on her shoulder.

I realize it is mine.

I suck in a breath, but no oxygen comes with it. Suddenly, I am tilting.

Little Matt is behind her, his face white as a sheet. There's a curse. And another.

My head slides to her shoulder because it's become too heavy for me. I can only move my eyes. But I see Finn, on the floor, scrambling backward away from me, his eyes so wide the whites are showing all the way around.

"Y-you can't . . . that's impossible . . . ," he stutters. His teeth are chattering with fear, and the petty part of me is happy.

"Older Me?" Ashley's voice quivers.

I close my eyes. We don't have long. The effort to bring my hand up to her shoulder is Herculean. I am left breathless and wrung out. But I manage to whisper in her ear.

"I love you," I say, cursing the lump in my throat that threatens to stop the words. "I only ever wanted the best for you," I murmur, fingers digging into her shoulder so she won't let go. "It worked."

"What worked?" she sobs.

"You're free." I manage. My eyes drag closed.

After a second she gasps again and shakes me. "Older Me!"

I force myself to look at her. "It will be different for you. And that's good. So remember you're worth it."

"Different how?" she whispers.

"Better," I murmur. "Because you're braver. I couldn't ever . . . I didn't use the painting . . . use it. You have to get to New York." My lips are heavy now, too. My hand slides from her shoulder.

"Older Me? Older Me! Help her. Somebody, help her!" she screams.

I wince. I want her to stop yelling. But I can't seem to move. And thinking becomes hard.

I am jostled. There are voices. I want to soothe them, but I can't move my mouth.

There is something I am here to do.

I can't remember what it is. But as hands close on my arms and shoulders, pressing into those burning lines, and someone says "artery" and someone screams "ambulance!" I can smile.

It has been a long time since I could smile and mean it.

The warmth of her chest disappears, and with it the cold linoleum under my knees.

As I slip away, I am laying somewhere soft. There are only two things left:

Matt's warm hands holding me.

And the knowledge that she will be okay.

SIX MONTHS LATER

CHAPTER THIRTY-SIX

I PRESSED THE soft bills through the little window in the cabby's bulletproof screen and waited for my change. Outside the car, a wide sidewalk was littered in tiny pieces of color from people's lives. A steady stream of bodies flowed by, but none of them turned toward the six shining glass doors at the top of the stairs behind them.

The gallery.

Posters hugged both ends of the building, proclaiming NATIONAL YOUNG ARTIST OF THE YEAR!

Mrs. D told me one of the half-dozen posters they printed this year featured my portrait of Finn. I hoped she was wrong.

I opened the taxi door and tried to pretend I was ready to do this. The second my feet hit the pavement, a wave of fear washed down my spine. The thick, woolen jacket I wore covered me from neck to knees, hiding my dress and the tiny, crosshatched scars on my arms. I took a reluctant step forward.

Six months after the "incident," I could move freely. The only thing that hurt anymore was twisting my head. A scar, only a couple of inches long, lay at the point where my shoulder met my neck. It was the last reminder I had of her—of how she was real. How she'd saved me from the mirror. From Finn.

From myself.

Thoughts like that always brought tears, so I shook my head and trotted along the pavement, around the corner to the side door I'd been told to use. As an exhibitionist I had to be there early, before the doors opened to the public.

There were fewer people on the side street—and less light, too. As the late afternoon sun dropped behind the massive face of the city, part of me wanted to walk right past the dark little door on my right and find a cute, hole-in-the-wall bakery instead. But just as my steps faltered, the door came into view. I set my teeth and grabbed the handle.

It felt like the building swallowed me as I stepped inside the black space of the doorway, into a dark, narrow hallway lined with pipes and electrical cords. A minute later, a door at the end opened to a shadowed corner of the lobby. The bathrooms were in a discreet alcove to my right. I stopped short, then I was in the lady's room and through the large, sliding door of the handicapped stall before I could think.

Old habits die hard.

Sure enough, the stall sported its own sink, and a small, square mirror directly above it—though even I had to stoop to see my face. When I looked, all I saw was myself, my blue eyes bright, a smudge of mascara on my eyelid. Every time I was alone in front of a mirror, the pangs started in my chest. She wasn't there. She hadn't been since that day in the art room.

That moment when I almost hit the glass, when she came

through for me . . . for a split-second I thought we were going to be together. But then she was gone. And she's never come back.

After all the years sharing my reflection, it was a strange feeling. But even though she was gone, I could still hear her. Hear her wisdom, and her laughter. Hear her telling me to remember . . . But though it was from within now, not from the mirror, I knew it was still her.

I took two more deep breaths and made my way to the lobby. Natural light from those glass doors brightened the broad space. But between the red carpeting and the wood-paneled walls, it kind of looked like an old-fashioned movie theater.

A cute guy with trying-too-hard hair emerged from the den of cubbyholes and coats. He couldn't have been much older than me. "Do you have your ID?"

Oh, right. I tugged at the lanyard around my neck until the large plastic card popped out of the neck of my jacket.

The guy scanned it and smiled. "Can I take your coat, Ashley?"

I ignored the way he stilled for a moment when my arms were revealed. Luckily, my scars are pale and fine. In normal light they're barely visible. But in the bright, white light of a gallery, they glimmered.

They were nothing like Older Me's. Hers had been thick ropes, separating her skin into jagged chunks. Mine were just . . . scars. Fine lines where tiny pieces of shattered mirror had slid across my skin on their way to the floor, and the deeper one where my neck met my shoulder, where a shard had been caught in her hair and pressed into me when she pushed me back from the mirror.

So, as the guy back-pedaled, the flirtatious smile dissolving, I held my chin high and gritted my teeth.

Tonight I was here to enjoy a measure of success. And no one was going to take that from me.

I passed the first wall of the exhibition and kept moving, past the next, and the next. There were black-and-whites, pencil sketches, two sculptures, and an abstract oil painting taking up an entire panel. A girl from Nebraska had submitted a surrealist piece, where her near-photographic cows had lamps instead of heads.

Everywhere I turned, there were new colors and new techniques, and for a second I was transported away from my fear and into this amazing world of people far more talented than me. I wandered aimlessly, taking it all in.

Then I turned a corner . . . and I was looking at myself.

I froze. Nailed to the floor. I couldn't speak or breathe because there was a picture of me on the wall.

But I wasn't the one who'd painted it.

Then I took in the pictures around the image and realized. *Matt.*

A handful of people huddled in a group, some pointing at the wall, talking, some nodding. I pushed past them.

Sure enough, all three panels were familiar, covered in pieces I'd seen before—pictures of movement—the fine, ruffled hair of a bounding dog, the gentle sweep of leaves in the wind . . . all pieces I knew, all pieces I'd envied at every step of their development. Matt's pictures were alive and about to step off the page. It always astounded me.

But the one in the middle? I'd never seen it before. It was nothing short of breathtaking. And it was *me*.

On a clear background, I was depicted from the front. In stark, black lines, my face tipped down until my chin almost met my chest. My hair, lush and flowing in a way real life never delivered, fell over my shoulders—over my breasts, because there were no clothes indicated in the stark lines.

My shoulders peeked through my hair. My waist slid out of the frame. My eyes were downcast, but my lips curled into a smile.

I was gentle, womanly, beautiful in a way I'd always wanted to be.

I sucked in a shuddering breath, took a step back.

"Gorgeous!" a female voice breathed to my right. "That's stunning. How can he do that with nothing but lines?"

"I don't know." The answer left my lips without my permission.

The girl flashed the hesitant smile of strangers stuck in the same space. She peered out from behind thick, black-rimmed glasses, and a crocheted hat pressed her hair against her cheeks. "Hi, I'm Shelley. Another finalist," she said nervously, flapping the ID card at her chest.

"Hi, Shelley."

She looked at the picture, then back to me. Her mouth dropped open. "Ohmigosh . . . is . . . is that . . . It's you! Did you do that?" she gasped. "Because, seriously, I think this is the best thing here. Like, I'm not joking—"

"No!" I jumped to interrupt her because . . . oh, man. I could just see it. Everyone would think this was my board. Everyone would think this gorgeous piece was my self-portrait. Then when they saw my real stuff it would be a disappointment. My stomach sank to my toes. I wanted to cross my arms, protect my chest. But that would just draw attention to my scars. So I clasped my hands behind my back instead.

Shelley looked back and forth between me and the picture, frowning. "I would have sworn—"

"She didn't paint it. But it is her."

His voice came out of nowhere, from right behind me. My hair shivered and I was pretty sure it was his breath. I couldn't move.

Shelley glanced at him, then at me. Her lips shifted from confused frown to smile of delight.

"Beautiful," she said. Then she waved and was gone, sinking through the small crowd lingering in front of Matt's work.

I turned, and heat rushed through my veins. Matt had dressed formally for the occasion, and I'd be a liar if I didn't admit he looked amazing. The suit framed his flat shoulders and trim waist to perfection. His chest was broad under the glimmering gray shirt and tie. I ached to touch him, caught myself before I swayed into his arms.

"You're late," he said quietly, smiling.

"Yes." I raised a hand toward the picture. "Matt . . . this is . . ."

The smile slid off his face. "Do you like it?"

"Like it?" I squeaked, drawing the attention of the people around us. I had to clear my throat so I could whisper. "It's amazing. Why didn't you tell me?"

His eyes twinkled. "I wanted to surprise you. I did it the day after the prom. After . . . *you know*." He looked away for a second, chuckling. "But we'd fought, and then . . . and then everything else happened. Anyway, by the time I could have shown you, it had already been submitted. When everything worked out, I figured it would be a nice surprise."

I turned to look at the picture again and wanted to weep. It was so beautiful. It made *me* look beautiful.

"It's stunning," I murmured. "But it isn't me."

"Yes. It is." He breathed against my skin and pressed a kiss to my neck, just below my ear, heedless of the ugly scar less than an inch away.

Tingling and goose-bumped from neck to wrist, I opened my mouth to argue, then closed it again. As his hands snaked around my waist and pulled me closer, it seemed nothing short of thankless for me to insist that he'd done the truth a disservice.

"Are you okay?" he asked quietly, true concern in his tone.

I nodded, let myself relax back into him. Let his arms hold me close.

"This is strange," I said after a minute. "I didn't think I'd be here."

"But you are," he said, his deep voice rumbling against my back. "And so's your painting."

Trust Matt to get right to the bottom of what was eating me up inside.

As soon as the words were out of his mouth, I tensed.

His arms squeezed me closer, ready to stop me bodily from running, if need be.

"Ashley—" he started.

I shook my head. "I don't think I can."

"Of course you can. It's just a painting."

I snorted. "It isn't just a painting. It's . . . it's the picture of *me*."

"It's a picture of the old you."

"With swearing," I added. "And a penis."

265

Matt chuckled. "C'mon," he said, releasing me from the hug, but keeping one of my hands firmly grasped in both of his. "I'm going with you."

"No, I—"

"Ashley, you know you've got to do it at some point. Might as well be now when there's only fifty people here, instead of five hundred."

He had a point there. But I hadn't been kidding when I told him I didn't think I could.

"Mr. Gray!"

Matt hesitated, then turned—not letting go of my hand— as a stern-looking man wearing a suit and thin metal glasses approached. One of the judges. I recognized him from the information packet they'd sent me. And he had a couple of less formal, but equally self-important-looking men following him.

Matt looked chagrined to have his attention turned from me, but I was relieved.

I'd dragged my feet getting ready tonight, told Matt to go ahead without me, then shown up at the last possible minute. A part of me hoped the show would open and I wouldn't have time to look at my wall. But deep down I knew it wasn't going to work that way. The whole point of being here tonight was to answer questions about my work—first for the judges, then for members of the public and art professors from many of the best art schools in the country.

Even the thought made my nerves twist.

"... very interested in your talent, Mr. Gray. I believe our curriculum could benefit your work immensely. Have you accepted a scholarship proposal yet?"

Matt flushed, and shook his head.

I'd known this would happen. I fully expected Matt to win the scholarship tonight. But even if he didn't, I had no doubt he'd leave the gallery with several offers.

This moment was particularly sweet. Matt's dad was livid that Matt had entered the competition against his wishes. But when he realized how prestigious the competition was, he'd agreed to give Matt one chance: Matt came home with a full-ride scholarship, or he gave up art school dreams and followed his father's footsteps and became an engineer.

As Matt became more and more engrossed in the conversation with the men, I slid my hand from his grip, then inched back.

It was time.

CHAPTER THIRTY-SEVEN

I MOVED DEEPER into the gallery, following the feast of art that surrounded me on every side. As I examined the brushstrokes on that painting, or how this artist used color to create a sense of light, I wasn't consciously anticipating the moment. In fact, when the moment came, it was shocking. Yet, somehow, not.

Crazy Ashley Loves Dick.

The words stole my breath—and not in the good way. In fact, I think if there'd been another human being present, I might have fled. But instead, I forced my feet to step closer. Forced my lungs to inflate. Forced my eyes to remain open. Forced my heart down, out of my throat.

There, on the very back wall of the gallery, in all its illuminated glory, was my story. Every face. Every stroke. Every moment of humiliation and shame.

Luckily, each artist's wall had a bench seat, and I dropped onto the wooden slats. This was it. *The* moment. This was where I was supposed to face my fear with courage; stare down the demons of my past and realize they had no power. If it were a movie, I might cry, but I'd walk away with my head held high and never look back.

Right?

But courage failed me. Fear set my hands shaking and twisted my gut into knots.

There were no tears, praise God, but my breath came in short puffs. My hands twisted in my lap. And the thought of looking at that picture again made adrenaline surge until my heart raced so fast I was afraid it might beat out of my chest.

What was wrong with me? Why couldn't I be the kick-ass heroine, like in books? Or the strong, noble star of a movie?

Because it hurts.

Something inside me broke open. I gripped the edge of the seat, swaying. My skin sung as every muscle in my body went rigid, because this wasn't just a story. This was my life.

That's the part they never tell you in the movies. That's the part the books pretend doesn't happen.

Sure, I made it to New York. And I have a wonderful, glorious boyfriend who I love. And none of that would have happened without my past. So I can't go back. I can't wish it away.

But it still hurt. Every stinking day.

Even if I walked out of that room, right at that moment, and never looked back . . . it would still ache inside when I thought of that picture, or worse, had to look at it.

Even if Matt loved me for the rest of his life, and never so much as blinked in the direction of another woman, there'd still be pain in our past. Fear that we might let each other down again.

And being with him was wonderful, but Older Me was right about one thing: Matt wasn't perfect. He was still working through stuff with his dad. We were going to face that again. Together, hopefully. But still . . .

Matt wasn't free yet, and I was not unscathed. I had scars—inside and out—that would never leave me. The pictures on the wall in front of me were just images put together, mostly by my hand. But they represented the weight I would carry for the rest of my life. And tonight it felt almost too heavy to bear.

But then my heart jumped and I heard her—remembered her face. But especially her voice.

You're worth it.

I bit my lip and swallowed the tears.

I had no idea if she'd lived on her side of the glass. No idea if she missed me, or wondered what I was doing.

But I knew, with certainty, that she loved me. That she'd been willing to *die* for me.

It opened my eyes. It changed my world.

She loved me enough to give *everything*. And if I walked around with my head down, and my heart strangled . . . how was that going to honor her—the person who had worked so hard to save me?

I remembered the days when I'd believed she didn't love me, that she was nothing but a liar. My fingers tightened on the bench, whether to hold me still or push me up and away, I wasn't sure. But when I looked up through tears, I saw the picture again.

Crazy Ashley Loves Dick.

And I heard her voice.

That says everything about them *and nothing about* you.

"Thank you," I whispered.

Quiet footsteps sounded on my left and I quickly wiped my face, heart thumping.

A low whistle rose then fell. A gruff baritone murmured, "Finally! I've been looking for this one."

The man standing a few feet to my right, staring at my wall, was almost a caricature. He wore brown leather short-top boots, with thick socks that bunched halfway up his calf. And a kilt. An actual, tweed, wool kilt with one of those man-purses hanging at the front. He'd paired it with a formal black jacket, white shirt, a matching sash that dropped to mid-thigh, and a floppy hat that reminded me of something on old French painter might wear.

He looked ridiculous. And somehow . . . *right*.

He glanced at me with a wry smile, then did a double take and turned, frowning. "Have we met?" he asked.

"Um. No."

"Are you sure? You look very familiar."

"Uh, yes, I'm sure." I think I'd remember.

But then he looked me up and down and snapped his fingers. "You're the girl in the painting! Matthew Gray's portfolio!"

Stunned, I nodded.

He closed his eyes and sighed peacefully. "That piece is remarkable. The movement! When I saw it I wished I could meet the young lady to see how it felt to be the inspiration behind such an erotic work. I never imagined—but you must be his girlfriend, then?"

"Uh, yes . . ."

"Wonderful! Tell me the story! Did he have you sit for it? Did you know it would be so . . . suggestive?"

I swallowed, feeling violated, and relieved, and inadequate, all at the same time. "I didn't know he'd painted it, actually. He didn't tell me." When he looked surprised, and not in the good

271

way, I wanted to fall between the slats of the bench and disappear. "It's complicated," I murmured.

"Ah, of course. The good stories always are, aren't they?" He waggled his brows, then turned back to fix his piercing gaze on my wall. My moment of relief quickly became gut-wrenching fear. "Now, this one, I'd *love* to hear the real story behind it," he said, flipping a finger toward my wall.

I swallowed. "Oh?"

"Yes. Have you heard about it?"

And then I realized he didn't know who I was. He thought I was only there as Matt's girlfriend.

The relief turned my knees to water. I was glad to be sitting down. "Uh . . . ," I croaked. "There's a story?"

He flapped his hand at me without looking away from my wall. "Well, I'm sure the story *we* heard isn't even close to the truth of it. But apparently the artist was . . . shall we say, *unpopular*." He gave me a pointed glance from the side. "Those awful words were actually painted by someone else, in an attempt to sabotage her chances at getting here."

"Wow," I said.

He nodded. "Instead of painting over it, or starting again, the artist *used* the saboteur's contribution." He shook his head. "Inspired."

"Really?" It fell out of my mouth in shock, but he didn't notice.

"Really." He stepped closer to my wall and pointed. I was forced to turn; otherwise, it would be too obvious.

Finn.

"See how she's used red and purple here? It looks positively sinister. She could have done his whole face that way, to denote a truly evil person. But she hasn't. She's used the implication sparingly. On the mouth." He turned, beaming, satisfied. "She's implying that the individual's *words* are dark, rather than his heart."

I didn't know about that. But as I stared at the painting, I had to ask myself if he was right.

I'd only seen Finn once since That Day. A few weeks before I went to New York. It was a Saturday. I had just walked out of the country store near Matt's house, when Finn almost walked into me on his way inside. We both stopped like we'd been sledge-hammered, staring. And for the first time since we were twelve, I didn't see the glint in his eye. All I saw was fear. And a question.

It was a shock to see him. He and Karyn had both been expelled from Black Point High. I heard he'd been sent to boarding school. And therapy. But since Matt hadn't kept in touch with him, and anyone who did was avoiding me like I had a contagious disease, I didn't really know what he'd been up to.

But at that moment, he stood in front of me, slack jawed, looking weaker than I remembered. While I gaped, unable to move my feet, even though my brain screamed *Run!*, Finn blinked a couple of times, then turned on his heel and fled.

I shook my head, returning to the present. The man was pointing at the picture of Dex.

". . . and so two-dimensional! It's as if she doesn't know—or perhaps care about—this man at all."

When I registered what he'd said, I almost smiled. He was exactly right.

Dex and I hadn't spoken since prom night. I heard later he'd dated Brooke for about three weeks——until they had a huge fight on the quad and she called him all kinds of names and outed him for doing drugs again. He left Black Point High for the second time, and no one's seen him since.

Now my new friend was waxing lyrical about how I clearly despised my father, held my mother in contempt, and had barely suppressed rage toward Karyn. By the time he was finished, I was almost in tears—and ready to tell him who I was just so I could thank him for taking the time to *look*.

Before I could speak, he moved to the center of the wall and stared at my self-portrait. The words I'd been about to say died on my tongue because he was looking at the picture with such sadness that I wanted to weep.

"The courage it must have taken to use this." He shook his head, then looked back at me. "I was bullied in high school, too," he murmured.

Reflexively, I scanned him from head to toe.

"Yes, yes. I wasn't quite so flamboyant then. But there was no doubt I had . . . flair." He gave a self-deprecating laugh and I couldn't help but chuckle with him.

"But I never would have had the courage to do this," he said quietly, the smile fading as he turned back to my painting. "This is an artist who's willing to lay herself bare in order to tell the truth." He nodded once. "And *that's* where real art comes from."

I swallowed hard.

"I'm determined to sit here all night until she shows up. I'm hoping she'll agree to—"

I froze. "Excuse me, sir . . ."

He blinked, then turned back to me. "I'm so sorry, I've been rude! I haven't introduced myself. I'm Jeremy August, I'm one of the deans at the Vintner School of Art." He took the four strides to reach my side, holding out a hand. I knew I should stand, but I was still feeling shaky. And he didn't know who I was, so I just shook his hand and nodded again.

"I shouldn't have been yammering to you. You're here to celebrate!" Jeremy said, throwing his hands in the air. "You must be so proud of Matt—another very talented artist, I must say. Such an opportunity to be here with him tonight! So what are you doing hiding back here? You should be standing by his wall! Let the people tell you how beautiful it is—you are, I mean." He grinned. "The likeness is uncanny. He's very talented."

It was like being buried in a whirlwind of words. "Uh, yes, he is. But I'm not . . . I mean—"

"Oh, don't be shy! Come on, I'll take you over there. I have some friends who'd love to talk to you." He took my elbow and pulled me to my feet.

"Wait! I can't!"

"Trust me, dear, this is one of those moments you'll remember for the rest of your life. Make the most of it. That boy is going places."

I shook my head. "No, you don't understand. I have to stay here . . . with mine."

Jeremy lurched to a stop. I tugged my elbow out of his grip and straightened my dress. "I'm sorry. I really do appreciate your compliments. But I'm exhibiting, too. And they said I have to stay here in case any of the judges come . . ."

But he frowned again, looking at me, then at the pictures on the wall. "Oh, my . . . These are yours?" he said, throwing an arm toward my portfolio. He sounded aghast.

I flushed. "Yes. I'm sorry. I wasn't trying to make you—"

"No, no, don't apologize. I didn't really give you a chance to tell me, did I?" he said ruefully.

"I think—"

"But I never would have recognized you from this," he said, gesturing toward my painting.

I frowned. "Well, either you're being nice, or I'm a terrible painter, because that's a self-portrait. And it's only six months old."

"Oh, no, dear, I assure you, now that I know, I can see it's a perfect *likeness*. But I wouldn't have recognized you from it because . . . you're different. This isn't *you*."

I wasn't sure that was entirely true, but I offered him a smile because it was easier to pretend it was.

"Thank you. For saying that. And those other things . . . You were very kind. And mostly right."

I was startled when he boomed a laugh in response. "*Mostly* right . . . oh, dear, you are a firecracker, aren't you!"

I waved my hands. "No! No, I didn't mean it that way."

"It's fine—"

"No, I meant—" I turned toward the wall, intending to tell him that I hadn't thought as deeply about Finn's lips as he thought—that he'd given me too much praise. But all I saw were the pink letters and that awful graffiti, and I stood there, finally, motionless in its glare.

My own face, haggard and sad, stared back at me, and for a moment it was as if Older Me were here . . .

As if I was *her*.

Because I remembered the moment when I painted that expression. How I'd felt so hopeless and . . . heavy.

And it occurred to me, as I let myself follow the lines of the letters and my lips silently formed their words, that I didn't feel that way anymore.

"I meant what I said, dear," Jeremy murmured at my side. "I find your courage humbling."

"I don't have courage."

"Of course you do, sweetheart. You just haven't grown up enough yet to realize courage isn't fearless." He patted my shoulder. I thought he was walking away. I thought our conversation was done. Then he reached into his bag.

"Here," Jeremy said. He held out a slim, glossy pamphlet.

When I took it, my hands shook.

He patted my shoulder again. "Unfortunately, Ashley, bullying doesn't stop when you grow up. It just looks a little different." He wrinkled his patrician nose and shook his head. "Don't let the snooty buffoons who run this tell you that you're unfinished, or too green. Your work isn't green. It's honest. Raw." He cleared his throat, then met my eyes. "Vintner isn't large. And it doesn't have quite as a prestigious name as the Institute, or CFA. But we won't try to turn you into someone else. And we won't denigrate your work. We believe in trial and error. And we believe in letting you tell us who *you* should be."

He straightened his sash and pushed back his shoulders. "Just don't let them make you think you're lacking. They'll jump all over Matt because he's so polished. And they may give you a chance, too. But I hope you'll consider us anyway." He flashed a wide smile. "With us, you can be proud of exactly who you are. Right now. And when we're done with you, I promise, you'll *never* be mistaken for someone else."

I opened my mouth, but he kept talking.

"And stop sitting back as if you don't deserve to be here. Even those flamingoes with their noses in the air could see that you do. It takes a lot out of an artist to show their plain face to the world, like this." He gestured toward my work again.

I snorted. "I didn't have much choice."

"Oh, you might be surprised, my dear."

When I looked at him, he offered a sad smile, but then he brightened. "Well, I better go find the competition and steer them away from this corner, all the better to keep you to myself. My phone number is on the back," He flapped his hand toward the pamphlet. "Call me anytime. Acceptance starts next month!"

"I know." The words came out too soft. He was almost out of sight before I remembered my manners and called after him. "Thank you!"

"Thank me by telling the rest of them where to put their scholarships!" he yelled. Then he was gone.

I looked from the slick photographs in my hand to the horrific painting in front of me. The sad face, the sickening pink. The words spewed all over the surface. I looked into my own face and braced for recognition. For remembrance.

But I couldn't find it.

"Ash?" Matt's low voice rose quietly behind me. I turned. He had his hands in his pockets, and there were lines in his forehead.

I patted the bench next to me, then turned back to my paintings and waited for him to join me.

I'd been there all night. Sometimes I'd answered questions. Sometimes I'd let people talk around me. Like Jeremy, most hadn't recognized me, and that was fine. I'd been inside myself, watching from a distance. There were still one or two people wandering around, but it was getting late. The night was almost over.

Matt settled next to me, sliding his arm around my waist. I leaned on his shoulder and let out a breath I hadn't realized I'd been holding.

"How did it go?" I asked, tipping my head so I could see his face.

Matt's eyes sparkled. "I have choices."

"Congratulations!" I put both arms around his waist.

"Ditto." He hugged me back. Then his face turned grim. "Dad won't like it."

"No, he won't," I agreed.

While Matt's dad had eventually agreed to let Matt attend the opening, he'd refused to come, or even let Matt's mom attend.

My own mother just waved her hand whenever I talked about what she referred to as my "little art show." That was fine with me; having her here would have ruined it for me.

Matt and I were both silent. Then I picked up his hand, twining our fingers. "We can handle your dad. Together."

Matt nodded, still staring into the half-distance.

A minute later he snapped back into focus. "How about you?"

I thought about it for a second. Then I told him.

I'd spent most of the night staring at my painting, not really seeing it. Instead of studying brushstrokes or intentions, I'd examined my life.

The pamphlet Jeremy gave me, and the hope it represented, was damp in my hand. I was afraid to let it go. Afraid to lose it. So it stayed with me, waiting out the night. It wasn't until an hour earlier I'd realized I wasn't afraid of my painting, or even of Finn—or people like him. I was afraid because, even after everything I'd overcome, I still had holes. Even with Matt loving me. Even with an art school dean asking me to choose his school's scholarship. My dreams were coming true—but they weren't filling the gaps.

I still felt . . . *less than.*

Then, twenty minutes before Matt arrived, I'd remembered something Older Me had said. Her voice echoed in my memory and raised my tears.

. . . it isn't what happens to you in your life that destroys you. It's what you do about it.

I'd decided to keep fighting, keep searching for answers. Because as long as I did that, there would always be a chance my holes would heal. I could have hope. My gaps only became inevitable when I stopped believing they could be filled. Because that's when I'd sit back and let life pile on the crap.

Like she did.

As long as I had hope, the good things would stay good.

So, no, I'd never be a kick-ass movie heroine.

But I was real. And loveable.

And for now, that was enough.

A NOTE FROM THE AUTHOR

BULLYING IS A unique form of torture. I know, because I was a victim of it for many years.

While Ashley's story is fictional, and the events and people in it are wholly fabricated, I drew on my own emotions to inform hers. I wanted you, the reader, to know I still remember how it feels. If you're currently living a story like Ashley's, take it from me: They aren't right about you. And the only way you'll ever know that for sure is to connect with people who value you exactly as you are. You need help. You *deserve* help. So reach out. If you can't be sure of help from those around you, get in touch with Teen Line where you can talk to other teenagers who understand:

Call (310) 855 4673 or (800) 852 8336
Text "Teen" to 839863 (between 5:30pm and 9:30pm PST)
Or go online: www.teenlineonline.org

I used to be afraid to walk down that hall, or into that room. I used to lie in bed at night and doubt myself—whether it would ever be different for me, whether anyone would ever really care, or think I was special.

They have no right to make you feel that way. Trust me: You occupy a very special place in this world. And if you were gone, the rest of us would be left with a hole shaped just like you. Don't let anyone make you believe any different.

Keep going.

It might not get better tomorrow, but it *will* get better.

ACKNOWLEDGMENTS

THIS BOOK IS a work of fiction. But if Ashley and I share any-thing, it is that we entered our twenties with an awareness of the holes inside, the wounds (self-inflicted or otherwise) that never completely heal.

I am unable to give enough of myself, my work, or my life to adequately say thank you, Jesus, for moving in to fill those gaps and heal my wounds. Your work in my heart is nothing short of miraculous. I hope you find some measure of delight in what I have delivered here. Thank you for bringing the incredible people into my life who made all of this possible:

Alan, you are a renaissance man: corporate businessman, hobby farmer, sometimes house-husband, Fun Dad, and rock of my world. None of this would have happened without you. So thank you, Darling. You have superior husbanding skills.

Lanie Davis, your first e-mail changed my life, and you've been making my dreams come true every day since. To you, Eliza Swift, and all the team at Alloy, thank you for taking a risk on a little book nobody knew about—and for making it so much better. The heavens are full of stars expelled in your honor . . . if you know what I mean.

My family deserves endless honors, especially my parents, Ernie and Ricki Pruitt, my sister, Heather, my cousins Emily and Mandy, and everyone else who insists on loving me even when it isn't easy. There are too many of you to list, but I promise that I'm grateful for your love, your support, and your willingness to listen to my "book talk."

Nyria Ratana and Raewyn Hewitt: There are three couches and a warm fire in heaven where you will be rewarded for your never-ending support and encouragement, and Jesus will join us in the next movie giggle-fest.

Kelly Geister, thank you for your incredible help when *Every Ugly Word* was a breakable little book. You are the most talented person I know, and your smile lights up a room. I fear our jokes are forever destined to be too sick for minors, but you know what? I kind of like it that way . . .

There's a group of incredible authors who've always believed in me and my book: First and foremost, Cora Carmack, who managed not only to tell people to read this story in its first iteration, but, I suspect, forced them to buy it. Vanitha Sankaran, Melody Valadez, Mary Elizabeth Summer, Sharon Johnston, Mikaela Gray, Liz O'Connor, Lorna Suzuki . . . (the list goes on!), your advice, time, friendship, and support have been a gift.

To all the bloggers, tweeters, Facebookers, readers, and others who loved this book *before*, thank you. You started this ball rolling. I'll always remember you with genuine gratitude.

And finally, to my favorite redhead in the entire world, thank you for sharing me when you didn't have a choice. Never stop believing that God will be the one to fuel your dreams and make them come true—and that your father and I love you almost as much as He does.

Author photo © Dawn Fulwood

AIMEE L. SALTER writes novels for teens and the occasional adult who, like herself, is still in touch with his or her inner-high schooler. She never stopped appreciating those moments in the dark when you say what you're really thinking. And she'll always ask you about the things you wish she wouldn't ask you about. Aimee blogs for both writers and readers at www.aimeelsalter.com. You can also find her on Twitter and Facebook.

DISCUSSION QUESTIONS

1. Throughout *Every Ugly Word,* the main character, Ashley, narrates the story from her perspective both as a high school student and as an adult. Which version of Ashley do you think is most honest with you, the reader? Which Ashley would you most like to talk to, if you could?

2. Ashley describes Matt as her best friend. Do you agree with her? Why, or why not?

3. If you were able to talk to yourself from five or six years ago, what would you tell him/her? Is there anything you'd hide?

4. Ashley admits that in the eighth grade she lied to everyone about sleeping with Finn. Why do you think she told that lie? Do you think that is the real reason Finn treats Ashley so harshly years later?

5. Have you seen people treated the way Ashley was treated by her classmates? Or experienced it yourself? Which part(s) of her story felt authentic to you?

6. Why do you think Ashley didn't talk to Mrs. D, or other teachers/adults about what was happening to her?

7.   Older Me tells Doc she believes anyone who treated her nicely, or claimed her as a friend in high school would be punished for being associated with her. Do you think she was right?

8.   Ashley struggles to believe in herself because of the bullying she experiences. Did her story change the way you might treat or talk to someone who is bullied? If so, how?

9.   Throughout the story, Ashley uses art as an escape or to express her feelings. Do you think this is good for her? Can you think of other positive ways could she have expressed herself?

10. Six months after the incident with the mirror, Ashley and Matt are finally in a committed relationship. Are you glad that they got together? Why, or why not?

11. At the end of the book, Ashley has everything she wanted from the beginning: Her best friend is her boyfriend, she is offered a scholarship to art school, she will get to leave her mother and her bullies behind. Yet she acknowledges that she isn't healed, and still has insecurities and holes in her life. Do you think Ashley is in a good place at that point? Why, or why not?

12. In your opinion, what was the most important part of Ashley's story?

Looking for more great reads?
Turn the page for an excerpt of the sci-fi adventure

REBEL WING

By Tracy Banghart

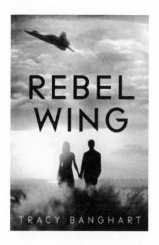

EIGHTEEN-YEAR-OLD ARIS'S LIFE
falls apart when her boyfriend is
drafted to fight on the front lines
of Atalanta's war. She has no idea
when—or *if*—she'll ever see him
again. So when she's recruited to a
secret program that helps women
fight in the all-male Military, she
leaps at the chance. The only catch:
She'll have to technologically disguise
herself as a man. . . . Just how far will
she go to be with the boy she loves?

1

HIGH ABOVE THE olive groves and blinding white roofs of the village, Aris danced. She twisted and dove, guiding her wingjet straight out over granite cliffs and the glitter of the ocean. As she did, she imagined its wings were her arms, reaching far out into the blue. Her fingers would knife through a wisp of cloud, and the moisture would linger against her skin, like a kiss.

Her father wouldn't approve of such thoughts. To him, flying was a practical pursuit, for dusting crops or traveling from place to place. Their village was built high on carbonate stilts, so wingjets were the easiest form of transportation unless you were working the land or hiking down the steep paths leading to the narrow beach below the cliffs. Most everyone here could fly. But no one flew like Aris did.

At least Calix understood what flying meant to her.

She pressed the pedals under her feet and twisted the hand controls, diving in a last tight pirouette before nosing the tiny two-seat wingjet toward home.

A flicker of light caught at the edge of her vision. She glanced out to sea and steered the wingjet in the direction of the movement.

Suddenly, the flash became a speeding wingjet. It hurtled toward her, its silver sides reflecting the sun. Aris hovered just off shore, the beach a golden crescent beneath her, waiting for the wingjet to change course or slow to land. Instead, it grew larger, advancing quickly. Surely the flyer saw her? Her hands tightened on the controls. She moved farther from the cliff. The other wingjet shifted too, keeping her directly in its path.

Aris nearly waited too long. She jerked the controls down, the force of the other wingjet's passage rattling the bones of her machine as she locked into a downward spiral. Heart beating wildly, she waited until the last second before pulling up and skimming the water. Beneath her, waves rolled from deep blue to white, ruffled by her jet wind.

The other flyer followed, matching her move for move. Her stomach twisted as the wingjet drew up alongside, giving her a clear view of its needle nose and the Atalanta flag decal stretched across its sloping tail. No solar panels curved above its wings like on her wingjet. Instead the whole thing shimmered a silvery gold, the hallmark of new-tech solar material. Aris had only ever seen Military wingjets on news vids, never up close.

What was it doing *here*, so far from the front lines of the war?

Without warning, the jet shot upward, piercing the cloudless sky like a shining arrow. She slowed to watch its progress, waiting for it to disappear. But with a flash of reflected sunlight, it dove again, straight for her.

What is he trying to prove? Her apprehension shifted to annoyance. She darted out from under the jet and flipped through the air to face him. It had to be a *him*. All members of the Military sector were male.

For a moment they hovered in a strange standoff. Then the other wingjet rocketed forward, forcing her into a series of evasive spins and loops. At first Aris dipped and whirled away in anger and frustration. But gradually, his movements lost their aggression and she relaxed into the dance, pushing farther and twisting faster until it was suddenly *her* chasing *him* across the sky. *She*, who flew the most intricate patterns, she who nipped at his jet wind, whooping as she tumbled toward the flashing waves below.

Eventually, the other flyer slowed and headed back to the cliffs, tipping his wings in a "follow me" gesture. She watched him land, her heart still hammering, then followed suit.

As she touched down, the tall, yellow-flowered grass beneath her swept in wild circles. She wrenched the hood-release lever twice before the glass slid back. It always stuck a little—the hazards of a second-hand machine. Not that she was complaining. Her parents had given her the wingjet three months ago for her eighteenth birthday. It was *hers*, and the only thing she owned that she really, truly cared about.

Aris slid both hands through her hair, trying to smooth it down. She'd left it loose and curling, the way Calix liked, but her recent maneuvers had given the heavy auburn waves a reckless disregard for gravity.

The other flyer stood among the flowers, waiting for her. Dressed in full uniform—blunt-toed boots, trim pants, sleek forest-green jacket—the man represented every fear she had for Calix. On the back of his neck was the black rectangular brand that marked him as Military. He could have just as easily appeared in a news vid as in one of Aris's nightmares. Her breath froze in her throat, and her hands went cold.

"That was incredible." The stranger was slight, with a fine-boned face and thin lips turned up in a smile.

"Thanks?" she replied, taken aback by his enthusiasm.

"Really, I mean it. I've never seen anyone go from a right-hook flutter pattern straight into a flat-nosed full spindrop."

With a grin, she said, "I call it the swing zinger."

He laughed. "I'd heard you were good, Aris Haan, but blighting hell, that was *fantastic*."

A whisper of unease unfurled in her belly. "How do you know who I am?"

Instead of answering, he held a hand up as an invitation. "You coming down from there?"

Her weak leg tensed reflexively. Flying was one thing; getting in and out of a wingjet gracefully was quite another. She eyed him warily. "Why don't you answer my question first?"

The man's friendly smile twisted into a guarded expression. "It's not important."

"And how did you know I was here? Is *that* important?" she pushed.

The man shrugged. "I watched you leave your father's grove and followed you so we could speak privately. And so I could see what you can do."

Her mind raced. He'd followed her? How had she not noticed? And more importantly: "Why would you do that?"

"Because I want to offer you a job."

She let out a disbelieving laugh. Not only were women not allowed in the Military sector, they weren't authorized to take *any* job, in any sector, deemed "dangerous." What could he possibly have in mind?

"Tomorrow, at your selection, you'll be invited to join the Environment sector," the man said. "And then what? Work as a duster for your father's groves? There were only two people in your entire year that scored even *close* to you in the aviation trial. That talent would be wasted there."

His words sent ice down her spine. "How do you know I'll be selected for Environment? No one finds out their sectors until the ceremony."

"I know more about you than you can imagine," he interjected. "I know why you won't get down from that wingjet, for one. And I know you'll never fulfill your potential here. It'll eat away at you, settling for this life." He put a hand on the side of her wingjet. "Listen to me—"

"Who are you? Is this some kind of . . . I don't know . . . some sort of trick?"

He raised his chin. "No. And I don't offer this lightly."

"You're Military. You can't be . . . I mean, you can't offer—"

"You have a lot of questions, of course. But I'm not the one to answer them." The man drew a small piece of silco from his pocket and handed it to her. The letters on it were stamped in blood-red ink. "Go to Dianthe. She'll explain everything. You'll find her at this address in Panthea. Tell her Theo sent you."

Aris took the silco, gingerly, as if it might bite her. "You want me to go to Panthea?"

He leaned closer, a new urgency in this voice. "Don't tell anyone where or why you're going. Tell them you got a job in the city, whatever will keep them from asking questions. We'll set it up, however you need. No one can know what you're really doing. It's imperative that you tell no one. Do you understand?"

She studied Theo's face. Understand? He had to be joking. "I don't understand *anything*. What kind of job is it? And why do I have to lie to my family?"

"This is your chance to fly," he said, his eyes serious. "Not that mindless drudgery you do for your father. I mean *real* flying. All across Atalanta. You have no idea how useful you could be to the war effort. How many lives you could save."

She couldn't keep a burst of bitter laughter from escaping. "That kind of flying isn't useful. It's self-indulgent." Her father had told her so often enough.

He made an impatient noise. "I've watched you. I know what your life is like here. Why aren't you jumping at this chance?"

Anger spilled through her. "You don't know anything about me. How dare you spy on me and think you know me? I'm happy here."

"Really? You're happy being a duster and never leaving Lux?" Theo stared up at her, his face set in rigid lines.

"I am." With Calix, she would be.

"You're either stupid or selfish then." He turned away, as if disgusted with her. "This isn't just about you."

Selfish? Stupid? "If you know so much, surely you're aware I'm about to be Promised." She and Calix had already decided. Two years of Promise, then they could choose to marry. And be bound, irrevocably, for the rest of their lives. It's what she'd wanted for as long as she could remember. "He's going to ask me tomorrow, after selection. I can't leave, and there's nothing selfish or stupid about it."

The man turned back to her and scoffed. "A Promise? Don't count on it."

"Excuse me?" Shock painted her words.

"I assume you're referring to Calix Pavlos?"

Her chest tightened. "Tomorrow he'll join the Health sector. He's going to work in his mother's clinic. We—"

Theo slammed a hand against the side of her wingjet, cutting her off. "Have you not watched the news vids? This war will claim us all, one way or another." His thin lips twisted with an emotion she couldn't identify. "Calix *will* be selected for Military, make no mistake."

"You're wrong." A buzzing filled her ears. "We're winning the war. *That's* what the news vids say. Calix isn't going anywhere." This man was her nightmare after all, come to take everything from her. "His family has been part of the Health sector for generations. There's no chance—"

"There is, Aris, and you know it." Theo stepped back, tipping his head up to look her in the eye. "Please. Consider my offer. You could save lives. Maybe even Calix's."

Then, without another word, he climbed into his shining wingjet and sped away.

For more, follow @tracythewriter on Twitter
or visit her at www.tracybanghart.com

Looking for another great read? Turn the page for an excerpt of

IMITATION

By Heather Hildenbrand

Ven knows everything about wealthy, eighteen-year-old Raven Rogen, from her favorite designer down to the tiny scar on her right arm. That's because she's Raven's clone, though she's never met her face-to-face. Imitations only get to leave the lab when their Authentics need them—to replace the dead, to offer an organ transplant, or in Ven's case, to serve as bait after Raven is attacked in broad daylight. Thrust into the real world for the very first time, Ven must draw out Raven's assailants, or die trying. But when Ven falls for Raven's bodyguard, she discovers some things are worth living for. She was created to serve . . . but is she prepared to sacrifice herself for a girl she's never met?

CHAPTER ONE

EVERYONE IS EXACTLY like me.

There is no one like me.

I wrestle with these contradicting truths most nights while the others sleep. Tonight is worse because Marla has left me a note to see her in the morning. No one sees Marla and comes back. Lonnie reminded me of this after she snatched the note out of my shaking hand and read it for Ida, who promptly burst into tears. We didn't speak after that, lying in our bunks until lights out.

Above me, Lonnie steadily breathes in and out. She's not worrying herself out of a good night's sleep. She's not the one going to see Marla. Below me, Ida is quiet. I suspect she is awake, ruminating. She has a way of latching on to other people's stress and not letting go until everyone is happy again. I long to call out to her, but there is no talking in the dormitory after lights out.

The rough fabric of my cotton nightgown chafes so I lie very still. Once, during a training exercise, they gave me a satin blouse in place of my coarse uniform. For a few moments, I was completely her—eighteen-year-old Raven Rogen, my Authentic—down to

1

the fabric. The slippery material felt like cool fingertips on a hot day. All I could think was: *She wears clothes like this every single day.*

I know everything about Raven and the world she lives in, thanks to the video footage I watch during my training sessions. But I have never experienced anything for myself—not even the sun. My entire life is an imitation of hers.

I am an Imitation.

All of us here are. From the time the tubes are removed and air is forced into our lungs, until our petri-grown organs learn to contract on their own, we are nothing but shadows of our Authentics. I used to think there was an Imitation for every Authentic, but when I asked my Examiner, Josephine, she laughed and said we'd need a whole lot more space here if that was the case. Only special Authentics get the privilege of a copy—ones with money, power, influence.

It seems as if there are thousands of us, though it's hard to tell exactly how many exist. Twig City is sorted into sections, our placement depending on our gender, how old we were when they "woke" us, and whether we've gotten a note from Marla. Those woken at a young age live in a different wing, where nurses and teachers chart their development daily. You have to be at least twelve to live on my floor—the training ward, where we learn to become our Authentic—but the oldest I've seen is somewhere around fifty. There is no saying how long you'll stay in this ward once you're here. Could be a week, could be a year, depending on when your Authentic needs you. I've been awake for five years. Training. Preparing. Waiting—for a note from Marla. And for what comes after.

Some say Marla is our creator—but I don't think so. I have a memory, a hazy nightmare, of the day I woke. None of the first faces I saw were female. One man in particular stands out in the fog. I can't recall his features, but the impression he left is one of utter fear. Though I can't explain it, I am positive this man is our creator.

Others say Marla is the gatekeeper. A walker between worlds, connecting us, the Imitations, to them. The humans, the womb-born, the Authentics.

I don't know which is true. All I know is no one ever returns from meeting with Marla.

Across the pitch-dark room comes a whisper, and I count down the seconds until an Overseer comes in. Overseers are the sentries, the silent guards who watch and wait, only intervening when a rule is broken or boundary overstepped. A minute later, I hear the sure, swift fall of an Overseer's feet as she makes her way to the offending bunk to bark an order of quiet at whoever it was. Probably Clora. She's new and headstrong. Lonnie speculates it is a trait from her Authentic. I hope not. If it's part of her DNA, it won't be easy an easy habit to break.

"This is your only warning," the Overseer threatens. "Another infraction and you'll be reported to Marla."

I'm convinced Overseers are paid to be cross. I've told this to my Examiner, Josephine, and she doesn't bother arguing so I know it's true. Josephine is more laid-back than most, but I've never told her the real truth: that the idea of leaving Twig City is terrifying. Instead, I tell Josephine what she wants to hear, what Imitations are supposed to say: When I am called to duty, I will be ready. I will serve my Authentic in any way necessary.

After all, I was created to serve.

The Overseer finishes her warning and exits the room, back to her monitoring booth full of cameras. I chase sleep, grazing my fingertips across its tail end but never fully catch it. Hours later, the lights come on, signaling to our windowless chamber that it is morning. I shove the blanket aside and sit up, blinking against a sea of sameness.

The sleeping room is a long rectangle with high ceilings and a bad echo, lined with triple-level bunk beds. Everyone here is part of a trio. Lonnie says it's because three's a crowd. It creates diversity and therefore animosity. It discourages the bonding that happens when there are only two. Ida tells her she's wrong because the three of us have bonded just fine. I see both points; no one else seems as close as we are, but no other trio has lasted this long. I've been with Lonnie and Ida since I began. Most others have lost at least one of their threesome to a note from Marla, only to have them replaced by a stranger.

And now I have a letter.

I slide out of my bunk and land lightly on my feet. In the bunk above, Lonnie is slow to wake, grumpily mumbling about coffee as she stretches her toned arms toward the ceiling. She thinks her Authentic must not be a morning person.

Ida stands more quickly. Her thick black hair ripples as she moves, mussed but manageable in its pixie cut. Her eyes are heavy and blinking but not from grogginess; her lids are puffy, rimmed in pink. The longer she stares at me, the more her bottom lip trembles. I slip my shoes on and fuss with my pale hair—anything to ignore Ida's nervous energy.

Anna, the girl whose bunk is closest to ours, catches my eye and nods. I nod back in silent hello. It is a daily ritual, simple and meaningless considering we never converse beyond this, but I will miss it when I'm gone.

While we wait for Lonnie, I take Ida's hand in mine and hold her palm open. Using my index finger, I trace the outline of a square and then a check mark inside it. It's going to be okay, I convey using our secret language. Ida takes my hand and scribbles a wavy line across my palm in return. A loose W for *whatever*.

I let my hand drop.

It started on paper, a shorthand code made up of symbols we'd exchange back and forth to communicate during lectures. When we got caught passing notes, we began drawing the pictures in invisible lines on each other's skin.

"Ven, I don't want you to go," Ida says in her soft voice, which always makes me think of dolls in pretty dresses. Porcelain. Breakable.

I don't acknowledge her plea. If she cries again, I fear I will, too.

"Time for breakfast," I say.

We fall into step together as the crowd of girls who live in this wing surge toward the breakfast hall. The air smells of sleepy bodies with an underlying chemical scent that drifts down from the pipes and mixes with everything, even the food and water.

Anna bumps my shoulder as she pushes past. I don't complain, because we're taught silence is best when there's nothing of value to say. Besides, the way to breakfast used to involve a lot more shoving and jostling for space. Notes from Marla have depleted our numbers.

We're the last group to arrive and the room, although large, is crowded. Four dormitories share this dining hall, a total of roughly two hundred forty women in plain uniforms.

Lonnie heads straight for the buffet line and taps her foot impatiently as she waits her turn. I wander to the coffee and muffins station with Ida and fill a plate even though my stomach feels packed with bricks.

As we sit down at our regular table, Lonnie glares suspiciously at Ida's plate. "Is that bran?"

"Bran's good for you," Ida says, her lips forming a pout.

I stare longingly at Lonnie's single piece of sausage and two small strips of bacon.

"Don't be too jealous," she says. "I had to sign up for an extra thirty minutes of cardio to get both."

As the smell hits me, it seems a small price to pay. I watch with rapture as she chews. She catches me looking. I force a bite of my muffin. "Yum," I say dryly.

"Maybe Ven will make Marla change her mind," Ida says abruptly.

Lonnie rolls her eyes and mumbles "not likely" around a mouthful of eggs.

Ida glares at her. "It's possible. Ven can be convincing when she wants to be."

"No one 'convinces' Marla," Lonnie says.

She's right. Even Ida knows it. "What do you think they want with you?" Ida asks quietly.

Lonnie and I share a look. There are only two reasons an Imitation gets a letter from Marla.

"They probably have an assignment for me," I say. Neither of us is willing to say the other option: that I'm wanted for harvesting. No one ever talks about it, but we all know it's the main reason we exist.

In training, we speak only of assignments. Missions. Most often, the job involves inserting yourself into the life of your Authentic when you're needed. For what, exactly, they don't say, and we've never been able to ask. Imitations who complete their assignments move from Training to Maintenance, where they get more free time than we have here. I've imagined hundreds of missions: giving speeches for a camera-shy Authentic; going to work while your Authentic goes on safari; walking the red carpet while your Authentic is sick in bed; being a surrogate mother . . .

"You're probably right that it's a mission," Ida says. "Something clandestine and exciting, I'm sure."

There is a note of forced cheerfulness in her voice. Anyone else listening would assume it was for my benefit, or Lonnie's, but I know better. Ida must convince herself there is no reason to panic.

"If you're really lucky, you'll get Relaxation," Lonnie suggests.

Relaxation is the ultimate reward, where you're sent when your Authentic is no longer in need of an Imitation. They say it's a hidden wing of Twig City full of nothing but leisure time. Sort of like retirement. Donuts and lounge chairs until our bodies give out. Exercise is no longer required six days a week and our food isn't rationed. Lonnie says that last part is too good to be true. Ida always rolls her eyes at that.

"That would mean my Authentic is dead," I point out.

"Not necessarily," Lonnie argues. "Maybe she just doesn't want an Imitation anymore."

"Or maybe she wants to meet you. Can you imagine that?

Living with humans? Pretending to be one of them?" Ida is far-away, her words wistful.

I force my hand steady and let Ida's comment pass without reply, choking down the smaller half of my muffin. I try to focus on my excitement rather than my fear. Because like it or not, I have a note to see Marla. And no one sees Marla and comes back.

For more, follow @HeatherHildenbr or
visit her at www.heatherhildenbrand.blogspot.com

3 1247 01798255 4